CW00671171

SHE WAS AT RISK

SHE WAS AT RISK

ZACHARY GOLDMAN MYSTERIES #10

P.D. WORKMAN

ISBN: 9781774680162 (IS Hardcover)

ISBN: 9781774680179 (IS Large Print)

ISBN: 9781774680155 (IS Paperback)

ISBN: 9781774680124 (KDP Paperback)

ISBN: 9781774680131 (Kindle)

ISBN: 9781774680148 (ePub)

pdworkman

ALSO BY P.D. WORKMAN

Zachary Goldman Mysteries

She Wore Mourning

His Hands Were Quiet

She Was Dying Anyway

He Was Walking Alone

They Thought He was Safe

He Was Not There

Her Work Was Everything

She Told a Lie

He Never Forgot

She Was At Risk

Kenzie Kirsch Medical Thrillers

Unlawful Harvest

Doctored Death (Coming soon)

Auntie Clem's Bakery

Gluten-Free Murder

Dairy-Free Death

Allergen-Free Assignation

Witch-Free Halloween (Halloween Short)

Dog-Free Dinner (Christmas Short)

Stirring Up Murder

Brewing Death

Coup de Glace

Sour Cherry Turnover

Apple-achian Treasure

AND MORE AT PDWORKMAN.COM

To all those who are vulnerable
Which is all of us

Zachary gazed out Kenzie's living room window at the pleasant, suburban view. He hadn't realized how much he was missing by living in apartment buildings instead of a nice little house like Kenzie had. When he stared out the window at his apartment, he saw nothing but sky, or looked down at the dirty parking lot, complete with homeless people going through the trash for bottles. He didn't know his neighbors within the apartment building well. They were familiar enough to nod to in the elevator, but that was about it.

What he was missing was the green lawns, the children walking to school, the flower borders and gardens. People smiling pleasantly at each other when they passed on the street or even stopping to talk to each other. It was a postcard picture day and, unlike when he looked at the Vermont trees and hills covered with snow as Christmas approached, Zachary could enjoy the scene.

Maybe he should have moved into a house like Kenzie's. Maybe sometime in the future, he would. Maybe with the way that his relationship was progressing with Kenzie…

He pulled his thoughts away from the possibility. He didn't want to be dependent on anyone's kindness. He had lived with Mario after his previous apartment had burned down, and it was better to be on his own two feet. He got lazy relying on someone else to do the work and keep him on track.

The thought stirred Zachary, and he got up and went into the kitchen. He put in a pod and made himself a cup of coffee and poked his head out of the kitchen for a moment to listen and try to decide whether Kenzie was up yet. He couldn't hear her stirring. No point in making her coffee before she was up; it would just be cold by the time she got to it.

But while he was in the kitchen, he rinsed the dishes that were sitting in the sink, put them into the dishwasher, and wiped the counter, eliminating the rings from his previous cups of coffee. He put the washcloth back in its place and gave himself a mental pat on the back for at least doing something to help keep Kenzie's place tidy.

Fresh coffee in hand, Zachary returned to his place in Kenzie's living room. Since he was there most weeknights now, he had asked Kenzie whether she minded his getting a mobile laptop table that he could use while he was sitting on the couch or in the easy chair, if he kept his space tidy and it didn't detract from the decor of the room.

Kenzie shook her head, bemused. "Sure, of course. You should have some kind of desk instead of sitting hunched over that thing all the time. It's not good for your body."

He was often sore after a couple of hours sitting with it, so he knew she was right. "I just… didn't want to presume."

Kenzie shrugged. "Of course. You're here. I like having you around, having… a few touches that remind me of you when you're out. I don't mind at all."

So he had browsed online until he found one that he liked, and it had been a good purchase. He could sit and type, read documents, or browse databases with better posture, which helped to keep him going for as long as he needed to.

Zachary's phone vibrated in his pocket. He slid it out to look at it, and felt frown lines crease his forehead.

Gordon Drake.

Gordon didn't have any reason to be calling Zachary. Zachary had stayed away from Bridget, his ex-wife. He hadn't been following her or spying on her. They hadn't accidentally run into each other anywhere.

Not lately.

Zachary had cleared everything up at Drake, Chase, Gould after Ashley's death. There was no reason for Gordon to call Zachary back. With the killer behind bars, there shouldn't have been anything else for Gordon to call Zachary about.

Unless there had been another death.

Unless something else untoward had happened.

But even if it had, Zachary would have expected Gordon to go somewhere else to get help. Bridget had not been happy with Zachary looking into Ashley's death, and Zachary didn't think that Gordon would do anything he knew would antagonize her.

Especially not since she was pregnant.

———

Zachary slid his finger across the phone screen to answer the call.

"Gordon? Is everything okay?"

"Zachary, it's been a while since I saw you last. How are things with you?"

Zachary chewed the inside of his cheek. "I'm fine," he said cautiously. "What's going on with you? Everything okay at Chase Gold?"

Gordon chuckled. The nickname for the investment banking firm left out his name, which was a bit of a slap in the face considering he was the principal partner and owner. But he appreciated the appropriateness of the name.

"Yes, everything is fine at Chase Gold," he agreed. "Better than ever. And I have… put some extra controls in place as far as the interns are concerned. We don't want any more… hospitalizations."

"Yeah, that's good." Zachary waited for Gordon to explain why he had called. It wasn't just for a casual chat and to catch up on each other's lives. They didn't have that kind of relationship. Although Gordon had always been very cordial toward Zachary, he knew how much animosity Bridget had toward him. He usually respected her desire to have nothing to do with him anymore.

Unless he needed something.

"I guess you're wondering why I called. I was hoping that the two of us could get together."

"I suppose," Zachary said slowly, feeling his way along. "What did you want to meet about?"

"I would… prefer to leave that for our meeting. It's a rather delicate matter. I prefer to discuss it face to face, somewhere quiet and discreet."

"Okay. If you're sure. Where would you like to meet? Your office?"

"Heavens, no." Gordon was silent for a moment as if considering, though surely he must have known before he called Zachary that they would need an appropriate place to meet. "I can book a private meeting room at my club. Do you know the Ostrich?"

Zachary knew of it. He wasn't a member and had never been there. He wasn't aware of anyone in his circles who was a member. Other than Gordon, clearly.

"I know where it is. What's the dress code?"

"They are fairly relaxed now. No blue jeans or track pants. Clean, neat, and pressed. Collared shirt. No tie required."

Zachary didn't think he even owned a tie. When was the last time he had attended an event where he had needed one? Probably not since he and Bridget had broken up. He had gone to fancy dress parties with her. Lots of places that had required a tie or even a tux with a bow tie. Not the clip-on ones. They had to be proper tie-up bow ties, Bridget had informed him. No shortcuts. People could tell when they looked at you whether you had taken the time or not. They could see right through you.

If that were the case, then he didn't know what point there was in wearing a bow tie of any kind. If people could see through his clothing to what kind of a person he really was, then why try to masquerade as a society man by wearing clothes that didn't suit him?

But he didn't say that to Bridget. He had shaved and dressed up and stood still while Bridget tied his bow tie and made sure that it was straight and everything else was in its proper place.

But he could manage business pants and a polo shirt. He didn't have to go out and rent or buy anything for that. Gordon would be in a three-piece suit if he were coming from work, but he had not told Zachary that he had to be formally dressed. He would probably just stand out more if he tried to look like an upper-class businessman anyway. People paid no attention if he looked like he was working-class or a bum.

"Okay. What time do you want to get together?"

"I have a rather full schedule," Gordon said, a note of apology in his voice. "But I would like to see you as soon as possible. Could you do lunch today? I just had someone cancel on me."

Lunch at Gordon's fancy club.

"Sure. Lunch at the Ostrich Club. Do I… check in with the maitre d' when I get there? I haven't been anywhere like that before."

"There is a reception desk. You can tell Danielle that you are meeting me. She will direct you to which room I have booked or someone will escort you up."

Zachary nodded to himself. He looked at the system clock on his computer. He'd better start getting cleaned up if he were going to look presentable by lunch.

2

The Ostrich was pretty much as Zachary expected it to be. Dark woods, plush carpets, polished waitstaff right there whenever you looked for them. He was escorted to the Roosevelt room by a pleasant young man who didn't try to make conversation or ask him what he was doing there.

Gordon was already seated at the table, his laptop out, working on some document or project. His expression was serious and focused. He didn't look up for a few seconds, but then he closed the lid of the computer and looked into Zachary's eyes, giving him a warm smile of welcome.

"Good to see you, Zachary. Have a seat. What do you want to drink?"

Zachary looked at the young man who stood attentively. "Uh… just a Coke, please."

The man nodded, acting as if that were a perfectly normal drink order. Apparently not everyone at the club was ordering hi-balls or tea. Or if they were, the waiter would never give it away. Gordon ordered some kind of French wine and the waiter nodded and wrote it down, expression not changing. Zachary couldn't tell if it was an expensive vintage or something out of a box. Given the setting, he assumed the former.

"And what would you like to eat?" Gordon asked.

"Uh…" Zachary looked around for a menu. "I don't know…"

"They're equipped to make any popular dish. What do you feel like?"

Zachary cast around for a suitable dish. "I'm not that hungry yet. Maybe just... a sandwich?"

Gordon nodded. "Sure. What do you like? Roast beef? Chicken?"

"Maybe cheese? Grilled cheese?" He felt a little silly ordering something juvenile at such a fancy place. But he didn't have much of an appetite. His meds made him nauseated for a few hours after taking them.

"How about a Monte Cristo?" Gordon suggested. "Grilled cheese and ham?"

"Sure," Zachary agreed. "That sounds good."

"Would you like salad or fries on the side?" the waiter asked.

Zachary shook his head. "Just the sandwich."

He nodded. Gordon ordered some kind of skillet. After the waiter was gone, he turned his attention to Zachary.

"So, things are going well for you?" he asked. "How is business?"

"Going pretty well." A few big cases had padded out his bank account and gotten his name out in the media, so he was doing all right.

"Anything interesting? Haven't captured any serial killers recently?"

"No. I think I'm going to put in all of my listings that I don't do serial killers. Too much time and effort," Zachary deadpanned.

Gordon looked at him uncertainly, then smiled. "Well, you might as well advertise the kind of cases that you actually want to get," he agreed. "I haven't seen much in the news lately. Has there been anything big?"

"I just finished with a man who was looking for his childhood home. Which ended up being where his brother was buried. So that was pretty intense. And the main one before that was a missing girl. Human trafficking. Prostitution."

Gordon shook his head slowly. "You do get around, don't you? Nasty business."

Zachary shrugged. "Yeah. Most people don't come to me because they won the lottery."

"I imagine not. People are coming to you at the worst, most vulnerable times of their lives."

"Yeah. Exactly."

Gordon stared off into space. He looked like a man with something heavy on his mind. Zachary waited for him to spit it out. Since he wanted to meet, Zachary had to assume that there was something he wanted to be investigated. He wouldn't be going to Zachary with personal problems.

Some people were much better qualified than Zachary to sort out relationship problems.

Gordon looked at his watch. A big, highly-polished gold number. "This is rude, but do you mind…" Gordon gestured to his laptop. "There are a couple of things I'd like to put through while I still have the time."

Zachary shrugged. "Sure," he agreed. Gordon wasn't yet ready to present what it was that he wanted. Maybe he was waiting for the food to arrive so they wouldn't be interrupted partway through. Or maybe he would wait until after they were finished eating to turn to the business he'd asked Zachary there for. He hoped it would not take that long for Gordon to get to the point.

While Gordon opened his laptop again, Zachary pulled out his phone. He checked his email, even though there wasn't likely to be anything important that had come in since he'd left Kenzie's house. And he browsed through his social networks. He wasn't big on social networks, but sometimes he did find interesting news stories or something that impacted his work. It was a good way to connect with family or friends, but Zachary wasn't quite ready to put that much of himself on public display. As a private investigator, he didn't want people to be able to track him down too easily. And he knew from experience that people shared way too much on social media. He'd been on the investigating end of a lot of those.

He and Gordon worked independently until the waiter arrived with their dishes. Then they both put the electronics aside and thanked the waiter. Zachary took his first bite of the Monte Cristo sandwich. It was crisp but not greasy, with just the right amount of cheese and ham pocketed inside.

"Mmm. This is very good."

Gordon nodded. "Good kitchen staff. We have world-class chefs. They don't disappoint."

Zachary nodded to Gordon's meal of grilled vegetables and seafood. "That looks good too."

"Yes." Gordon took a few bites, then he pushed the dish a few inches away from him as though he were full. "Zachary, I know I can rely on your discretion. You've proven yourself eminently capable in the past."

Zachary nodded. "Yes. I won't share any company secrets."

"This one isn't for the firm." Gordon was staring off into middle space again, considering. Making his final decision as to whether to proceed or to jettison the whole thing. He swallowed and put his hands palms-down on the table to physically brace himself. "It's Bridget."

Zachary had been half-expecting this. He had tried to convince himself that it was about Gordon's firm, but Gordon was perfectly capable of handling his business without bringing Zachary in. He was the one who knew about investments and financial stuff and all of the ins and outs, not Zachary. Zachary would be hard-pressed to help Gordon with a case of fraud or some other business-related area. Maybe if he wanted to find out if one of his partners were out fooling around where he shouldn't be, but nothing about the business itself.

Zachary swallowed. He was going to have to tell Gordon no. He couldn't work on a case that had anything to do with Bridget. He was trying to put Bridget out of his life, out of his thoughts. He didn't want to be thinking about her when he was with Kenzie. He didn't want her creeping into his dreams or keeping him up at night. He just wanted to be able to leave that part of his life behind and to move forward.

"What about Bridget?"

Gordon traced a circle on the polished tabletop. He had a quick sip from his glass and poked around at the seafood on his platter. But he wasn't interested in the food. They weren't there to eat lunch. He was a man with something far more pressing on his hands than his next meal.

"You know that she's pregnant."

Zachary nodded.

"Of course you do," Gordon said quickly. "Of course. I told you that when she was in the hospital. She's been quite sick with this pregnancy. It hasn't been easy on her."

"Right." Zachary had, in fact, thought that her cancer had returned. He was relieved that wasn't the case, but he wished he didn't have to think about Bridget pregnant either. He had wanted children when they had been married. She had not. She'd had a pregnancy scare before her cancer was diagnosed, and she had no interest in carrying it to term. But she had not been pregnant, so that disaster had been averted.

"What I don't think I told you is that she is expecting twins," Gordon said slowly, enunciating his words as carefully as if he were being graded on his diction. "Two girls."

Zachary nodded again. He swallowed. His mouth and throat were very dry. He irrigated them with a good amount of Coke. "I guessed as much," he agreed.

Gordon looked at him for a moment, then nodded. He didn't ask how Zachary had guessed. That was not the point.

"In the beginning, Bridget agreed to try to get pregnant." Gordon couldn't have any idea the kind of pain that this disclosure caused Zachary. He had failed on so many levels with Bridget. "She was a little reluctant at first, but she agreed to give it a try, see how things worked out. Neither of us knew whether she would even be able to get pregnant and be able to carry the baby to term."

The doctors hadn't expected her to have viable eggs after the cancer treatment. Instead, she had banked them before she started treatment. She had been very sick, and it had taken a lot of coaxing on the part of the doctors. They didn't like leaving a woman with no options. She might change her mind in the future. She might decide, after the crisis was past, that she did want to expand her family or at least to have those choices open to her.

And apparently, she had done just that. They had fertilized a couple of frozen eggs and she had become pregnant with twins.

Gordon fiddled some more, not able to come to the point yet.

"The further along she has gone with the pregnancy, the more difficult things have become. She has had a lot of second thoughts."

But what was she going to do? Terminate the pregnancy? That was what she had threatened Zachary with after she had a positive pregnancy test. She didn't want her body ruined by pregnancy. Didn't want to be burdened by children who depended on her. She didn't think that Zachary would be able to man up and be a good father to them. He could barely take care of himself; how was he going to help with children?

"Has she decided... that she doesn't want to continue?" he prompted.

"She is getting older and we don't know how many chances she will have to get pregnant. How hard it will be to terminate and try again."

"Try again? If she wants to terminate, why would she try again?"

"It changes from day to day," Gordon sighed. "Maybe she's not ready. She could try again in a year or two when she feels more ready, though that will be pushing against her biological clock. Or sometimes she decides that twins will be too much and she should only carry one to term. They can do selective reduction... And other days, she is convinced that there is something wrong with the babies."

It wasn't that surprising that Bridget would be worried about her pregnancy. Many women had anxiety over such a significant change in their lives. It was something so utterly different from anything they had done before. For Bridget, it would mean a big change in the way she lived her life. Being a mother, tied down to two children, instead of being able to go wherever she wanted whenever she wanted to. Things were different for parents, even if she did get a nanny to help.

"What does she think is wrong?"

"Well, up until now, it has just been 'something'—'*What if* there is something wrong with the babies?' 'Something doesn't feel right.' 'I think something is wrong.'—But I'm not willing to operate on 'somethings.' I need answers. Concrete evidence."

And he had found something. But what? Why did Gordon need a private investigator?

"And... you found something?" Zachary ventured.

Gordon tapped his computer. He took a couple more bites of his grill.

"She decided to have prenatal DNA testing done. Just to make sure that everything was okay. It's not just Down Syndrome anymore. They are very sophisticated now. They can do all sorts of testing for genetic problems and predict a lot of developmental issues."

Zachary nodded.

"I went along with it," Gordon said. "I thought this would help her to move on. She would know that everything was okay, so she would feel better about continuing the pregnancy. I thought it was a good solution. Rule out all of those things that she was afraid of."

"But, something came up on the test." Zachary still didn't have a clue why Gordon would want him involved. He couldn't fix genetic issues with his magnifying glass.

Gordon sighed. "Both babies are at high risk for developing Huntington's Disease."

3

Zachary had heard of it before, but knew very little about what Huntington's Disease was. He chewed the bite of sandwich in his mouth slowly.

"What exactly is Huntington's?"

"It's a neurological problem," Gordon said in a flat voice. "Like having Alzheimer's and Parkinson's and Lou Gehrig's all at the same time. Dementia, tremors and movements and, eventually, total loss of control and inability to even swallow." He shook his head grimly. "Not a pleasant thought, both of our little girls ending up with this horrible disease."

"No. That sounds horrible. So… Bridget was right. There is something wrong with them."

"But the thing is, these girls could live normal lives until they are forty or fifty—even sixty or seventy in some cases. A long, fulfilling life before it eventually strikes. We all have a limited time here on earth. None of us knows how long we will be in this mortal sphere. You or I could drop dead tomorrow."

"Yeah, that's true."

"So really, we don't *know* anything. We have no idea *when* they are going to develop Huntington's. Just that someday, sometime along the line, they will."

"So you want to continue with the pregnancy, but she wants to terminate," Zachary summed up. "But she doesn't need your permission to terminate. She can go out and do it at any time."

"Yes. She's agreed to hold off a week or two while I look at some of the possibilities. A lot of people are saying that by the time they reach twenty, we could have a cure. Almost guaranteed, in fact. The research looks very good. They could be gene editing by that time, and be able to prevent them from ever getting Huntington's Disease."

"I don't have much knowledge about medical research." Zachary shifted uncomfortably. "I could talk to Kenzie and see what she knows. Or you could get a genetic counselor who could help you to work through this stuff. A professional."

"I'm willing to believe that we could have a cure in the next few years," Gordon said, making a movement with his hand to brush the comment away. "Especially where we are going with things like stem cells and gene therapy. We've come a very long way in the science, and it won't be long before they can treat this."

Zachary leaned back against his seat. Then what did Gordon want?

Gordon pushed his plate away again. "The genetics of Huntington's Disease are such that a child can only get Huntington's if one of her parents have it."

Zachary considered this. His knowledge of genetics was pretty thin, but he remembered some from high school biology. "But it could be that the parent is just a carrier, right?" he suggested. "Because everybody has two copies of each gene."

"In the case of Huntington's Disease, you can't just be a carrier. You have to have it to give it to a child. Maybe you haven't started having symptoms yet, but it's there, and typically it starts to develop between the ages of forty and fifty."

Which meant that Gordon could develop it at any time.

Things suddenly became more clear. Gordon himself was going to get Huntington's Disease sometime soon. Or perhaps sometime in the next couple of decades. But he would get it, and he wanted Zachary to track someone down for him. An absent parent. A sibling. An old sweetheart. Maybe a child that he'd never been involved with.

Zachary pulled out his notebook and laid it on the table. "Okay, so who are you looking for?"

"Who am I looking for?" Gordon repeated. "Well, I don't know that, do I?"

Zachary stared at him, frowning. "What do you mean?"

"I want to know who the father of the babies is."

It was the second shock of the meeting. Zachary stared at him. Who the father of the twins was? Did he think that Bridget had ended up having an affair with Zachary? That the babies might be Zachary's? Or did he have someone else in mind?

He swallowed and shook his head. "I'm a little lost. Who the father is? It's not you?"

"I just had myself tested for the Huntington's Disease gene. I don't have it."

"Oh."

"I didn't think that I did. It would have to be in my family in the recent past, and I don't have any relatives who have had dementia or Parkinson's or anything else that Huntington's might have been mistaken for."

"Does it have to come from the father?"

"No. It could come from Bridget. But we have the same problem there. There's no hint of Huntington's Disease in her family. No sign at all."

Zachary worked through the combinations and options, his brain whirling away.

"So if it didn't come from you or Bridget, then it came from somewhere else. Obviously, Bridget is the mother, since she's the one who is pregnant."

Gordon raised his finger, shaking his head. "Remember, she probably didn't get pregnant naturally. It was frozen eggs. And that means it could have been someone else's eggs."

"True. Right."

"The clinic might have mixed something up. A vial mislabeled or misfiled. It might *not* have been her eggs or my sperm. It might be someone else's fertilized embryos."

Zachary nodded. "But they must be able to test for that. If they're doing a DNA test for Huntington's, then they must be able to test for parentage at the same time."

Gordon was nodding. "Except that Bridget is against it and the doctors seem to have some sort of ethical dilemma. Or maybe it's legal; they don't want to get sued. Bridget says it shouldn't matter where they got the Huntington's gene from. We should be making a decision based on the risk factors that we know, not on who the biological parents are."

Alarm bells were going off in Zachary's head. *Bridget said it didn't matter who the parents were?* Bridget was the one who had said that she wondered if there was something wrong with the babies and had wanted to terminate before they had even proven it.

"Do you think she had an affair?"

Gordon cleared his throat. He poked at the food still on his plate but didn't eat anything else. He sighed. "What else am I to think? Her reactions and explanations up until now have been… improbable. She had IVF, so the babies should be the implanted embryos. But the other possibility is… the embryos didn't take, but she became pregnant naturally. By… me or someone else."

"She couldn't get pregnant naturally, could she? After the cancer treatment?"

"I've dug into that a little. She was told she *probably* wouldn't be able to. That's why she froze her eggs in the first place."

Zachary nodded. He remembered that part very clearly. How much the doctor had to argue to convince her to at least prepare for the possibility she might change her mind in the future. How she had just glared at the doctor and at Zachary and said that there was no way. But in the end, she had agreed.

"But I guess it wasn't a foregone conclusion that she would become sterile. There is still a slim chance that she would have viable eggs left in the other ovary after the treatments. Slim, but not impossible."

"Okay. So… you want me to investigate whether she had an affair?"

"Or whether she still is having one," Gordon said, his words painfully slow and precise. "I have to wonder… and maybe it doesn't matter. Maybe it makes no difference to anything. But I'm a man who likes to have all of the facts before he makes a decision."

Zachary nodded.

He knew that it was not a good idea.

He should have told Gordon right from the start that he couldn't meet. That he couldn't have anything to do with Gordon or Bridget. And now, he needed to say that he couldn't possibly investigate Bridget. It was a conflict of interest. Or something like that. It wasn't a good idea for him to be following her around, seeing where she went, who she talked to, who she might be meeting on the sly.

His heart raced just thinking about it.

And not the pounding heart he often felt from anxiety and the inherent risks of doing surveillance and possibly being caught.

This racing heart was from excitement and anticipation. His brain was being flooded with all of those feel-good neurotransmitters. He was going to be able to see her again. To follow her. To watch her covertly. And it was okay, because he wasn't doing it for himself. He wasn't doing it for his own kicks, because his OCD brain told him that he needed to follow her and know where she was at all times.

It would be for Gordon.

And for the babies.

4

Zachary told himself more than once that he was not taking the job for himself and that he could have refused if he'd wanted to. He would show Gordon, if no one else, that he was able to deal with his feelings for Bridget calmly and rationally. He could separate his emotions from the investigation and treat it just like any other surveillance job. He would be professional in every way.

That's what he told himself while he was still at the Ostrich Club, and in his car driving home, and throughout the afternoon as he started to put together his plan for the surveillance. It was distracting. He knew from the tightness and heaviness in his gut that he wasn't really fooling himself. He probably hadn't fooled Gordon either. Gordon had a way of seeing right through him. But Zachary's obsession for Bridget was to Gordon's advantage. That was undoubtedly why he had approached Zachary in the first place. He wanted to get the best surveillance possible on his wandering lover? What better choice than to hire the man who was obsessed with her?

Of course, there had been one more bump to get over in his conversation with Gordon.

"This is where thing get tricky," Gordon said, fidgeting with his fork. It wasn't like him to be nervous. Or at any rate, not to show it.

Zachary raised his brows and waited for Gordon to work out what he wanted to say. If it was difficult, Zachary wouldn't help matters by being impatient or pestering him about it.

"I suppose being direct is the only viable option." Gordon cleared his throat. "*You* haven't seen Bridget recently, have you?"

Zachary thought back. "The last time I saw her was at the gas station," he said. "We were both filling up at the same time. That was before I saw you at the hospital."

"I don't mean running into her around town. That's bound to happen from time to time, even if she thinks she can tell you to stay away from her favorite haunts. What I mean is… the two of you have not had any time with just the two of you…"

Zachary shook his head. "No. Why would we—" It suddenly hit him what Gordon was asking, and he let out a laugh of disbelief. "Am *I* having an affair with Bridget? Is that what you're asking?"

Gordon gave an uncomfortable nod. "You and she do have a history. I'm aware, of course, that you still have feelings for her."

"But she doesn't for me. She's made it pretty clear that she doesn't want anything to do with me."

"Yes. But what a person says, and what they feel, and the way they act do not always line up. I have often thought that she is too emotional about you. That she protests *too* much."

Zachary tried to laugh again, but it stuck in his throat. That was what Kenzie said too. That if Bridget really didn't have any feelings for Zachary, she wouldn't care what he did. She wouldn't care if they happened to run into each other somewhere. The fact that she flipped out any time she saw him meant that she still had feelings.

Unless, of course, Bridget wanted something from him, and then she would show up at his apartment and pretend to be sympathetic and friendly.

None of that meant that she still had feelings for him.

"I am not having an affair with her," Zachary told Gordon firmly. He tried to keep his voice completely calm and level and to look Gordon in the eye. To give him all of the nonverbal indicators that he was telling the truth. "I haven't been with Bridget since we broke up. Not once."

"So you are one hundred percent sure that the babies are not yours."

"Yes. One hundred percent. It's been more than two years." Zachary shook his head. "When she found out that she had cancer… I was out the door. That was it. She didn't have time or energy for me in her life anymore. Things had been rocky before that, but we were trying to make it work. Once she knew she was sick, it was a whole different story. She needed to remove everything *toxic* from her life."

Gordon winced. "Understood," he agreed with a quick nod. "I just figured… you were the first one who came to mind when I thought about who she might be… emotionally involved with. The two of you have always had that dynamic. That tension."

"That's just because we used to be together. Not because we're together now."

"Okay. I'm going to trust you on that one. I'd look like a real idiot if I hired you to find out if she was having an affair, when it was you all along."

"It's not. If she's with someone… it's not me."

"I wondered because of some of the early symptoms of Huntington's too. Because the babies' father must have Huntington's, and some of the early symptoms… depression, anxiety, erratic behavior…" He trailed off.

Zachary cleared his throat and shook his head. "I don't have Huntington's Disease. I have PTSD, major depression, other stuff. I've always had it. Or at least, since I was a kid. It isn't from Huntington's."

Gordon nodded. He seemed relieved to have put this part of the conversation behind him. "We should discuss terms, then."

Gordon was a wealthy man, so Zachary had no problem charging him the high end of his usual rates, even though he would have been happy to surveil Bridget for nothing. Gordon agreed without trying to negotiate Zachary's rate.

So he was on the case.

He already knew Bridget's usual schedule and travel patterns. It would be easy for him to start surveillance.

No need to put an electronic tag on her car or to have Gordon install one under the mud mats or some similar out-of-sight location. If Bridget found a tracking device, she would know where it had come from. Zachary had used them in the past, so he couldn't afford to be caught doing it again.

But it was unnecessary. He'd be able to predict where she was going and to see any deviations from her usual practices. It was easy when he already knew her so well.

5

Zachary wasn't sure how to approach the usual dinnertime conversation with Kenzie. He decided right off the bat that he would not disclose who it was he was surveilling. She didn't need to know that. Gordon would expect confidentiality. If Kenzie knew that Zachary was following Bridget again, she might just blow a gasket. Even if it was a paid job.

When they sat down to eat and Kenzie asked him how his day had gone, he had prepared his answer and spoken in his usual voice, giving no sign it was anything other than a usual job. He'd done plenty of surveillance, after all. Couples who fooled around had been his bread and butter for a long time.

"Picked up a new case today," he told Kenzie casually. "Possible extra-marital affair. It will involve some surveillance. But from their usual schedules, I don't think there will be anything overnight. Just daytime."

Kenzie nodded. She didn't give him a second look. "Sounds good. Nice of them to keep their dalliances to the daytime for you."

Zachary gave a little laugh. "You'd be surprised. The majority of affairs that I have investigated have been during the day. When one spouse is supposed to be at work or looking after the kids. There aren't that many who are sneaking off to hotels at night. That would be too suspicious."

"If one of them travels a lot, though, they wouldn't have to worry about that."

"Yeah. When one travels a lot, they are usually *both* having affairs."

Kenzie speared a tomato from her salad and looked at him. "Do you get a lot of cases where someone who is having an affair hires you to see if their spouse is having an affair?"

Zachary nodded. "Frequently. People who are unfaithful tend to be more suspicious of their spouses."

"But isn't it sort of hypocritical to investigate your spouse, when you're the one messing around?"

"Sure. But they do it anyway."

Kenzie chuckled and shook her head. "We're a strange species."

"But I don't think, in this case, that the husband is having an affair. Could be, but I don't get that feeling from him."

"So what makes him think that his wife is having an affair?"

"Well... it actually might be a case that interests you. They have just found out that one of their children has Huntington's Disease. And neither parent has it."

Kenzie nodded eagerly. "And Huntington's is autosomal dominant. It doesn't skip generations."

"That's what he said."

"Has *he* been tested?" Kenzie leaned forward. "It tends to come from the father more often than the mother, for some reason. And sometimes it doesn't show up until late in life, so it can be missed if parents and grandparents died before showing any symptoms."

"He was tested. He doesn't have it."

"So then it has to come from the wife or she is having an affair. Has she been tested?"

"Doesn't want to be. She says there is no Huntington's in her family and, from what he knows of her family history, she's right. He's talked to her parents and they don't know of any cases of Huntington's Disease in the family."

"Well, I can see why he would be suspicious, then. I'll have to look up the genetics of Huntington's Disease, see if there can be sporadic cases, but I've never heard of any."

"Sporadic means that it just shows up without either parent having it?"

"Yes. A chance mutation rather than an inherited trait. Sometimes the cells make mistakes during fertilization or division. Something goes wrong in the transcription. We all have mistakes in our genes. It's not quite as clean as what you learn in high school genetics. All kinds of mistakes can happen during those processes. But there are redundancies so that, in most cases, one mistake doesn't cause any problems with your health."

Zachary nodded. "He didn't say anything about that. Just that one of the parents had to have Huntington's."

"It's a nasty disease."

"That's what he said. But they can have a lot of years before they are affected, too, so they could still have a good life."

"Yeah. It's usually a mid-life thing, but I know some cases don't show up until late in life."

"I wouldn't want to be the one making that decision," Zachary said, thinking about what Bridget and Gordon were going through.

Kenzie frowned. "What decision?"

"Oh… terminating the pregnancy."

"This was a prenatal test?"

"Yes."

"That's not usually done. I'm surprised."

"I guess it makes sense… if you can avoid having a child with a medical problem, but…"

"All kinds of ethics involved in eugenics. When is it okay to make decisions based on an embryo's or fetus's genes? At least we are past the point now when it is considered okay to kill or sterilize someone because they are less 'desirable,'"

Zachary shuddered at the thought. "But there are still medical practices where it is okay to decide not to treat someone."

Kenzie gave an uncertain shrug. "End of life care, maybe. Do not resuscitate orders. But other than that, doctors are required to treat people. You can't just decide not to help someone who needs it."

"But some people get prioritized. Triaged."

"In a mass disaster, sure. But again, that's based on who has the best chance of survival. Not personal feelings."

"Never?"

He could see the emotions chase across Kenzie's face. She wanted to say that of course not, doctors never made triage or end of life decisions based on their feelings toward patients. But she had probably seen situations where that was not the case. She was reluctant to share her thoughts on the subject.

"Not consciously, I don't think," she said slowly. "I'm sure that yes, people's prejudices do enter into care decisions sometimes. But doctors go through a lot of training, and there are ethics boards and all kinds of guidelines for making informed decisions."

"I've heard that the mortality rates for women are a lot higher for things like heart attacks."

"Yes. Probably more a function of men being studied more than women, though. Not doctors deciding that they'll just let the women die." Her tone was sarcastic. She knew she was exaggerating what Zachary had said, wanted to show him how ridiculous it was that a doctor would make *that* kind of decision.

"And Blacks have higher death rates with almost any kind of illness or injury."

Kenzie looked for a counter to this statistic. She ended up just shrugging and shaking her head. Zachary didn't believe that Blacks were somehow more medically fragile than whites. And he didn't think that their physiology was any different, unlike the biological differences between men and women. So why were their death rates higher?

"And look at the differences between the way someone with cancer is treated when they are fifty versus when they are eighty. Or the way that someone with autism or Down Syndrome is treated versus someone who is neurotypical. Some classes of people are considered more disposable than others. If you look at the guidelines for the people who decide how to prioritize people for transplants—"

"Don't talk to me about transplants," Kenzie said icily.

Zachary froze, his fork hovering, stopped between his plate and his mouth. He hadn't ever heard that tone from Kenzie before. They'd had their arguments and differences, but he'd never heard that level of controlled fury in her voice before. He just stared at her, not sure how to handle her reaction. He had clearly stepped over some line. He had thought that they were just talking about statistics. They often talked about medical science, especially death, because it was relevant to both of their professions.

"Uh…" Zachary shook his head. "I'm sorry…"

Kenzie stood up. She picked up her plate. She'd only eaten half of her dinner, and Zachary watched in shock as she scraped the rest into the garbage and left the room without another word. Clearly, the discussion was closed. They were done.

Zachary looked down at his plate, unsure what to do. He wasn't hungry. He had only been forcing himself to eat because it was suppertime and he knew that he had to continue to do so to get his weight up to where his doctor would be happy with it. He enjoyed talking with Kenzie and it was one of the things that helped him to get through a meal and to ensure he didn't forget all about eating. He didn't want to eat anymore, but he also didn't want Kenzie to think that he was refusing to eat because of the way she had reacted. He didn't want to make it a power struggle. He wasn't refusing to eat as a way to control her and shame her for what she had done; he just didn't want to eat any more.

He stayed at the table, listening for Kenzie. She went to her room, shut the door, and didn't come back out. She didn't bang around, slamming doors and drawers like Bridget would have done. Or call a friend to do something with her or go out on her own. She was still in the house, close by, but blocking Zachary out.

He sat at the table for another twenty minutes, until he was sure that she wasn't coming back out and wouldn't know how long he had stayed at the table after her. He got up, scraped his own plate, and put it in the sink. Then he changed his mind, rinsed it and put it in the dishwasher, and did the same with hers. It wasn't full enough yet to run the dishwasher, but he did it anyway, just to show that he was being a good partner and not expecting her to do everything for him. He was willing to help with the household. She probably wouldn't care about this while she was so angry with him, but the more he could do to appease her wrath, the better.

He reviewed the argument in his head, trying to find the point at which he had pushed it too far. She usually didn't mind his challenging what she had to say, giving different scenarios and figuring out if there was the possibility that a death had been homicide rather than an accident, or something like that. But there had been times. He had pushed it too far before, but this seemed to be a new line that he hadn't crossed before. Or the line itself had moved.

He went back to his computer, checked his email for anything new, and then returned to his surveillance plan.

He was going to follow Bridget. And not only was it okay, but he was actually being paid to do it.

When Kenzie didn't come out of her room for the rest of the evening, Zachary had to decide whether he would stay or should go back to his own apartment. If he were infringing on Kenzie's space, then he should leave. He wasn't sure if it were because he was in her private space too much, taking advantage of her hospitality. He didn't think he was, because she had given him no signals until then that anything was bothering her. But he should pay attention in case it was.

He couldn't exactly ask her whether she wanted him to stay or not. That would aggravate her further. He should be able to figure it out. He should be able to make a reasonable decision based on what he already knew. They had been together long enough.

Despite all of the criticisms he heard in his head, many of them in Bridget's voice, he wasn't sure how to make everything better. He couldn't read Kenzie's mind and know what he had done wrong or how he could fix it.

Eventually, he decided to sleep on the couch. He wouldn't go to her bedroom and incur her wrath for presuming he could sleep with her after a fight. He wouldn't go home and abandon her and make her think that she didn't matter to him or that the only reason he was there was to share her bed. Sleeping on the couch seemed like a reasonable compromise.

The warm blankets that they had used during the evenings that it got chilly beneath Kenzie's front window had been put away in the linen closet. He grabbed one and a spare pillow. Kenzie had a bedroom made up for guests, but she had never invited him to use it, so he didn't want to presume. He put the pillow down on the couch, lay down, and pulled the blanket over him.

He had slept on other couches plenty of times before. It wouldn't be any harder for him than sleeping on the bed.

Except that his thoughts were chasing around his head in an endless loop, asking what he had done wrong and why he wasn't fixing it.

He didn't know.

He would fix it if he could, but he didn't know what he had done.

6

_____

He had been tossing and turning for a while, trying to convince himself that he could sleep. It would be fine. He would sort things out with Kenzie in the morning when they had both had a chance to sleep.

But he wasn't having any luck in settling down the hamster wheel spinning in his head or the restless, skin-crawling feeling all over his body. He wanted to be with Kenzie, not fighting with her.

He heard her door open and went rigid, listening to see if she were getting up to the bathroom or for a snack to supplement her light dinner. She padded down the hallway toward him. Zachary wasn't sure whether he should pretend to be asleep so she didn't have to talk to him, or to see if she wanted to talk it out.

Which would she want?

Kenzie paused at the mouth of the hallway, looking toward him. She took a few steps toward him. "Hey. Are you still awake?" she whispered.

Zachary sat up. "Yeah."

She closed the distance between them and touched him on the shoulder. "Come on."

He hesitated at first. He'd been asking himself what to do, and now she had told him, but he didn't want to screw things up any worse. He'd had fights with Bridget that had ebbed and restarted several times over the next few days without warning. He remembered his parents having loud arguments and physical fights, subsiding to quiet, and then restarting again later. He didn't want to start talking with her and take the chance of saying the wrong thing.

She grasped his upper arm and gave a little tug. "Come. You don't need to sleep out here. Come cuddle."

"Are you sure?"

"Would I say to if I wasn't sure?"

Would he have asked if he'd known the answer?

"Okay." He followed her back to the bedroom and they got into bed, both moving slowly, unsure of the other's raw feelings, not wanting to upset the fragile truce.

Zachary settled with his arms around her and breathed in the scent of her hair. She was a strong woman. Passionate. She had a mind of her own and used it. They were bound to disagree on some things. And while he spoke from a place of ignorance, knowing only what he had heard and read other places, she was the trained medical professional. She knew how things really worked. She wasn't just going from medical dramas on TV and the screaming twenty-point spam-bait headlines of online news.

He should be more careful of what he said.

"It's okay," Kenzie said. "I was just tired. I overreacted."

"I'm sorry. I didn't mean… to step over the line."

"Shh." She kissed him and cuddled close, her face against his chest. "No more apologies. It's fine. And tomorrow is a new day."

Zachary let out a long, relieved exhale.

Tomorrow was a new day. And he would be more careful not to start any arguments.

The next morning, they both moved around each other carefully and spoke hesitantly, not wanting to renew the discussion of the day before or to challenge each other over their reactions. Zachary felt that he had done the right thing in choosing to stay there but to sleep on the couch. He hadn't deserted Kenzie after a fight, but had given her the space to decide for herself where she wanted him.

They didn't discuss his work, cheating spouses, or transplants. Zachary still wasn't sure what she thought of terminating a pregnancy due to a prenatal Huntington's Disease test. But it wasn't the time to discuss it.

"So, you start your surveillance today?" Kenzie asked.

Zachary nodded. His heart started thumping faster as he thought about it. "Yeah. I don't expect to find anything out the first day, but I'll start today and see what happens."

"You remember you have an appointment with Dr. Boyle today?"

They each kept their own schedules, but Zachary had recently given Kenzie access to his calendar, which she synced to her phone. He had marked any client appointments as private so that she could only see the block of time without seeing any labels or notes that might be confidential. He'd been good about keeping his therapy appointments with Dr. Boyle, so he wasn't sure why she was reminding him. Maybe she was just worried that he was going to get caught up in his surveillance and forget that he had to take a break to go to his appointment.

And the fact was, he didn't want to see Dr. Boyle. Not on a day when he was supposed to be surveilling Bridget. He would feel too guilty after the work that they had put into overcoming his compulsion to follow her. He was supposed to tell Dr. Boyle any time he broke his commitment not to stalk her location, which included just driving by her house and looking for her car or hoping to catch some glimpse of her in the yard. He couldn't very well tell Dr. B. that he had taken a retainer to surveil Bridget.

"I might have to reschedule this week," Zachary told Kenzie, pulling out his phone to look at his appointments. "I can't really pull out of the surveillance halfway through the day to see my therapist. I'll give her a call and see if we can swing a time when I don't need to be on this job."

Kenzie's forehead creased. She didn't like him waffling on an appointment. He'd skipped in the past when things were getting bad, and she probably saw it as a red flag.

"I'm okay," he assured her. "It isn't because I'm having problems. It's just a logistics thing."

"Well… I get that. But you need to make sure… don't let it go too long without seeing her. You don't want to lose the progress you have been making."

"No. Of course not. It's just one appointment. Everybody has to dip out now and then."

"Okay." She touched his arm briefly. "But don't lie to me. It's okay to tell me if you're having problems."

Zachary nodded, feeling even more guilty. He and Kenzie had been doing couples therapy to try to work through his issues with intimacy. They had talked a lot about open communication and role-playing, telling each other about their feelings or how to handle various challenging communication scenarios. And now he was intentionally not telling her something that he knew she would think was important.

But it was because of client confidentiality.

Not because he didn't want to tell Kenzie about Bridget.

7

Z achary knew that Bridget had been dealing with some pretty severe morning sickness during her pregnancy. Enough that it had landed her in the hospital at least once. She had not looked well when he had run into her at the gas station one day.

So he wasn't surprised not to see her leave the house until almost noon. She was a social person, and normally a morning person. She liked to get out early and be involved with her charities and other ventures. But that had probably ceased with her morning sickness.

He saw her exit the house from the back door. She took a few minutes to walk around the grounds, looking at the gardens with their colorful spring flowers. She looked pregnant now. She hadn't the last time he had seen her. She walked with an adorable little side-to-side movement, hand resting on her baby bump when she stopped to consider something, as if she were communing with the babies on what their thoughts were.

He felt a rush of endorphins when he saw her. He had been head over heels in love with Bridget Downy. Smitten with her. And the first little while had been great. She had been encouraging and attentive and had brushed aside his apologies and explanations about the difficulties that he had.

Those things that she had originally thought of as quirks or failings that he could fix had ended up consuming her. She couldn't believe that he couldn't just choose to stop being anxious or depressed, couldn't socialize with her friends without embarrassing her, would forget within five minutes which fork he was supposed to use for the salad course.

Despite her increasing impatience and vitriol, he still held on, loving her as much as ever, until she discovered she had cancer and concluded that Zachary had to go.

Maybe it was because it was cancer that had split him up that he still held out hope that her feelings would change. Cancer had split them up, and now that she was in remission, everything should go back to the way it was.

Even after everything, just seeing her still made his heart skip a beat and made him long for the life they'd had together, especially those early days in the first flush of love.

He watched her waddling slightly around the garden, fantasizing that they were together and the babies were his. He'd been mourning their antic- ipated children ever since the positive pregnancy test had turned out to be proof of cancer rather than of a child growing inside her. Seeing her obvi- ously pregnant was almost enough to convince him that the past two years had just been a nightmare and their life together was unbroken.

But he knew that it wasn't the case, and pain sliced through his chest at the disappointment and grief.

It would have to be enough just to watch her. He couldn't have her back again, but at least he could see her again. For the time that he had her under surveillance, he could watch her to his heart's content.

He was late getting home for supper, but Kenzie didn't say anything about it. She was looking tired and irritable and hadn't had a chance to start supper yet, so he suspected she had worked late too and just barely beaten him home.

"Kenz. You look beat. Can I take you out to dinner or order in? I'd offer to make you something, but... you probably don't want microwaved dinners."

Her expression softened. "You know what, ordering in would be so great. I don't even know where to start with making dinner tonight."

"What do you want? Pizza? Chinese?"

"Chinese."

Zachary went to the drawer in the kitchen that held takeout menus, and pulled out the one for the Chinese restaurant a few blocks away. They put their heads together and picked out the dishes they wanted to share. He wouldn't eat a lot of the Chinese food, but he enjoyed it.

"So you must have worked late too," Zachary said when the food had arrived and they sat down to eat. "Lots going on at the morgue today?"

She shrugged. "It's not like it's our busy time, but some cases just take longer than others, or are more... emotionally taxing."

Zachary nodded. "Accidents? Murder?"

She wouldn't give him any identifying details, but they had a mutual interest in homicide, something that wasn't usually accepted in polite society. Not the bloody details, anyway.

"Had a tough case today," Kenzie said, staring off into the distance. "A teenager with kidney failure. Those ones are always hard for me."

"Teenagers?"

She hesitated, then nodded. "Yeah. I guess."

Zachary had a feeling he had missed something. He thought back over the conversation and couldn't see anything else that he should have picked up on. But he sometimes let his thoughts wander and might have missed something she had said. Or he might have done something else, like taking the last dumpling when she wanted it. He scanned his plates and the remains of their dinner, but he hadn't taken the last of anything. In fact, he'd barely touched the food on his plate. And maybe that was bothering her. She thought he wasn't enjoying himself or wasn't putting the emotional energy into their time together.

"This was nice," he said, touching her hand for a moment, and then taking a couple more bites of the rice and the noodles.

"Yeah, I'm glad we did something. If you'd left me to make supper, it might just have been toast."

"I could have made *you* toast."

Kenzie smiled. "Yes, you are a pro toast-maker."

"Usually. As long as I remember to take it out and butter it." There had been more than one slice of toast tossed in the garbage after he'd left it to dry out in the toaster.

Kenzie gave a tolerant smile. "I think... I'm going to work on a few things in my office and have a bath. Head to bed early, so I'll be fresh for tomorrow."

Zachary searched her face to see whether she were telling him that she wanted him to go to bed with her, or that she wanted him to clear out so she could have a quiet evening on her own. He frowned, trying to unwind her words and decide what she wanted him to do.

"Should I head out...?" he asked tentatively.

"Head out? Where are you going?" Kenzie shook her head. "I thought this surveillance wasn't going to be night-time."

"No, not the surveillance. I just thought... you might want some space. I can head back to my apartment if you don't want someone else knocking around here tonight..."

"No. Stay." Kenzie put her warm hand on Zachary's thigh, which sent a sudden flush and goosebumps over him. "I didn't mean I'm kicking you out. I'd rather have someone around tonight."

Zachary nodded. His face was burning, wondering if she'd noticed his reaction to her touch. "Okay. You let me know if you need anything. And when you want to go to bed, I can come in for a while even if I'm not going to sleep right away."

"Yeah. That would be nice."

She bent to give him a brief kiss as she got up. "Can you clear up? Put things in the fridge and the plates in the dishwasher? And start the dishwasher?"

Zachary nodded. "Yeah. Of course."

She went down the hall to her home office. He didn't know what kind of work she was doing, whether she had something she needed to log in and finish for work, or she was balancing her bank account, or doing something else that he hadn't thought of. Not that it mattered, of course.

As he carried the takeout containers to the kitchen to put them away, he thought about his physical reaction to Kenzie's touch. It was a positive development.

He'd had such bad flashbacks after he was assaulted a few months back, flashbacks both to the assault and to abuse he'd experienced while in foster care, that he hadn't been able to react naturally to Kenzie. Everything was conscious and forced and, if he wasn't able to push through the flashbacks, he would dissociate, removing himself far from the situation until it was over. Not a great way to improve his relationship with his girlfriend.

So reacting to her touch was good. It was a positive sign. But he couldn't help worrying about the change. What if he was only feeling something because he had spent the day watching Bridget? What if it had been a reaction to being close to Bridget and Kenzie triggering it had just been a coincidence? What if the only person he could have a natural relationship with was Bridget? She was with someone else and would, he knew logically, never get back together with him again, however much he wanted it.

They'd had a good physical relationship, one that had not suffered with the same shortcomings as he had demonstrated in his relationship with Kenzie.

It wasn't fair. It just wasn't fair that he should have so many emotional problems when he was doing everything he was supposed to, going to all of his therapy appointments and doing couples sessions with Kenzie. Things should have been so much better with Kenzie. She was kinder and more understanding with him. She was willing to go at his speed. She was a much better match for him than Bridget had ever been.

So why did he continue to obsess over Bridget? Why was his relationship with Kenzie the one that suffered?

He retired to the living room and opened his laptop on the mobile desk. He took out the clipboard he had used to record Bridget's movements and started to transcribe them into a spreadsheet while they were still fresh in his mind. If he left the logs to pile up over several days, the information would all run together and if he had to decode his messy handwriting, it would be much harder.

Even just the process of transferring Bridget's movements from one medium to the other soothed him and made him feel better.

8

Zachary's phone vibrated. He slid it out of his pocket and put it on the desk beside him, but didn't look at it to see who had messaged him. He needed to stay focused on the job he was doing, or it would take him ages to get back into it. Once he was finished, he would reward himself with the distraction of a message from a friend or family member who was thinking of him.

Or maybe something from Gordon.

Zachary tried to remain focused on the task at hand, his attention starting to drift to Gordon. Was he calling already? Checking to see whether Zachary had been able to find anything out on the very first day of surveillance? It would take longer than that.

It was a struggle to keep himself from being sidetracked by these thoughts, but he got to the end of the log and saved the spreadsheet in a new computer folder set up under Gordon Drake's name. He wondered briefly if he should call it by a code name so that if Kenzie happened to glance at it, she wouldn't be suspicious of his activities. He needed to keep his client information private, especially when it was someone she knew.

He closed the file with relief and picked up his phone.

It was not a message from Gordon.

It was from Rhys, a young man whom Zachary had first encountered when he had investigated the death of his aunt, a woman Bridget had known when she was in treatment for her cancer. Even though Rhys's mother had gone to prison for her part in her sister's death, Rhys had stayed friends with Zachary.

He was selectively mute, saying only a word or two in the course of a day, and did not communicate with conventional language when he messaged Zachary or visited with him face-to-face. The trauma that he had suffered when his grandfather was killed when he was still a little boy had affected him deeply, stealing from him the ability to communicate easily.

Rhys often began a conversation with a GIF, meme, or other picture. His message to Zachary on this occasion was a sad-looking basset hound. It actually reminded Zachary strongly of Rhys's own face. His sad eyes would cheer briefly when he and Zachary were visiting, but would quickly fall back into the same sad, downward gaze as the dog's.

He tapped a message back to Rhys. *Hi. How's it going?*

It was a few minutes before Rhys wrote back again. He sent an emoji with a straight mouth, which Zachary assumed meant he was neither happy nor sad, or was still frustrated by his lack of progress in therapy and dealing with the memories that had recently resurfaced.

Before Zachary had any chance to react to the emoticon, Rhys had sent another picture. One that was becoming very familiar to Zachary.

Luke, the boy he and Rhys had helped to break away from the human trafficking syndicate that he had worked with since he was a teen younger than Rhys.

Zachary had only recently figured out—with Kenzie's help, admittedly —that Rhys was attracted to the older boy. There were plenty of reasons the two of them should not get involved with each other, from Rhys's age to the prejudices against biracial relationships that were still strong in Vermont, to the fact that Luke needed to do a lot more work to overcome his addictions and find his place in the world, unqualified for anything but the prostitution and recruiting that had been his only means of subsistence for the past five years.

But despite his many reservations about Rhys pursuing a relationship with Luke, he couldn't shut Rhys down and refuse to give him any information. Luke was living halfway across the state; it wouldn't be easy for Rhys to see him even if *he* knew where Luke was. And Luke's location was strictly confidential. The cartel thought that he was dead, and he needed to stay out of sight if he were going to have any chance of starting a new life.

Zachary sighed, blowing the air out between pursed lips. He couldn't tell Rhys much more than he had repeated the last few times they had exchanged messages.

Luke is okay. Still working on his recovery. He thought about what else to say. He wished he could give Rhys more. Information that would make Rhys see that Luke was going to be okay without him and that Rhys should be more concerned about his relationships with the kids his own age in his own school and neighborhood. It was so much safer.

But since when had either of them been able to make the safer, more reasoned decision? Rhys was a teenager. At an age when boys were not well-known for making choices that were good for them.

No news is good news, Zachary typed.

As long as Luke was working on his recovery, there was hope. Hope that maybe in a year or two when Rhys was older, Luke would be a safer option.

A thumbs-up graphic from Rhys. A safe reply. Like he was happy to hear what Zachary had told him and not that he would try to pry more information out of Zachary or try to make contact with Luke somehow. Zachary couldn't imagine how Rhys and Luke would connect without Zachary's facilitating it. Unless, of course, Luke decided to look for Rhys. Or gave up on recovery and went back to trafficking. Or both, maybe seeing if he could lure Rhys into the life as well. Zachary's stomach knotted at the thought.

Zachary's oldest sister, Jocelyn, was the one who was providing a home for Luke and trying to help him through the difficult transition period. She had personal experience in what Luke was going through and Zachary couldn't have found anyone better to help Luke. But she had warned Zachary. She had told him that staying away from the life would be difficult or impossible for Luke. It was just too tempting. It was the only life he had known since his grandma had died and, when people were struggling, they went back to what was familiar. Chances were, Luke would not succeed in separating himself from human trafficking. Even if he stayed away from his old organization, he would take up with someone else local and be entrenched again within a few days.

How's Grandma? Zachary typed to Rhys. Vera had been looking after her grandson since his mother had gone to prison. She had been the one constant in his life from the time that he'd been born.

"Zachary!"

Zachary was startled from his conversation with Rhys. He looked up to see Kenzie standing a few feet away from him. There were frown lines between her brows and, by her volume and the tone of irritation in her voice, it wasn't the first time she had tried to get his attention.

"Sorry. Sorry, I was focused on a conversation. With Rhys." Zachary turned the phone toward her, as if to prove what he'd been doing, even though he was sure she didn't really care. "What did you say?"

"You said you would put things away. In the kitchen. The food and the dishes…?"

Zachary pushed himself to his feet. He was pretty sure he had taken care of everything. He remembered putting a couple of cartons of food into the fridge. Maybe he'd just missed one thing—a forgotten soup bowl or condiment cup of sauce.

"I did… didn't I?" Zachary walked past Kenzie into the kitchen.

The dirty plates were still on the table, as were several takeout containers.

He had the illogical thought that someone must have come into the house and taken them back out of the fridge after he had put them away. Or Kenzie was trying to gaslight him. But he knew that wasn't the case. He had just forgotten or gotten distracted.

He grabbed a couple of containers and folded them closed, moving quickly so that he would get it done before Kenzie got too angry or he got distracted by something else.

"I really am sorry. I thought I had done it."

He shoved the containers into the fridge and went back to the table for more. Even after he had cleared all of the food away, Kenzie just stood there watching him, her arms folded in a closed-off gesture.

Zachary looked at her, then back around the kitchen to figure out why she hadn't relaxed yet.

The plates were still on the table. Zachary ran a stream of water over them and put them into the dishwasher.

Kenzie stalked into the kitchen and, before he could shut the dishwasher door, took a moment to rearrange the dishes he had put away. "You know they won't get clean if they are facing away from the spray."

"Yeah. Right. Sorry."

Kenzie pushed the door shut with a bang. She looked around the room and nodded. "Thank you."

Zachary grimaced. He held himself back from apologizing again. "Have you already had your bath?" he asked. "Are you ready for bed?" He turned his phone to look at the face to see what time it was. Sometimes when he was immersed in his work, he lost track of time.

"No." Kenzie pinched the fabric of her shirt between her finger and thumb to draw her attention to it. She was still wearing her work clothes. "You'd think that a detective might notice that I haven't bathed and changed for bed yet."

"Oh, right." Zachary laughed. "Yeah. You'd think, wouldn't you?"

9

————

After a few days on surveillance, Zachary strongly suspected that Bridget was not having an affair. That didn't mean she hadn't had one, of course. He would poke around discreetly to see what he could find out about any interests she might have had in the past year but, if she had been seeing someone, Zachary suspected they had broken it off and were no longer involved. It hadn't been long enough to be sure, but Bridget's routine seemed to have changed little since he had last tracked her whereabouts. She slept later and walked more slowly, but still went to the same places as she had previously—no noticeable deviations.

So what did that mean? Zachary brought it up with Kenzie as they got ready for bed. Zachary's thoughts were spinning too fast and he hoped that if he talked it through with her, his brain would settle down and he would be able to get to sleep quickly rather than lying awake for hours. He told her about the IVF, that the couple hadn't thought that they could conceive, and when his client had found out about the Huntington's Disease, he had assumed that his wife had been involved with someone else.

"But if she didn't have an affair, then what does that mean?" he asked Kenzie. "A mix-up at the fertility clinic?"

Kenzie nodded. She climbed into bed and applied cream to her hands and arms, rubbing the moisturizer in to keep her skin from getting chapped. "It does happen sometimes. You hear about a parent ending up with a child of the wrong color, or there's some other genetic red flag and they know the baby could not belong to both parents."

"Like Huntington's Disease."

"Not usually. Maybe a blood type mismatch, the wrong color of eyes, or obvious racial differences. But yes, Huntington's Disease could mean that there was a mix-up with either the eggs or the sperm. Most clinics have lots of controls in place now, so that the parents are shown the labels on the genetic material being used and can be assured that they haven't mixed up files or room numbers."

"But mistakes still happen."

"Yes, they do. Who knows how many have been made over the years that the parents never figured out."

"And it could be the eggs or the sperm. Either one."

"I don't know all of the ins and outs of running a fertility clinic. Maybe one is more likely than the other. But from a purely biological standpoint, then yes. They could have mixed up either the eggs or the sperm. Or they could have implanted the wrong embryos. So, three places they could have made a mistake."

"And if they used the wrong eggs, then the mother's body wouldn't... I don't know... reject the baby?"

"It isn't an organ transplant. It doesn't work the same way. The mother's body will accept an embryo whether it was created from her own genetic material or not."

Zachary nodded. "So I guess I'll talk to the clinic, find out on a no-names basis what their controls are, see where they might have screwed up."

"This client of yours... they haven't done any DNA testing to see if both parents are biologically related to the baby?"

"Is that something they can do before she is born?"

"They can. Most places will wait until after the baby is born, but it is possible to do it prenatally. I figured since they had done the Huntington's Disease test prenatally that they would check everything out before deciding whether to continue with the pregnancy."

"I think... the subject doesn't know that her husband has any doubts. She didn't want to do the Huntington's test herself, and I don't think he told her that he's had his done."

Kenzie nodded her understanding. "There is one other possibility. I hesitate to bring it up, but..."

"What?"

"There have been several recorded cases where… the fertility doctor has been using his own sperm."

Zachary stared at her. "You're kidding." He was repulsed by the thought. It felt like a violation. To fertilize the egg with his own sperm and implant it into a woman felt like an assault.

"Unfortunately, no." Kenzie stopped rubbing the flowery-smelling cream into her hands and looked off into space. She looked back at Zachary, then away again. "I guess it wasn't such a big deal back in the heyday, when they pioneered fertility treatment. Fresh sperm worked better than frozen, so doctors and students generously provided the genetic material in cases where women were using donor sperm anyway. What did it matter whose genetic material they used?"

"Well… I would think it made a difference to the parents. And maybe to the kid who goes through life not knowing his family medical history."

"Yeah. Can you imagine? I guess they didn't see anything unethical about it in the beginning. The science was new. They were setting up their own policies and procedures. There wasn't the regulation that there is now."

"But you think that maybe the doctor in this case could have… used his own stuff."

"It's just one of the possibilities if we are trying to narrow down what happened. It still happens every now and then."

"But now it's been determined to be unethical, right? So why would anyone take the chance?"

"Why does anyone break the law or society's taboos? Because they see a benefit, I guess."

Just like the psychologist Zachary had talked to when he was ten and they were evaluating him for the school and his foster parents. He observed that Zachary would break the rules if he saw it to be to his own advantage. Even though Zachary knew what the rule was, he would break it if he felt like he had a good enough reason.

And so did everyone, to some extent, the doctor assured him.

Some people broke the speed limit only when someone's life was in danger and they needed to get them to the hospital. Others thought it was okay to speed all of the time, as long as they stayed within ten miles per hour of the posted speed limit. Still others sped because of the thrill.

Did the same apply to a doctor using his own sperm to fertilize patients' eggs? Did he do it because he thought it was their best chance at maintaining a pregnancy? Because he wanted to spread his genetic material far and wide? Because it was a thrill?

"These doctors tend to have pretty big egos," Kenzie said. "I honestly think that some of them are doing it just because they think that their progeny will be superior to anyone else's."

"That's pretty... egotistical," Zachary admitted. "They really feel that way?"

Kenzie raised her eyebrows and nodded. "Believe it. Doctors in general are a very arrogant bunch. I've known some doctors..." Her focus drifted. Zachary was starting to wonder what was on her mind. She had seemed to be somewhere else a few times lately, and that was usually his domain.

"Doctors who would do that?" he prompted.

"Doctors who... would do anything they thought they could get away with. Anything to get better results, to exercise their power over death. Or in this case," her eyes focused back on Zachary again, "power over life."

He nodded slowly. He could see how that could be intoxicating. Power over life and death? What could prove their superiority better than that?

Zachary took one last look at his phone screen before putting it on the side table.

"So... how would someone figure that out? How do you know that the doctor has been... providing his own samples?"

Kenzie lay down beside him, her body relaxing. "In the cases that I've heard of, they have done private DNA testing, like for genealogical research, then submitted it to one of the public databases to see who popped up as relatives."

Zachary knew some of the ins and outs of that kind of testing from Heather's case. He nodded. "Okay, sure."

"And before those databases were around, it was a little more difficult. Finding other patients of the same clinic or doctor and seeing if they had the same doubts, or if the children had the same traits. Easier with some traceable trait like celiac disease. They would need to gather all of the data they could before anyone would look at it. Because who would think that one of these eminent doctors could do something like that?"

Zachary shut off the lamp that was still on beside him, then cuddled close to Kenzie, rubbing her back and hoping it would release some of the stress she seemed to be under.

"Is everything okay with you?" he asked in a low voice, nearly whispering. "And between us?"

She snuggled and didn't say anything. Zachary decided just to hold her. If she didn't want to talk about whatever was on her mind, that was fine. As long as she knew he was there and was ready to help or just to sympathize.

His mind wandered to his surveillance of Bridget, picturing her getting in and out of her car, the glimpses he had caught of her as she walked into different business establishments or met with friends to socialize. It still blew his mind that she was pregnant. She, who had said that she would never ruin her body by getting pregnant. He'd always thought that he'd eventually be able to talk her into it, but he hadn't.

Gordon had some real skills.

"Zachary?" Kenzie murmured.

"Mmm-hmm?"

"There's something I want to tell you."

Z achary's chest and stomach muscles tightened into hard knots. He tried to ease his breathing. She hadn't said it was something to do with him. But what else could it be?

She had found out about Bridget.

Or she had decided that things just weren't working between them.

She had given it a good long run, but Zachary couldn't shed all of his problems and conform to the person she thought he should be and, like Bridget, she'd decided to stop wasting her time.

"Yeah?"

"Do you remember a long time ago, I told you that I don't have any siblings?"

It was such a tangent from where Zachary thought she was going that he didn't answer at first. He tried to remember when he had told her this. Back at the beginning, when they had just started to see each other? He had probably told her about his five siblings and many foster families, and she had told him that she was an only child. Totally different life experiences.

He couldn't remember it happening, but she clearly did.

"I don't remember specifically," he said cautiously.

"Well, I did… and it's not quite the truth."

How could it be only partially true? A step- or half-sibling? A child who had been adopted out? Been disinherited?

"Okay. Do you want to tell me about it? You don't have to."

"I think I want to." Kenzie squirmed, and Zachary tried to give her room while at the same time keeping her close and letting her know that he was there for her.

He nodded, even though she might not be able to see him in the darkness of the room. He waited, allowing her to take her own time. Kenzie was quiet for a while, and he wondered if she were going to fall asleep without telling him whatever her family secret was.

"The case that we had this week reminded me of my sister," Kenzie said. She sniffled a little. "Amanda."

"Amanda. That's a pretty name. I like it."

"She was quite a bit younger than me, and we were really different in our personalities, but she was like… she was more like my own baby than my sister. I loved to help taking care of her when she was little. She was never my bratty little sister, you know? We never had that dynamic."

"I bet you were a great big sister."

"With Amanda I was. I don't know if I would have been with someone else with a different personality. But with Amanda… she was my baby sister."

She spoke of Amanda in the past tense. She clearly wasn't around anymore. "What happened?"

Kenzie had helped Dr. Wiltshire with a few cases that week; he wasn't sure which one had bothered her and reminded her of her sister.

"It was her kidneys. She had kidney disease. Started when she was really young. She couldn't keep up with her friends, was tired all the time. And then… they figured out that her kidney function was really low."

Zachary remembered the scar on Kenzie's abdomen. He rubbed the spot above her hip gently. She'd told him once it was a surgical scar, but she'd never said what it was for. He'd thought it might have been an appendectomy.

Kenzie nodded. He felt her head moving against his chest. "Yeah… as soon as I was eighteen, I donated a kidney to her. Mom and Dad wouldn't let me do it when I was younger, even though I wanted to. As soon as I could sign the permissions myself, I arranged to give her one of my kidneys."

"That was really generous."

"I would have given her both. Seriously. I loved her so much and wanted her to get better."

"Did the donation... not take?"

"No, it worked. She got better and could do the things she wanted to and not have to sit at the hospital on dialysis. For a while. But a few years later... well, it eventually failed as well. That happens sometimes. Donated organs don't always have the same lifespan as they would normally."

"I'm sorry."

"Yeah." She was quiet, squirming around to tuck her head into the hollow of his neck, breathing warmly on his throat. She smelled and felt so good. If he could just take that moment and stretch it out...

"Anyway. I'm sorry I told you I don't have any siblings. Because I did. I just... haven't shared that with very many people. I'm a private person. Too private, sometimes."

"You're allowed to share or not share, it's up to you."

They had agreed to that in therapy. Mostly in relation to Zachary. If she asked him something and he didn't feel comfortable answering, he was allowed to just tell her instead of trying to find an excuse. And the same applied to Kenzie. It was an equal, two-way relationship.

"And back around when you were working on the Lauren Barclay case, when I got mad at you for asking about that doctor wanting to screen organ donors based on what they said on social media..."

She had blown up at him. Zachary hadn't had any idea why she had been so upset. Except that they were on a break and he had gone to her with a question that he could have asked somewhere else. He'd thought it was because she didn't want to be his go-to for answering all medical questions when they weren't even together.

"That was... because of Amanda? Could she... not get another transplant because of something like that?"

"No, not something quite that close. Just... ethics and organ donations and some of the stuff that I went through with my dad..."

"Sorry. I didn't know."

"Of course not. You couldn't have any idea about it because I hadn't shared it. I can't blame you for something you didn't know."

"Well," Zachary rested his face against her hair, breathing in her scent, "you apologized later and we worked things out."

"It's like Dr. Boyle says, though, if we're open with each other… we don't have to try to read each other's minds."

"Yeah." He wiggled around a little, trying to get more comfortable. "And this girl at the morgue this week…? She reminded you of Amanda?"

"Yeah. So young. It was kidney failure, and something about her… just reminded me of Amanda." Kenzie shook her head a little. "It was such an awful time, Zachary. Losing Amanda and then finding out that my father had arranged for… a gray market medical procedure that contributed to her death."

"Ouch. That's why you're estranged from your parents?"

"I'm not exactly estranged. I'll still talk to them. But… I don't really have anything to do with them most of the time. My mom's personality is so different than mine; I can't really talk to her about anything I'm interested in. Only her fundraisers and social appearances. That gets tedious. My dad and I are more alike, but our opinions, especially on medical stuff…" Kenzie trailed off. Zachary rubbed her back.

He expected her to keep up the conversation, but in a couple of minutes he could tell that she had drifted off to sleep.

11

Zachary had never been to the Westlake Women's Health Center. Bridget had banked her eggs before her cancer treatment, but Zachary had not been welcome to go along with her. At that point, she had already started the break with him. Hints about how she couldn't handle any extra responsibilities or focuses. That he was taking too much of her time and energy. She needed to focus on her treatment and recovery, not on Zachary. But he was not welcome to go to appointments with her. He wasn't allowed to be a part of her medical decisions.

He thought at first that she didn't realize what she was doing, pushing him away but, eventually, she had made it clear. He came home to find his belongings packed into bags at the front door. Bridget had removed her wedding ring. When he had tried to talk to her about it, she just shook her head.

"It's not working out, Zachary. You know it's not. We're not happy together anymore. I need to focus on my treatment. You need to move on with your life."

"We can still make it work," Zachary had objected. "I thought we'd been doing better. I'm not going to abandon you in the middle of cancer treatment. I can help you."

"You can't help me. You can't even help yourself."

Zachary didn't think that being able to address all of his issues was necessary for him to help Bridget, but she was firm. She didn't want him there. She didn't want him anywhere near her.

"Can I help you, sir?" The young woman at the reception desk was looking at him expectantly.

"Oh. I was wondering... my wife and I have been talking about maybe... you know, trying some fertility treatments. Seeing if we can get pregnant that way. But she's nervous about all of this..." Zachary made a motion to indicate the clinic. "She's worried about mistakes, privacy, that kind of thing. I'm wondering if I could get a tour, sort of an orientation of how it all works. So I can help show her there wouldn't be any mistakes."

The receptionist gave him a reassuring smile. "Of course. Can I get your name?"

"Do you get asked this a lot?" Zachary asked. "People must have concerns."

"Yes, people naturally want to know how things are going to be handled when they have a procedure. It's a very personal thing, and our patients want to know that they will be handled with respect and discretion and that their genetic material will be well cared for." She stepped around the desk to shake his hand. "I'm Carole. And I didn't catch your name?"

"John," Zachary told her. "John Smith. And I'm not kidding, it really is. People always think I'm making a joke."

"You wouldn't be the first John Smith we had through here," Carole laughed. "Why don't you come with me to our welcome room. I'll give you some literature to look over while I see who is available to show you around."

Zachary was impressed. It would appear that she'd spoken the truth when she said that people often had similar questions.

"Thanks. That would be great."

He followed her to a small boardroom, where she provided him with a cup of fresh coffee and laid a glossy folder full of brochures and other pages in front of him.

"You don't have to read all of this," Carole gave him a pleasant smile, "It's just for your future reference, and something to get you started. Trust me; nobody reads it all."

Zachary was glad of that. It was an impressive amount of literature. Most of it would have little to do with his investigation. He looked through the various pages as he sipped his coffee and waited for his tour guide to make an appearance. He pulled out his phone and glanced through his mail and his social networks.

He remembered messaging with Rhys, and pulled up the stream to see whether he had left the thread too abruptly and whether Rhys had posted anything after Kenzie had pulled him from the conversation. He tapped out a quick message to let Rhys know that they could talk some more later, so if Rhys was feeling like he'd been brushed off, he would be reassured.

The door opened, and a man in a white lab jacket entered. He had on a collared shirt and dress slacks underneath it. He wore glasses with thin black rims and carried a clipboard. Zachary's overall impression was of a busy, competent doctor.

"Mel Banks," the man introduced himself, holding out a hand to Zachary as he approached the table. "John?"

"Yes. Hi." Zachary shook.

"So how can I help you today?"

Zachary again ran through his patter about his wife, shrugging and motioning at the clinic.

"Of course," Banks agreed. "People are entrusting us with one of their most precious resources. That isn't something we take lightly. I'm happy to give you a tour, but you should come back with your wife so she can see it for herself. That will help to put her mind at ease."

"Yeah, I'm sure she'll come next time. But we live out of town, and she wasn't feeling up to it today. I didn't want to put it off, and had some time today, so…"

"Well, why don't we talk about your journey so far. Do you have any other children?"

"No. We decided to start trying about a year and a half ago, and it was fun at first and we thought that everything would just happen naturally, but… well, it didn't, obviously. By the time a year was up, my wife was getting anxious and had me set up an appointment with a specialist. I forget the name… it's foreign-sounding. Starts with B, or maybe an M? She would be able to tell you."

"Mbatha?" Banks suggested.

Zachary lucked out on that one, beginning with both an M and a B. He had learned that people would go out of their way to provide missing names, especially if you said that they sounded foreign. Throw in a couple of possible starting sounds, and they would throw all the names you could possibly need.

"That must be it," Zachary said with a nod. If challenged on it later, he could say that he had thought that was the right name, but he wasn't very good with names and it was his wife's domain. He could easily have mixed up two foreign-sounding names. It was understandable.

"And what did Dr. Mbatha find? He did a full fertility workup for the two of you?"

Zachary nodded. "Yeah, and he said that probably if we did this...." He indicated his surroundings again. "There was a specific procedure that he recommended. He said we had a good chance of success. I'm afraid... I didn't get all of the medical details." He rolled his eyes toward the ceiling and shrugged his shoulders. "It all makes me a little uncomfortable, you know. All the stuff about women's reproductive systems. I mean... I know my part, but the rest... that's kind of her job. She's the one who knows all of the... female side."

Banks laughed. "You're certainly not the only one who feels that way," he assured Zachary. "We're raised to see women's bodies as something dirty. Messy periods, water breaking, things coming out of orifices. We do our part, like you say, and try to avoid thinking of the rest."

Zachary nodded, his eyes down.

"But you're here. That's a good step. Good initiative, especially since your wife isn't with you. Do you have specific concerns, or is she working...?"

"The timing wasn't good for her, and we live out on a farm. I think... she wanted me to ask the initial questions. She says doctors talk down to women. They're more likely to answer men's questions without treating them like they're ignorant. She's really smart, you understand, but men treat her like she's a child and doesn't know what she's talking about."

Banks sighed. "Well, I hope you will assure her that she won't be treated that way here. I understand it goes on, but... we are very patient-oriented here. We will treat her questions with the same respect as yours."

"I'll tell her. Although... maybe I wasn't supposed to tell you that part. I'll have to think about how to bring it up."

"You take her home those brochures and tell her she can call with any questions. If she prefers to talk to a nurse or a female doctor, of course that can be arranged."

Zachary nodded. "Okay, yeah. I can do that."

"Good. Do you have any questions before we begin the tour? What are your concerns?"

"There was an article we saw, well, several articles, actually, about cases where the wrong sperm was used. Parents ending up with children who they were not both biologically related to. My wife doesn't want to adopt or to have someone else's baby. She is very determined about having a baby that is genetically ours. So… I suppose we want to know what controls are in place to make sure that doesn't happen."

Banks was nodding along seriously. "Of course. It's perfectly understandable she would be concerned about it. Those stories do hit the news every now and then, and we always experience repercussions here. There is an increase in calls from patients; we see a downturn in the number of people signing up for procedures. It's really too bad, because those cases are very few and far between. We have never had a mistake at this clinic. There have been no lawsuits over the wrong genetic material being used. Never, in the two decades this clinic has been open."

"That's great. I'm glad to hear that."

"We are very careful, and of course whenever a story like that comes out, we do an audit of our procedures, try to find any weaknesses. Find out the details of how the mix-up came about at the other clinic and make sure there is no way the same thing can happen here. And it hasn't. We're always doing our best to stay ahead of the game and be absolutely rock-solid on our procedures."

Zachary gave a grateful nod and smile. But of course, he would hear the same thing from any clinic he went to. They would all claim to be rock-solid in their procedures. What doctor or businessperson would admit to being sloppy and frequently trying to recover from or cover up mistakes?

"Let's take a walk around, then," Banks offered, "and we'll talk about procedures and audits that we have in place. I'll show you everything."

Banks led the way. Zachary followed, sometimes keeping up with Banks and sometimes lagging behind to have a second look at something or to see just how good their security procedures were.

12

"Samples are collected in vials that are already labeled with patient identification numbers," Banks showed Zachary the cupboard where the collection vials for the day had been set aside for use. "Each donor is asked to verify the number before beginning. Names are not used for privacy reasons."

"And do people check the numbers? What if they can't remember what their number is or would be embarrassed to look it up?"

"Well…" Banks looked troubled at this suggestion. "We find that people are generally concerned enough about avoiding any mix-ups that they will check." He shook his head. "It's impossible for us to know whether someone has really verified it or not. But that's our procedure. It helps to… protect everyone."

Which wasn't true, of course. It was designed to put the onus on the patient. A way for the clinic to cover their butts. It protected them, not patients who were too excited, nervous, or embarrassed to remember their patient number or to look it up.

"We ask the patient to check at the beginning of every procedure," Banks went on. "Every time we collect a sample or remove it from storage, the patient must verify it."

"What about in the lab? They can't verify everything that is done there."

"Good point," Banks admitted. "Of course they are not involved in any of the lab procedures, washing or prepping specimens, fertilization, any of the work done in vitro. We do have procedures in place in the lab as well, to ensure that a worker never has more than one couple's genetic material out at the same time, and there is always a second worker to check the numbers to ensure that they have the right ones."

Good if they wanted to prevent cross-contamination or innocent mistakes. Not something that would help if a doctor were interested in spreading his own seed.

"What kind of security is there for samples while they are in storage?"

"We have excellent security. Nothing is accessible by the public at any time. Someone could not break in here and steal embryos, for example. People are often worried about that. Those embryos are your potential children, and we treat them like your most priceless possession."

"So who does have access to them?"

"Only medical professionals. No couriers or janitors or any non-professional staff would have access to the freezers. Or to fresh specimens."

"But any of the doctors or nurses would be able to access any of the samples."

Banks cocked his head, frowning. "Well, yes, they would be able to. They need to be able to access them for procedures."

"And what procedures are in place to make sure that a doctor couldn't access them for their own purposes?"

"What do you mean? The only reason they would need them is to perform a procedure for you."

"What if he wanted to… sabotage them. Or contaminate them. Swap them. I don't know. It seems like these things could happen."

"Our doctors and staff are professional and very well trained. Something like that… would never happen."

Zachary took a deep breath. He tried to look reassured, but he certainly was not. While they might be protecting themselves from accidental mix-ups, contaminations, or lawsuits, there didn't seem to be any procedures in place to prevent intentional tampering. They just trusted that no one would try.

"We have check-out procedures," Banks said tentatively. "Anyone removing a sample has to put their name on the sign-out sheet."

"Who controls access to it?"

"To...?"

"To the sign-out sheet. Or the freezers or cupboards or wherever stuff is stored."

"Well, there's just a clipboard with a log, so we can keep track of who has accessed what..."

"So it's just voluntary. You expect people to comply."

"Yes. We've had no trouble that way. There wouldn't be any reason for people not to sign the log..."

Zachary could think of a few. The rule-followers would be diligent about always signing the log, but others would be too lazy or distracted, or willfully disobey the rule to avoid detection.

"I guess that's good," he acknowledged. He didn't want to put Banks on the defensive or for him to think that Zachary was anything other than what he claimed, a potential client who just wanted to make sure that the clinic was following some kind of procedure that would help prevent mix-ups.

Banks nodded.

As they continued the tour, Zachary watched for locks and other security measures, counted the number of people he saw back and forth, and assessed what other security measures they had in place. There didn't appear to be any surveillance cameras to monitor the staff. And despite what Banks had said about the janitorial staff not being able to access the freezers, he didn't see any measures that someone with a bump key or set of lock pickers could not get past. The janitorial staff probably had master keys for everything in the clinic anyway. Who else kept the lab and the sample room clean?

After the visit to the clinic, Zachary, as John Smith, promised to come back with his wife when she was available. He returned to his surveillance of Bridget. By this time, he didn't expect to see her doing anything other than her usual meetings and social events. She seemed to have cut back on them, maybe finding the schedule too tiring now that she was pregnant. There did not appear to be another man in her life. Gordon would be happy to hear that.

But he had not answered the question as to who had fathered the babies. Had it been Gordon? A mix-up at the clinic? An intentional switch at the clinic? If it was the result of a mix-up or intentional switch, then which had been swapped? Bridget's eggs or Gordon's sperm?

Which of them was a biological parent to the twins?

And who had Huntington's Disease?

1 3

While he was watching for Bridget to come back out of the grocery store with her purchases, his phone rang. Zachary didn't generally answer while he was on surveillance, not wanting anything to distract him from the job. But he didn't think there was any danger of his getting distracted from Bridget. And he didn't think she was going to do anything suspicious anyway. Even if she were having an affair, why would she meet her fling at the grocery store?

It was Mr. Peterson, one of Zachary's old foster parents and the only one he had ever kept in touch with. Even though he had only been with the Petersons for a few weeks, their relationship had survived the decades. Mr. and Mrs. Peterson had divorced a few years after Zachary had been with them, and Lorne Peterson had gone on to meet Pat, the younger man who would become his permanent life partner. They had been together for so long that it was hard to remember sometimes that Mr. Peterson had ever been with anyone else. It seemed like something that had happened in a different life entirely.

"Hi, Lorne." Zachary tried to call Mr. Peterson by his first name like he was always told to but, in his mind, he was always going to be Mr. Peterson.

"Zachary. Is this a good time? I should probably have waited until the evening."

"You never know when I might be working in the evening anyway. This is fine, or I wouldn't have answered."

"Good. How are you and Kenzie getting along?"

"We're fine. Maybe even better than usual," Zachary said cautiously. Yes, he still screwed stuff up regularly, but he felt like he and Kenzie were getting closer in their relationship. Something that was evidenced by Kenzie telling him about Amanda and hinting at a few things about her parents. She had always kept those things out of their relationship before.

"That's wonderful to hear. You know how we feel about Kenzie. I think the two of you are a great match."

"Yeah. Things are working out well right now. I hope… they'll continue that way…" Zachary was anxious about putting these thoughts into words. He was always afraid that saying something aloud about his relationship would somehow jinx it. He didn't want to take any chances on messing up anything about his relationship with Kenzie.

The knot in his stomach reminded him that he had already taken a rather large step that he knew could cause a rift between him and Kenzie. She would not be at all happy to hear that he had taken a job from Gordon. Even less so when she discovered it involved him surveilling Bridget.

"Zachary?"

"Oh, what? Sorry, I was just…" he trailed off and left space for Mr. Peterson to just pick the conversation back up again, not wanting to explain or give an excuse.

"It's fine. I'm wondering about next weekend. If you would be able to come for a visit."

"Uh, sure, I think so. Let me just look at the calendar for a minute." Zachary picked up his phone and switched over to the calendar app. "Yeah, that looks fine."

"And how about Kenzie? Could she come too, or is she working on the weekend?"

"Might be working. I'll have to ask her."

Though he had given Kenzie the information she needed to add his calendar to her phone, she hadn't given him hers. That didn't particularly bother Zachary. She might have confidential stuff on her calendar to do with her job. Or they might not allow her to share her calendar with people outside the medical examiner's office as a matter of policy. He hadn't asked. He didn't need someone else's information on his phone; it would only distract him from his own. If he didn't keep his calendar simple and clean, his dyslexia made it impossible to read and comprehend it.

"Well, if she can come, she is invited as well."

"Can they come?" Zachary heard Pat's voice in the background and thought he detected a note of excitement.

"What's going on?"

It had been at Mr. Peterson's house that he'd met Joss, his older sister, a reunion set up by Tyrrell and Heather, the two siblings he'd already met. And he still hadn't met the youngest two siblings, so he wondered whether they were trying to set up yet another reunion. He wasn't opposed to it, but wasn't sure he liked them doing it behind his back. They didn't want him to feel anxious about it ahead of time, but he preferred to have some time to mentally prepare.

"Pat's mother and sister are going to be over," Mr. Peterson explained. "He'd like you to meet them. We talked about that before… Christmas time…?"

Zachary remembered. Pat's father had died the previous year, and he had finally been able to reconcile with his mother and sister, after being shunned by the family for many years for being gay.

"Yeah. Of course. I remember."

"She wants to meet her grandson," Pat called out.

Zachary chuckled. He'd never had a grandparent that he could remember. He didn't know if his parents had been estranged from their own families, or if they were orphans, but he didn't know any blood relations other than his siblings in his biological family. And while Pat had never been one of Zachary's foster fathers, he and Mr. Peterson had both been the only ones in a parental role since Zachary had aged out of care.

"I would be glad to meet them."

"He's up for it," Mr. Peterson relayed to Pat.

"Perfect! I'm going to make ravioli. No one in my family was ever a cook. They haven't had anything but the canned stuff."

"They'll love it," Zachary told Lorne. "Is he making the cheese ones?"

"Is that a request?"

"If he feels like it." Zachary wasn't about to insist. He wouldn't be eating much, and Pat should make something that his family would enjoy, not cater to Zachary.

"Zachary wants the cheese ones," Mr. Peterson reported to his partner.

Zachary laughed and didn't try to correct him. There wasn't any point.

Bridget picked that moment to leave the store with her cart of groceries. Or rather, one of the grocery store staff was pushing Bridget's cart of groceries.

Zachary studied the store clerk as he and Bridget walked across the parking lot to Bridget's yellow Volkswagen bug. He reached for a camera with a telephoto lens and carefully focused on the man pushing Bridget's cart.

Did he think the man was the father of Bridget's babies? Zachary mentally shook his head at the thought. He did not. But his full report would need to include pictures of anyone he saw Bridget with, especially if it were out of the ordinary.

Bridget walked slowly, and halfway to the car she stopped to rest, pressing her hand against the small of her back. The man pushing the cart stopped and waited, chatting with her. They moved on again, and Bridget climbed awkwardly into the car as the man unloaded the groceries into her car.

Just someone helping her with the physical chore of getting her groceries from one place to the other when she was already carrying a heavy load.

Zachary snapped several pictures, then put the camera back to the side.

"Sorry," he said, realizing that Lorne was still on the line and was probably wondering what was going on. "Needed to get a couple of pictures. I'm sort of on surveillance."

"You told me you could talk," Mr. Peterson reproached. "I don't want to keep you if you're on the job."

"It's fine. She was in the store, so I was just waiting."

"But she's out now, so I'll let you go. I'll email you."

"Okay. But it's a yes to dinner. I'll make it work, whether Kenzie comes or not."

"Excellent. Pat is eager for them to meet you."

14

Zachary waited until after supper to bring up his questions, giving Kenzie all of his attention while they ate. She seemed to have had a better day at work, whether that was because she hadn't had to work any more on the teenager who had died of kidney failure or because she had opened up to talk to Zachary about it. He was glad that she seemed to be less stressed about it.

"I'll be reporting to my client on the surveillance so far," he told Kenzie as they cleared the dishes, uncertain whether it would lead into what he wanted to discuss or not.

"Yeah? How has it been going? Is she having an affair?"

"I don't think so. Haven't seen any sign of it."

"She could have had one a few months back and ended it since," Kenzie suggested.

"Yeah, it's possible. I'll see whether I can find anything out, but I don't know if there is anything there."

"Which means you're back to whether it was a problem at the fertility clinic she had her procedure done by."

"Yeah. Spent some time there this afternoon checking out security procedures."

Kenzie motioned to the couch, and she and Zachary sat down. "What was it like? I haven't ever been to a fertility clinic."

"Nice place. Dark wood and artwork in the waiting room. Looks more like a lawyer's office than a doctor's. Except for the pictures of babies on the walls, of course."

"So that's the outside. That doesn't really tell you what the inside is like."

"No. Good staff. Prepared to answer questions and do an orientation."

"And...?"

"The fellow who gave me a tour... he looked like a doctor, but he didn't introduce himself as one. Just first and last name. When was the last time you heard a doctor do that?"

"Never," Kenzie said, shaking her head immediately. "Doctors expect to be addressed as 'doctor' even if they aren't practicing anymore. It's a big deal. You don't 'mister' them. And even if one introduced himself to me with his first name, I would probably still call him doctor. It's just one of those things."

"Yeah. So he must not have been a doctor, right?"

Kenzie considered for a few moments. "I can't see it. Even if they're trying to make people feel relaxed and at home... people will be more reassured by someone with the title of doctor, even if he says 'Call me Paul' or whatever after introducing himself. If I was getting an orientation—as a patient? Did you say you were a patient?"

"Yes. That my wife and I were trying to get pregnant and had been referred there by our specialist."

"If I was getting an orientation for the fertility clinic, I would expect to be taken around by a doctor, not some office lackey. It would make me feel better. I would want to know that I was in good hands, that the doctor was there to help me, and I wasn't just going to be pawned off on the receptionist or a nurse."

"So you agree. Not a doctor."

"No. I wouldn't think so. If he was, he would have told you. So what was he?"

"I'm not sure. He didn't give me a title, just his name. He was dressed like a doctor."

"Scrubs?"

"No. A white jacket over dress shirt and slacks. You don't see lab workers or nurses dressed like that, do you?"

"I wouldn't expect to."

Zachary rubbed his jaw, thinking about the day and everything he had learned at the clinic.

"What was it like?" Kenzie asked. "Do you think it could have been an innocent mistake?"

"They have pretty strict procedures. For the routine stuff. So no... I don't think it was an accidental switch."

"What does that mean, for the routine stuff?"

"Collecting samples, doing implantations, or whatever it is called. They have procedures for all of that stuff, lots of checking ID Numbers on the tubes."

"Okay, but...?"

"But I couldn't see any controls to prevent people from sabotaging samples. Contaminating them, replacing them, that kind of thing. They have a checkout log, but just a paper sign-out sheet. Nothing that tracks it electronically, no person who administers it. Not like the evidence room at the police station, where someone makes sure you are authorized to take out a sample and keeps track of everyone who has touched it."

"Well, I wouldn't expect them to have anything as stringent as the police department. But... I see your point. Preventing intentional sabotage would be different from preventing accidental mix-ups or cross-contamination. But someone like we talked about, a doctor with a god complex, he's not doing it by accident. It doesn't matter what ID Number is on the collection vial."

"Yeah. That's what I thought too. And the security controls to make sure that no one other than the medical staff can access the specimens are pretty lax. A locked door that pretty much any petty burglar or someone watching online videos could get past. It's not secure. They may say that they haven't had any burglaries or any mix-ups in all of the time that they've been in operation, but I can't just take their word for that."

"If there was a burglary, you can at least check that with the police department. They should be able to tell you whether that part is true or not."

"Yeah. But we're not actually interested in whether anyone has stolen anything, but whether they have swapped, replaced, or contaminated anything. And that could be done by someone inside or outside the clinic."

"What are you going to do? Will your clients do DNA testing for paternity and maternity?"

Zachary shrugged. "I think he will. The wife... I don't know."

"If she's not having an affair, then what is the downside? She finds out whether the baby is hers or not. And her husband's or not. Wouldn't she rather know before making the decision to terminate or not?"

"I'm not sure. She didn't want to do the Huntington's test. I mean, she did DNA testing for the baby, but not herself. The husband went and did his own. But she didn't want to know. She said it wasn't from her because it wasn't in her family. Would she want to find out for sure that the baby isn't hers?" Zachary shook his head slowly. "I don't think she does. But I don't know. Emotions..."

"Emotions aren't logic," Kenzie agreed. "Just because something seems logical to us, that doesn't mean someone would accept our recommendation. There are all kinds of other factors involved. Past experiences, fears, worries about the relationship, how it might affect the child's life. A lot of sticky emotional issues get involved."

Zachary nodded. If it were him, he didn't think he would want to know. He would want to have the child, to raise it as his own whether she were biologically related to him or not.

But he wasn't like Bridget. Gordon said she had been talking about terminating before she even knew the results of the DNA test. That sounded more like the Bridget he knew. Regretting the decision to get pregnant and looking for a way out. He didn't know how Gordon had talked her into it in the first place.

It would make sense to him that Bridget would want to have the babies' parentage tested, even if she hadn't wanted her own DNA tested for Huntington's Disease. Maybe Gordon could gently talk her into it.

If the babies weren't his, then he would concede to Bridget terminating the pregnancy and try a second time.

15

Zachary had been putting off reporting to Gordon. When he reported back that Bridget was probably not having an affair and that his best guess was someone at Westlake was intentionally mixing or swapping samples, that would be the end of his retainer. Zachary would no longer be able to justify following Bridget around and watching her every movement.

Maybe Gordon would want him to make further inquiries about the possibility that she'd been having an affair when the babies were conceived. He could talk to some of her friends and find out whether she was seeing anyone other than Gordon. Or could he? How many of them would know about him? Or would report back to Bridget about the man asking all of the questions. Bridget would immediately recognize the strange man as being Zachary, and he would be outed.

He could involve a subcontractor. Maybe Heather. She hadn't done anything like that in the past, but he had been training her in private detective skills, and perhaps it was time to take it to the next level. She was brilliant on the computer. She had taken immediately to skip-tracing. How would she do on the ground, talking to people face-to-face? Could she find a way to talk to Bridget's girlfriends naturally? So that it seemed to be part of a normal conversation?

Zachary sighed. He had to know that the retainer was going to come to an end sooner or later. And it would probably be sooner. There wasn't any evidence that Bridget was having an affair. It was far more likely she had become pregnant with the implanted embryos than naturally. Not after the cancer treatments. Not coincidentally in the same month that the embryos were implanted. That was just too much of a stretch. He understood that was where Gordon's imagination had immediately taken him, but the truth was probably something much less intimate.

His phone rang. Zachary knew without looking at it that it was going to be Gordon. He swiped the call after verifying that it was, in fact, his latest client.

"Gordon, I was just thinking about you."

"I was expecting a report before this," Gordon reproached.

"Yeah... sorry about that. I was just gathering my thoughts so I could give you a call."

"Gathering your thoughts... that sounds serious. Does that mean that you found something?"

"Well, I made some progress, but I don't have a definite answer for you."

Gordon sighed. "So, you don't know if she is having an affair?"

"Now? I would say not. Nothing in her behavior or daily patterns would indicate that. She's doing the same things that she always did, going where she used to go. Nowhere new, no changes in her routines, other than not getting out until later in the day. Obviously she is still not feeling very well in the morning."

"No," Gordon confirmed. "Not as bad as it was in the beginning, but she's still not herself. Pain and nausea. Mood swings. Irritability."

Zachary didn't tell Gordon that maybe that wasn't because of morning sickness. Bridget's emotional behavior wasn't likely to stop when she was no longer pregnant. Not if Zachary's life with her was any indication.

"So I don't think she's having an affair. I could watch for a few days, just in case it isn't someone she sees very often. And I could dig into her background, her behavior around the time that the twins were conceived."

"No... I think you're probably right. What are the chances that she would become pregnant the same month as we had the embryos implanted?" Gordon didn't know he was echoing exactly what Zachary had been reasoning to himself before Gordon had called.

"Yeah. That's what I'm thinking. And that takes us to the next possibility. That the wrong eggs or sperm were used in Bridget's IVF procedure."

"I hate to think that could be true. I mean, you hear stories, but it can't be very common, can it? That kind of thing must be so rare…"

"It is rare. But not impossible."

Gordon swore flatly. "Have you looked into the clinic? Have there been any other cases where this has happened?"

"I've ordered a courthouse search to see if they've been sued for it in the past. And I'm going to check with the police department to see whether they have had any break-ins or other security breaches there the last little while. But that's a long shot. What are the chances someone broke in to swap samples around or substitute their own genetic material for what was banked? I think that would stretch the bounds of credulity."

"Yes. I've never heard of that happening before. Embryos being stolen, but not… switched."

"Right. What we usually hear about in the media is mix-ups being made by the clinic. Wrong genetic material being used. I had a tour of the clinic and talked with people there, and their controls for making sure that they are using the right specimens for each procedure are reasonable. Did they talk to the two of you about always verifying the identification numbers on the collection vials? About always making sure that everything in every procedure is listed with your file number?"

"Sure. I could even tell you what our number was. But that assumes that they don't make any mistakes in the lab. Unlike during the natural process, we are not present for the fertilization or monitoring of the embryos for the first few days."

"Right. And I talked to them about that. They always have two people verify that the right specimens are being used. Or so they say. They do have internal controls for that."

"So there isn't any chance of an accidental mix-up. That's what you're telling me, right?"

"I wouldn't say no chance, but I think the chances are pretty small. It could happen if someone is sloppy and doesn't follow the proper proce-dures. But I'm more concerned about the possibility of something happen-ing… on purpose."

"Something goes wrong in the fertilization process, you mean? They use all of the right material, but something is… damaged? I understand that genetic mistakes are more common with fertility technology. The chances of mutations increase every time you touch the genetic materials."

Zachary hadn't looked into that, but it made sense. Mess with Mother Nature, and she would get even with you.

"Maybe… but that's not what I meant. What I mean is, they don't have controls to prevent someone from intentionally contaminating or replacing the samples."

"Intentionally? But who would do that? Do you think I have an enemy who would do that? At the fertility clinic?" His voice dripped with disbelief.

"No. I mean one of the doctors or staff… they sometimes decide to use their own sperm. It's happened a few times. Big lawsuits. Who knows how often it happens without the doctor getting caught."

"Really?" Gordon considered this. "But why would someone risk that? I can understand if there was something to be gained, or they wanted to get back at a rival. But just for the heck of it? People that they'd never even met before? Why would anyone do that?"

"Apparently, some doctors have a god complex. They have huge egos and think that the world would be better populated with their progeny."

"Really? Good grief."

Zachary nodded and waited. There wasn't really anything else for him to investigate. The case was over.

"So, what is your recommendation?" Gordon asked. "I mean… there's no way for us to find out what happened. Who might have mixed up or intentionally switched samples? Is there?"

"Are you willing to do DNA testing to find out? We can do maternity and paternity tests to see which of you, if either, is biologically related to the babies. And who is not."

"Bridget is against doing any testing of her own DNA. I'm not sure, but… I think she's afraid of finding out that she has some bad gene… that breast cancer one, maybe. For someone who has already been through cancer treatment… well, you can see how that could be devastating."

Zachary hadn't even thought about that. And it would be. Bridget was strong, or she wouldn't have survived what she already had. But she didn't need to be told that she was going to develop another kind of cancer. Or one of the other big diseases. Some kind of degenerative disease that they didn't have any cure for. He could understand why she would not want to face something like that.

"Yeah, okay. I can see how she might feel that way."

"Don't say anything to her about it. She hasn't told me that. She's only said that she won't do any kind of DNA testing. I can only surmise."

"I'm not exactly going to be talking to her about it."

Gordon chuckled. "No, I don't imagine you will be."

"You could still test the babies' DNA against yours, see whether or not you are the father. That may not be a full answer, but it could be a beginning. Prove whether you are or are not the father of the babies."

"But to do that prenatally, Bridget has to have another procedure. She would have to know about it. They would have to do either amnio or blood testing. We can't exactly do that covertly."

"No, I guess not. You might have to wait until after the children are born. Then get a cheek swab."

"I don't know whether she is going to carry them to term. She agreed to give us some time to think about it. But I suspect I know what her decision will be. She's going to want to terminate."

A wave of nausea passed over Zachary. How many people in the world would have given anything to be able to raise those babies? Including him. He'd always been more baby-hungry than Bridget. He remembered helping to raise his younger siblings. There was nothing like holding a new baby in his arms. Nothing else in his life had come close.

"What if she carries them to term… and then adopts them out?"

Gordon didn't answer immediately. When he did speak, his tone was bemused. "Why would we do that? If she carries the babies to term, we will raise them. We wouldn't give them to someone else."

"I just meant, if she didn't want them because of Huntington's Disease. I'm sure there would still be couples out there who would want to adopt them."

"Adopt a baby with a fatal disease?"

"A disease that won't kill them until they are middle-aged or older? Sure. I remember hearing about people adopting babies with HIV, back when it was a death sentence."

"No. We're not interested in doing that. I would prefer Bridget carry this pregnancy to term, but if she doesn't want to, then… I guess we'll try again."

Or not.

Bridget might decide that there was no way she was going through it all again. The morning sickness, the weight, all of the aches and pains that she suffered because of the pregnancy. And whatever was going on inside that made her worried that there was something wrong with the babies.

"What if she doesn't want to try again?"

"She may not. She wasn't too sure about it the first time. It might be too much to ask for her to try again. And she doesn't have a lot of eggs banked. I don't think we could try again more than once."

Zachary was glad to hear of that. He didn't know how he would handle it if he had to watch Bridget go through multiple pregnancies, trying again and again for the perfect baby. Or having however many children Gordon wanted, her body getting stretched and soft, turning into a matronly figure.

He had wanted her to be the mother of his children as much as she had wanted him to be the perfect spouse and partner for social functions. They each had a very distorted picture of what the other could be. He knew it had been unrealistic to expect her to be the perfect mother he had imagined. Even if she went on to have Gordon's children, she wouldn't be the kind of mother he fantasized about. The type of mother he had always longed for. That was as much a product of his imagination as the Easter Bunny.

It wasn't possible and it never had been.

"I don't know what else I can suggest," Zachary said slowly. "I can ask the clinic for some references, and investigate whether anyone who had babies recently has a family history of Huntington's, but that would be a long shot. It's not exactly the kind of thing that people advertise. But I probably can't even find out the names of everyone who works there, down to the receptionist and janitorial staff."

"Let me think about that. It may depend completely on whether Bridget has made a decision yet. If she is still determined to have the pregnancy terminated… well, there's not much we can do about it, is there? Not much point in investigating any further. If she did decide to have a go at another IVF implantation… I would insist we go to another clinic."

"Yeah. That makes sense. Okay, then, I'll wait to see what you decide."

16

Zachary went on with other investigative work. There wasn't anything more to do about Gordon's case. His surveillance of Bridget was done. He was both disappointed and relieved about it at the same time. He was disappointed because Bridget was like a drug he was addicted to. He loved to see her and follow her. He could spend all day every day just following her around like a puppy.

And he was relieved for the same reason. He knew he shouldn't be indulging his compulsion to track her and be close to her. He had been able, with medication changes and therapy, to stop once. He wasn't sure he would be able to stop again. The more he saw of her and followed her, the harder it would be to stop again.

He didn't want to end up in jail because she spotted him one day. She would take out a restraining order. He wouldn't be able to stop. He'd get arrested and thrown in the clink and, as soon as he got out, he would be watching her again.

He couldn't let that happen. So it was a good thing that the retainer was at an end and he didn't have any more excuse to follow her.

He wasn't expecting to get a call back from Gordon so quickly. It took him by surprise. He looked at his phone face and then glanced across the table at Kenzie's face. He hesitated, trying to decide whether to reject the call and try Gordon back later, or whether to be rude to Kenzie and take it in the middle of the meal.

She clearly saw the dilemma in his face. "If you really need to, then go ahead."

He waited for one more instant, but was afraid that Gordon would hang up and Zachary would miss the call.

"Just be a minute," he promised, getting up from the table and swiping the call at the same time. He didn't put it up to his face and answer immediately, waiting until he could duck into Kenzie's bedroom and shut the door for some privacy.

"Gordon?"

"Ah, Zachary. I was afraid it was going to voicemail. Sorry to bother you tonight, I know it isn't exactly office hours."

"Yeah. No problem. I wasn't expecting to hear back from you so soon."

"I had a thought."

"Yes?" Zachary was inexplicably relieved that it wasn't because Bridget had already made the decision to terminate.

He hated to think about how sick the possibility made him. He needed to let Bridget go.

He had to let her go.

He shouldn't have taken the job in the first place, and he had known it at the time.

"You already started an investigation into the clinic."

"Right. Only preliminary. I have the brochures and such, did a tour to check out their security procedures. If there is something else you want me to ask, I can do a follow-up call."

"Yes. What if you do background checks on the doctors? At least the main ones? It probably isn't likely that a brand-new doctor would have the guts to do something like that, intentionally swapping sperm samples for his own. More than likely, that's one of the more established doctors, right?"

"I'm not sure. If it was one of the older doctors, then it's probably been going on for some time. If it's been going on for a long time, wouldn't someone have figured it out? There would at least be some investigations made by whatever the governing body is. Maybe a reprimand or some black mark against his name. Directions that he had to follow some specific procedure, or had to undergo counseling. Something."

"That's what I'm thinking," Gordon said. "He must have left a trail. If this has been going on for some time, there must be some rumors, some reprimand, like you say. Maybe even previous lawsuits. Not necessarily against the clinic, but against one of the doctors. Maybe it's someone who has just recently started at the clinic, so they haven't had this happen before. Because they don't know his background, what happened to him before."

It could be challenging to catch unethical doctors. The profession didn't want people to mistrust doctors, so they didn't like to make everything public. They would keep it low-key, trying to keep the public's trust. Discipline the doctor quietly and impose some penalty. Maybe even take away his license to practice medicine. Then the doctor moved to a different state and tried again. Zachary knew some of them turned into serial offenders.

If a doctor had a compulsion to impregnate as many women as possible, then, like Zachary's compulsion to follow Bridget, it would be hard to resist the impulse. And the more he indulged the desire, the harder it would be to stop. He wouldn't stop just because he'd been caught once. He would keep going until he was behind bars.

"Yeah, you may have something there," he admitted. "I have the brochures, that will give me the names of the major players. I can start with them, see who the most recent additions to the clinic are. If they're telling the truth and have never had any issues before, he might not have reached the tipping point where enough parents have started to ask questions. Most couples don't do prenatal DNA tests. But there might be some traits that don't fit in the family. Why does Johnny have blue eyes? Where did he get celiac disease from? That kind of thing."

He could imagine Gordon's piercing eyes and his eager nod. "Yes. Good man. You have it. Can you do that for me? See if you can figure out who did this. It may be too late for us, but if we can stop him from impregnating someone else…"

Zachary was struck again by how much of a violation it was. He was furious at whoever had done this to Bridget. Even if it had not been a violent, personal attack, it still felt like it. Even if the man who had mixed or substituted his own sperm to fertilize the eggs had never been in the same room as Bridget, he had still violated her. Zachary gulped, trying to keep his anger under control.

He would find out who had done it. All it would take was a little detective work.

17

The next morning, Zachary spent an hour pulling all the names that he could from the brochures and the website for the clinic and then going over them with Heather. They split the names up so that they could get through them more quickly. Zachary explained what he was looking for, and gave Heather some pointers on the searches she would need to have done and the people or organizations that she would have to talk to. How to best get the information they needed from people who might be under a gag order or have signed a confidentiality agreement. While the beginning steps would be ones that Heather was familiar with, she needed a few more pointers on the steps to take after that.

Kenzie called him midway through the morning while he was running one name after another through the databases. Zachary was surprised. Usually, when she was at work, she wouldn't call him, except maybe at noon to see how he was doing while she had her lunch.

It must have been a slower day at the morgue.

"Hey, Kenz. What's up?"

"I was wondering if you were still working on that Huntington's Disease case. Or have you already put that one to bed?"

"Still working on it." Zachary tried to pull his attention away from the list of names. Switching gears could be a problem when he was deep into something. "Did you think of something?"

"Well, I had been doing a little bit of research into whether it could be sporadic, you know, and I've been talking to Dr. Wiltshire about it this morning."

Zachary didn't know how much the medical examiner would know about Huntington's Disease, but he would take what he could get. They would both have more experience than he did about the ins and outs of the genetics.

"Yeah. Did you find anything? Everybody I've talked to says that if one parent has it, the kids each have a fifty percent chance of getting it. If both parents have it, then the kids have a higher chance of getting it, but still not one hundred percent."

"Right."

"But if neither of the parents have it, then there's no way the kids would, right? Or did you find out something different?"

"Well, I discovered it is a little more nuanced than that. You have to change your thinking about how it works."

"Okay." Zachary closed his laptop screen so he wouldn't be distracted by it. He closed his eyes, trying to focus all of his attention on Kenzie's words. "I'm ready."

"When we're talking about genes to the general population, we are usually talking about a binary model. Right? You think of someone as either *having* the gene or *not having* the gene."

"Yes… except I know that you can have different versions. Dominant or recessive. You can have a gene, but if it is recessive, then you don't see it."

"And with something like Huntington's Disease, then it is autosomal dominant, which means that you don't have to inherit two copies of it, like you would for something like cystic fibrosis. You only have to inherit one copy of it."

"Right."

"But I want you to forget the binary model. It is not a matter of having the HD gene or not having the HD gene."

"It isn't?"

"No. It's a matter of how many CAG repeats you have."

Zachary opened his eyes and frowned at the phone. Kenzie wasn't kidding when she said he would have to think about it in a different way. He didn't have any idea what CAG repeats were.

"Stay with me, Zach. I'll get you up to speed."

"Okay. CAG repeats."

"So, everyone has CAG repeats on the Huntington's allele. That's normal."

"Uh-huh."

"Some people have just a few repeats. If they have under twenty-six repeats, then they do not get Huntington's Disease."

"Okay." Zachary could understand that so far.

"Some people have lots of repeats. If they have over forty repeats, they will synthesize a mutated huntingtin protein and develop Huntington's Disease. They start experiencing dementia and other symptoms mid-to-late life."

"Oh. Okay. So a few repeats, they don't get Huntington's, a lot, they do."

"And if they have an extremely high number of repeats, they might even develop Huntington's in childhood. That is very rare."

"I never heard of that."

"It isn't always diagnosed right away, because it is so rare. But in families that have seen multiple cases of Huntington's across every generation, it pops up. These 'super' repeats that cause Huntington's to show up early in life."

"That's really scary. So Br—my couple could have a child that develops Huntington's Disease as a child, not as a fifty- or seventy-year-old."

"If they are one of the few that ends up with this super-expanded gene, yes."

"Sheesh."

"Now, this is where it gets interesting."

Zachary waited.

"You know what happens when they have twenty-six or fewer repeats, and what happens when it is forty or more repeats, but what happens if it is *intermediate.*"

"Well… I would guess that you end up with someone who might develop Huntington's, and might not."

"Yes. Exactly. If they have thirty-six to thirty-nine repeats, they have only partial penetrance, and they may or may not develop Huntington's Disease. And there is one final possibility."

Zachary felt an itch, like when he had a word on the tip of his tongue, but couldn't quite reach it. He could almost predict what Kenzie was going to say. Another minute or two to think about it, and he might come up with it.

Kenzie told him. "If you have twenty-seven to thirty-five repeats, you have an intermediate allele. You may end up with a case where the parent *will not* develop Huntington's Disease, but the child *will*."

"How does the child get it, if the parent doesn't?"

"Because the fertilization and division processes are not perfect. The cells may 'mistranscribe' thirty-five CAG repeats as forty CAG repeats. So the parent was too low to get Huntington's Disease, but the child is high enough that they do."

"What are the chances of that? How common is this 'intermediate' gene?"

"A lot more common than you would think. It is rare for it to result in the expanded form in the offspring. That's why it is often left out of the conversation."

"Huh. So it is possible. My couple *could* both be below the range where they will get Huntington's, but still have children who will get it."

"Possible, yes. Not likely, but… possible. I would still pursue the fertility clinic angle as the more likely explanation."

"That's what I'm doing right now. So I'll continue to push in that direction."

"And you should know that sometimes people with this intermediate allele do show some of the Huntington's behaviors. Even though they don't have what would be diagnosed as full-blown Huntington's, they may have some of the behavioral characteristics, movements, and so on. It's like… mild Huntington's. But not diagnosable as Huntington's."

Zachary leaned back, rubbing the center of his forehead. "So there may still be some of these behaviors in the family even if they don't have a family history of Huntington's Disease."

"Yes. Possible."

"So I should watch for some of those behaviors in the doctors I'm doing background on."

"I would. Are your background checks going to be that detailed?"

"Not at first. But I'll delve deeper into the ones that seem suspicious. And sometimes, things are reported in the news or social columns about eccentric family members. Or people act erratically on social media."

Kenzie laughed. "How can you tell?"

"You have a point."

"Yeah. I'd better get back to work, but I thought I'd give you those details while they were still fresh in my mind."

"Thanks! I appreciate it. I'll put them to good use."

18

Zachary decided to meet with Heather face-to-face to collate their research and see where they needed to do more. He enjoyed highway driving, so he went to her house. He sat in the car outside the house for a moment, just looking at the house and remembering the various times he had been there while investigating her cold case. It had been an emotional time and had stirred up a lot of bad memories for both of them.

But that was in the past now. He had helped her to figure out who her attacker had been, and the man was now in jail awaiting trial. For the first time, Heather had been able to shed her fear of running into him again. She started thinking about herself and what she wanted to do with her life. It might seem like it wasn't worth it for a woman her age to just be starting out in a new direction, but how could it ever be too late to start living? She had blossomed since she had freed herself from the chains of the past. She was a new person. Not different from her old self, but better. It was hard to find the words.

The front door opened and Heather stood there looking at him. Zachary pulled the charging cable out of his phone and opened his door. He remembered to grab his messenger bag before getting out. He got his feet a little tangled trying to get out of the car, flustered by her watching him and trying to get out quickly so he wouldn't look so awkward. But he managed to get out without falling on his face. He pressed the switch to lock the doors and slammed his door shut. He tried the handle and it was locked. He looked at it through the window to make sure, and tried the handle of the back door. He pressed the lock button on his key fob a couple of times to make sure that the security system was set, then pressed it once more for good measure. He stood looking at the car.

"Come on, Zachy," Heather invited. "I'm waiting for you."

Zachary turned away from his car and walked up the sidewalk to the front door. "Sorry. Just had one thing to do…"

"Come on in. Let's get right to it."

He was glad that she didn't make a big deal of his delays. He followed her into the house. He could smell fresh coffee and something gingery. He glanced toward the kitchen as they passed the doorway. But Heather led him directly to the dining room table where her laptop sat, surrounded by piles of paper and folders. She had already set out coffee for both of them, and a small plate between the two settings with a circle of ginger snap cookies.

"Those smell good."

Heather nodded. "Help yourself. When my son was on meds for ADHD when he was still at school, I had a terrible time getting him to eat enough. But something like these cookies, they helped. They just smell so good that he wanted them even if he didn't have much appetite."

Zachary sat down and took one from the plate. "I didn't know your son had ADHD. I don't think you mentioned it before."

"They both did. Or do, I guess. But as adults, they're better at managing it. It's so hard when they're in school, supposed to be sitting still in the middle of a whole class full of distractions. It's easier now that they're in the workplace and can adapt their environment. Change things around to make it easier to work. Go for a walk. Take stuff home."

Zachary nodded. It had been a big relief for him to get out of classrooms. Even though he had known that he was jumping into the adult world with no supports, it had been so good to get away from classrooms, from teachers and foster parents or supervisors who thought that he should just be able to turn his attention on and off like a switch.

Even with all of the training that was out there on dealing with students or children with ADHD, they never seemed to have much sympathy or workable solutions. They should have been able to help him with accommodations, but what they offered was always minimal. Or nonexistent. Once he was over fifteen, they thought he should have his brain whipped into shape and be able to do everything that everyone else could.

Even if Zachary had been able to beat the ADHD, to find that miracle pill that would fix his brain or the therapy that would allow him to access that on/off switch that must exist somewhere in his head, he had other learning disabilities on top of it. And PTSD and other mental health issues.

School had been pretty hopeless. It had been good to get out.

Zachary refocused on Heather and looked at the table at the various folders. He delved into his bag to pull out his papers as well.

"Let's get to it, then," he said, knowing that Heather wouldn't mind him skipping over the small talk. They could chat on the phone anytime. He was there to do a job and, if he wasted a lot of time talking, they wouldn't have time to get everything done. "Should we start with… the list, I guess? This will be our master list."

He flipped through his papers, looking for the list of doctors and other staff he had assembled from the brochures and the clinic's website. He probably should have alphabetized it, but he hadn't. He'd just gone with the order he had found them in.

Heather gave a quick nod. "So you want Dr. Weaver first?"

Zachary nodded. Dr. Weaver was one of his names, so he went through the stack again until he found Weaver's various reports, all clipped together with a handwritten cover page summarizing what he had been able to find.

"Looks like Dr. Weaver is one of the owners of the clinic. He was one of the original partners that set it up, so he has been there from the beginning."

"Is he still doing procedures?" Heather asked with a frown.

"No. He's semi-retired, from what I can tell. A figurehead."

"I was going to say; I don't know if I would want an octogenarian doing my procedures. Some people are still razor-sharp at that age, but…"

Zachary nodded. "Yeah, I can understand that. He's also old enough that if he had Huntington's Disease, he should be showing symptoms by now. So I think we can probably eliminate him. If he's been there for twenty years and they've never had a lawsuit over the wrong sperm being used, then it isn't him. And it doesn't look like he has Huntington's, even a mild form."

"Okay. So we can start a pile for 'no' or 'unlikely'?" Heather picked up the sheaf of pages and moved it toward the middle of the desk to start a pile.

Zachary nodded his agreement. He looked back at the master list. He put a checkmark beside Weaver's name. One down.

"Dr. Carrie Ryder is next."

"Man or woman?"

"Man. Not one of the original partners, but he has been at the clinic almost from the start."

"Yeah. I couldn't find very much online for him. He's an older guy. Not an octogenarian, but I don't think he's much into social media or anything to do with computers."

"Any red flags? Anything suspicious?"

"No. And like Weaver, he's been there for a lot of years. If there was a problem, I think it would have shown up before now."

"More than likely. No recent changes in his credit score? Or other changes in behavior?"

"Nope."

"Nothing to indicate that he's had any problem behaviors? Fights with neighbors or the clinic?"

"He seems like a pretty quiet guy. Nothing that makes me think he's been in any trouble."

"Lawsuits?"

"One a few years ago over some kind of property dispute. Nothing professionally."

"I think we can probably put him in the 'no' pile."

Heather agreed. She put her folder on top of the reports on Dr. Weaver.

The first few were easy, but Zachary knew they were going to get harder. The doctors who were listed the most prominently on the website were the ones who had been there the longest, and they were unlikely to be the culprits in any intentional contamination of DNA specimens. If they had been the type to do that, they would likely have started much earlier and it would already have come to light.

He put a checkmark beside Carrie Ryder and they went on to the next person.

19

It was tedious work, but they ended up with most of the files in the 'unlikely' pile, and a handful of names to do further research on.

"So how deep do you want to go?" Heather asked. "Are we just looking for doctors who have been sued or accused of unethical behavior, or are we looking for anything negative? Deep background? Family relationships? Early history?"

"Everything we can get. If there are lawsuits, that's a big red flag. But also things like a change in behavior in the last year or two, someone who is known for unpredictable or inappropriate behavior. And then, whether they have family members who are. I want obituaries wherever we can get them. Start putting together a family tree and marking whether there have been any relatives that might have had Huntington's Disease. Does anyone in the family participate in Huntington's research or post on bulletin boards or discussion groups about it? Are there any legacies or 'please send donations to' Huntington's Disease researchers in the obituaries?"

Heather nodded, scribbling down some notes for herself. "Genealogy sites, obituaries, Huntington's sites. Any runs or sports fundraisers for Huntington's Disease. Any mentions in social media…"

"Someone with Huntington's might also have some strange or erratic social media posts. Overemotional, forgetful or confused, angry, posts showing wide mood swings."

Heather added details to her list. "Marriages? See what behavior has been mentioned in divorce documents?"

"Good idea. Yes."

"What about police files? Can we find out whether any of these people have had assault charges? Or has been the subject of a missing persons report, even for just a short time?"

"Yeah. I'll see what I can get on that front. Mario might be able to do some preliminary searches and point me in the right direction."

They looked at the small pile of files and clipped papers. Heather teased one out of the pile. "I like this guy for it. Forest McLachlan."

Zachary raised his brows. "Why?"

She hadn't known a lot about him when they had done their first run-through of the files.

"I'm not sure I can put my finger on one thing in particular. He hasn't been there for very long, just over a year. Usually, when I am doing a preliminary search, previous employment comes up. Usually, you can trace at least the last three jobs. But there wasn't anything earlier than Westlake Clinic on his LinkedIn profile, or in his social media profiles. Some people just don't have any online media presence." She flicked a finger over to the bottom files in the 'no' pile to indicate the older doctors. "You know, they don't have anything on any of their profiles, if they have a profile in the first place. But Forest has social media profiles. He's filled in things like hobbies, religion, and political affiliations. But he's silent on previous jobs. So, where did he come from? What was he doing before he went to Westlake?"

Zachary took the file from her and looked through what she had already collected on him. "Did he move here from out of state?"

"Yeah. I think I read somewhere he'd been in Minnesota before? Something like that. But no listing of what he did there."

"Okay. Double-check the state, and start getting some searches done. Courthouses especially. Look for a name change, not just lawsuits. See if he's got an ex-wife there who might talk about him. Kids, maybe. Let's do him first. If you've got an instinct about him, let's make sure we do a really good job on him."

"I could be wrong."

"Yeah. But if you have a feeling about him, then there's probably a reason for that, whether he's our guy or not."

Heather shrugged.

"Maybe we'll get him for something else," Zachary said. "I've had it happen more than once. Start doing deep background on someone and realize that it's not the guy, but he's guilty of some other crime. Sometimes worse than what you were initially looking for."

"Yeah?"

Zachary nodded. He grabbed another ginger snap and washed down a bite with coffee that was past being lukewarm.

"Do you want me to get you another coffee?" Heather asked grimacing.

"No. I should be getting back home. Don't want to keep Kenzie waiting. Let's just divide these up…" He went through the 'maybe' pile, handing Heather the files she had already started and balancing them against the ones that he had worked on, taking a couple of her files himself so that she wasn't overloaded. "There we go. Start on McLachlan. Let me know what you find. We'll keep each other apprised."

"Are you going to work on it tonight?"

Zachary hesitated. He tried to make time for Kenzie during the evening, but he was eager to get started on the deeper background on their suspects. If the man who had impregnated Bridget was in that pile, Zachary wanted to find him. He didn't want to wait another day to get started.

"I might do a little tonight," he admitted. "You?"

"Yes." She laughed. "Grant doesn't mind. I do work while I watch TV with him all the time. I won't spend all night on it, but…" She shrugged again. "Some of it."

"You're sure he doesn't mind?"

"He says he likes seeing me working. Engaged in something instead of just… sleeping or vegging in front of the TV."

Zachary nodded. She had a life to catch up on. She had spent too many years inside herself, afraid to move forward. He was glad that Grant understood that on some level too.

"I'm going to be down to Mr. Peterson's on the weekend." He watched for Heather's reaction, still wondering whether they were planning another reunion for him. Mr. Peterson had said it was to meet Pat's mother and sister, but that didn't mean they couldn't have a second meeting up their sleeves. He wouldn't put it past them. "You're not going to be there, are you?"

"No, not this time. Are you doing something special?"

He watched her eyes, but she seemed to be telling him the truth.

"Pat is having his mom and sister over. I just wondered… whether anything else was going on."

"Nothing I know about, sorry. I'm not a part of any plans."

"Okay. Just… checking."

20

Maybe Grant didn't mind Heather doing work in front of the TV as they passed their evening together, but Kenzie definitely noticed Zachary's distraction and commented on it.

"What are you working on? Still the Huntington's case?"

Zachary was correlating names on the page, looking for any sign that the Jacqueline Merrit listed there was the same person as Dr. Jackie Merrit on his list. While he didn't think that they were looking for a woman, it was always possible that someone had just been intent on causing chaos and had mixed sperm samples between clients. There was nothing to say that it had to be a man using his own DNA.

Kenzie prodded Zachary's arm, making him startle. His jump made Kenzie jump as well. Zachary put his hand over his heart, trying to tell himself that there was no need to be freaking out over a love tap from his girlfriend. He wasn't being attacked.

"Sorry," Kenzie laughed. She gave his arm a squeeze and cuddled against his shoulder for a moment. "I didn't mean to scare you."

"No, no, it's fine. I was just focused. What did you ask?" He realized belatedly that he had heard her talking to him, but had tuned her out. He tried to run back the tape in his head, but had been too focused to know what she had said.

"I asked what you're working on. Is it the Huntington's case?"

"Oh. Yes. Background on the doctors and staff that could be our culprit."

"Ah. I guess they're probably in a rush for the information to decide whether to terminate or not. How far along is she?"

"Um, yes. Probably. I think she's probably going to terminate whether we figure out what happened or not. I think she was already looking for a reason to."

"Oh?" Kenzie's eyebrows went up. "Why would she do that? I would think that if she's doing IVF, she's pretty invested in getting pregnant. Why would she want to terminate? Especially before she even knew the baby has Huntington's?"

"I don't know. People can still get cold feet. Decide that they're not ready for it, even though they have been waiting for a long time."

"I guess. I just think if I had decided I was going to spend all of the time and money and mental resources on IVF, I'd make sure it was what I really wanted before going ahead."

Zachary nodded. He looked down at the work he had been doing, rubbing a crick in his neck that he hadn't noticed before.

"How far along?" Kenzie prompted.

"I don't know, exactly. She's... big." Zachary made a movement suggesting a large pregnant belly.

"So, not early."

"No. But I don't know how many weeks or when she is due. Still a few months away."

"Not that it's any of my business," Kenzie admitted. "I'm just curious. It's hard to imagine what they must be feeling like right now. You think that you're going to have that baby you wanted, that everything has worked out and your dream is going to come true... and then you find out that the baby has a potentially fatal disease. A genetic disease that he didn't inherit from either of you. It would be pretty tragic."

"I guess." Zachary fiddled with the keys on his laptop, tapping lightly. "I really can't imagine deciding to terminate, though. I know..." He tried to put the words together in a way that would make sense to her. "I know... what it's like to hold a newborn, and to love her... even though it's the first time you've ever seen her. To decide that you won't let that child be born... I'm not a woman, but once she's felt the baby moving and heard her heartbeat... I don't know how she could make that decision."

"You can't know what you would do if you haven't been there." Kenzie stared off, thinking. "It's funny, you know, that we've both had that experience, with helping to raise a sibling. Not just entertaining the baby or giving her an occasional bottle, but actually being one of her caregivers."

Zachary nodded slowly. "I hadn't thought about that. But yeah. I guess we have. What was it like for you?" He hesitated to ask, but did anyway. "What kind of home did you grow up in? Was it hard on them? Having another baby? Or did they want to?"

Kenzie gave him a quizzical look. "Yeah, of course they wanted Amanda. They had been trying to have another baby. There was at least one miscarriage between me and Amanda. They never intended for me to be an only child, but I almost was. I'm glad they didn't decide that it was too late to have a second baby."

"And your mom... I guess if she didn't have the two of you close together, like with my family, it wasn't so hard on her to be pregnant and to take care of Amanda."

"No. I don't think it was too bad. I don't remember her complaining a bunch about how hard it was to be pregnant. Some women do have a really hard time, feel really bad, but I don't remember her throwing up or being overly tired, or complaining about a lot of pain."

"That's good. So it was easier for her to take care of a baby."

"I don't think it was really very hard for her. I loved helping with everything, even changing diapers. And Dad liked babies too. A lot of men don't get very involved with babies. They figure they'll bring in the bacon and leave that part to Mom. But he was always involved if he was in town."

"He traveled a lot?"

Kenzie nodded. She didn't tell him anything else about what her father did. Zachary assumed he must be a doctor from what Kenzie had said earlier. But doctors didn't usually travel a lot, as far as he knew. Maybe her father had clinics in several different cities that he rotated through. That could be a thing.

Zachary closed the lid of his laptop, deciding that further research could wait until morning. He didn't want to shut Kenzie out. He wanted to have this conversation with her.

"You don't have to do that," Kenzie said immediately. "I didn't mean to interrupt you. If you need to get it done right away..."

"It can wait. I shouldn't have been working on it tonight."

"You can," she repeated.

"No. It's okay." Zachary took a couple of deep breaths and returned to their discussion. "My mom... she didn't do so well with babies. I'm not sure why she kept getting pregnant. I mean, after the first two or three of us, she must have realized how hard it was on her body and that she wasn't cut out to have a big family... but she still did. Six kids. I don't know why she would do that."

"Was she Catholic? Some religions don't believe in birth control. They think it's a sin."

"I don't think so. I don't remember either of my parents being religious. We didn't go to church. I'd never been to church until I was in foster care. Some of the families I was with would drag everyone off to church. But at home... I don't think they were religious."

"Maybe she still thought that it was wrong. What was it like? She just didn't like having kids around? She was overwhelmed?"

"I think... she probably had postpartum depression. I didn't realize that there was anything really wrong at the time. I mean, I was just a kid. Only eight when Mandy was born. But she..." Zachary put his computer aside, shaking his head. "She wouldn't get out of bed. I just thought that's how it was when you had a baby. When you break your leg, you have to have a cast on for six weeks, or a few months, whatever. Or stay in bed if it's really bad. And when you have a baby, you can't get out of bed for weeks."

"Yeah, sounds like she must have had it really bad. Or she might have lost a lot of blood and was anemic. Just having so many children in such a short period of time... she might have had other vitamins and minerals that were really depleted. Essential fatty acids. Deficiencies can cause a lot of psychiatric symptoms."

"Maybe that was it. I just know it was bad... We took care of the babies, me and the older girls. Gave them bottles, changed them, rocked them to sleep and tried to keep them from crying and waking my mom up. She would take them a couple of times during the day when she had to. When we were at school. I always hated going to school, worrying about if they would be okay while we were gone."

"Someone should have involved child services. Gotten her some kind of help. It's pretty dangerous, letting kids so young be in charge of taking care of a newborn."

"I guess so. It was always a relief when she was able to get up again, and I knew that at least the baby wouldn't starve while I was at school."

"How long was it before she could be up and around?"

"I don't know. Seemed like a long time. Weeks."

"Sheesh. She's lucky she had the help she did. If one of you had ever had an accident with the baby because she couldn't take care of it…"

Zachary wasn't thinking about his mother anymore. He was thinking about Bridget. Worrying, as he had many times over the previous weeks, how she was going to take care of a baby.

He worried too much. Bridget wasn't his mother. She wasn't going to have depression that kept her in bed for weeks after the twins were born. If she even went ahead and had the twins.

If she did decide to go ahead, if Gordon somehow managed to talk her into having the twins, she would have help. Not from children who were eight or ten years old, but maids and nannies and whatever else she or Gordon thought she needed to get through. She wouldn't be lying in bed, her babies neglected.

Kenzie cuddled up to Zachary, sliding her arm around behind his back, her touch warm on his back.

"A movie?" she suggested. "I think you could use the distraction. Something light and fun to get your mind off the case."

She knew, of course, that he wasn't just thinking about the case. But he appreciated her putting it that way anyway. He didn't need to be reminded how easily he sank into obsessive thoughts about his past.

Or about Bridget.

But Kenzie didn't know that was what he was thinking about. He at least hadn't given that away.

2 1

H eather had turned up several facts about Forest McLachlan. She went through what she had discovered point by point over the phone. Zachary made notes in his notepad that he would later expand upon on the computer.

It wasn't an airtight case, but there were plenty of reasons to be suspicious of McLachlan. So far, everything they had discovered was circumstantial, but many cases started that way. Then he gathered the evidence needed to prove his case. Or at least to get the police involved, and they could gather the evidence needed to charge a suspect.

McLachlan had previously worked at another fertility clinic, and it was one that had been in the news for irregularities. It had been under investigation for sloppy or unethical practices. Heather hadn't been able to find any verdict or resolution in the media, but the fertility clinic was no longer in existence. McLachlan had good reason for not wanting that clinic to be on his resume. More than likely, he had lied on his resume, but simply left it off of his social media.

He had left an ex-wife in Minnesota. She would be a good source for them to check in with. Find out what had gone on at the clinic, why she had divorced him, and whether he happened to have Huntington's Disease in his family tree. Heather promised to send him her information via email, so he didn't bother to write it down.

"That's great. Is there anything else?"

"I put in for some courthouse searches, here and in Minnesota. But they will take a few days to get in."

"Right."

"Before the fertility clinic, he was at a hospital. I haven't been able to find any hint of scandal there. So maybe nothing. Or we might need to talk to people he actually worked with to find anything out."

"Sometimes there are non-disclosure agreements," Zachary said. "They promise not to put anything in the media or to talk about what went on, if he'll just go his own way and they don't have to take him to court or deal with the fallout of people knowing what they allowed someone to get away with while he worked for them."

"Why would they do that? Don't they know the same thing is just going to happen at the next place?"

"Yeah," Zachary agreed. "Not exactly protecting the rest of society, are they? They're just getting rid of a problem. Covering their butts. They know that he's going to keep causing problems, but they don't really care as long as it is in someone else's back yard."

"If this sicko has been breaking the rules and doing... disgusting stuff like this for years, then they're partially responsible for that. They can't just say they didn't know. Or that they were gagged. Don't they have a responsibility to do something?"

"You'd have to talk to a lawyer. I couldn't tell you. I'm sure they had lawyers advising them exactly what they could and couldn't do. They probably had to make some kind of report to their professional board, whoever regulates doctors."

"Then why didn't *they* do something?"

"That's why he moved. So he could start fresh in a new state."

"And it didn't follow him? No one checks to see what his status was in Minnesota?"

"Probably not. Or he gave them forged documents. If you see something in black and white, you don't bother to call to find out if it is real or faked. You just assume that what you were given is legit."

"Not me," Heather vowed. "I'm never trusting anything anyone gives me again. It's crazy that he could get away with this."

"So far, we don't know that he has gotten away with anything. All that we know is, he used to work at a clinic that had some issues. We don't know that he did anything. We're just speculating."

"I suppose so," Heather said grudgingly. "But I really think he's the one."

"Probably. But we can't assume that until we find some more evidence. I'll talk to his ex-wife, see if I can talk to anyone who worked with him at the clinic and hospital. Then we'll have a better idea of whether he's done this before. Still not proof of him fathering my client's baby, but maybe enough that the police will investigate."

"Will your client cooperate? Do they want to know? If I had a new baby, I don't know if I'd want them to confirm who fathered the baby. Does it matter?"

"Well, there is always medical history and that kind of thing. They might want to know that." There was a knot tightening in his gut. If Bridget terminated the pregnancy before they caught the biological father, that might prevent them from proving what he had done. Hints and rumors wouldn't get them anywhere in actually prosecuting the guy or preventing him from going on to another clinic in another state and doing the same thing over again. "Uh, listen, Feathers, I have to make a couple of calls. Make sure that we don't lose any vital evidence. Will you send me the info on the ex-wife, and anything you know about who he worked with at the previous clinic and hospital?"

"I don't have much, but I'll send you what I've got. Do you want me to make a few calls and see if I can find out who he was friends with and who else he might have associated with?"

"Yeah, that would be great if you can coax them into giving you any information we can use."

"All right. I'll see what I can wheedle out of them."

Zachary looked up Gordon's numbers on his contact list and tried his direct work line. He wanted to avoid, if at all possible, the chance that Bridget might overhear Gordon on the phone.

He had considered sending Gordon a text to tell him to call back at his earliest convenience—code for when it was safe—but he didn't know whether Gordon had his phone set to show the full details of his text on his lock screen, where there was the possibility that Bridget might see it.

He should have asked Gordon for the best protocol for getting in touch with him when they had first met.

The work line rang a couple of times, and Gordon picked it up. "Zachary. How are you?"

Zachary didn't bother answering the inquiry. It was just a social nicety and Gordon probably wouldn't even hear his answer. "Are you free? Or is this a bad time?"

"Actually, it's a good time. I have a few minutes to myself, for once."

"I wanted to check in with you on... well..." Zachary's face got hot, and he was glad that Gordon couldn't see him. But it didn't make the question any easier to ask. "Whether you and Bridget have made any decision yet on whether to terminate."

"Well, that will be Bridget's choice. I, unfortunately, have no say in the matter. If she doesn't want to talk about it anymore, she can just go ahead and deal with it herself."

Zachary remembered that helpless feeling. When she'd had a positive pregnancy test, the false positive that had been a sign of cancer rather than a pregnancy, she had told him that she was going to terminate, and she wouldn't even talk about it. It was her body, her life, and her decision. He didn't get to have any say in it. She wouldn't consider anything he might have to say about it.

It really didn't make him feel any better that she had told Gordon the same thing. She had at least discussed it with him, allowed him to talk her into waiting while they gathered more information and thought about it but, in the end, it would be her decision, not his.

"I'm worried that if she terminates, we won't have the evidence we need to prove that someone else's genetic material was used to create the embryos. The lab that did the prenatal screen and found the Huntington's Disease, did they do a full genome map? One that could be used for a paternity test?"

"I don't think so. I think it was just for certain anomalies."

"Then if she terminates... we won't have the evidence we need—unless they keep samples. Do they do that? I don't know if you can ask."

Gordon cleared his throat. "I'm not sure how I can suggest that to her unless you've come to a landing on what happened. Do you have something to report?"

"Not yet. I'm still following up. But it occurred to me that if we get enough evidence on this guy—the guy that I think may have sabotaged the samples—to start a police investigation, they're going to need proof of his wrongdoing. If we can establish him as the... uh... sperm donor, then he could be charged with fraud?"

"You have identified someone, then."

"It's preliminary," Zachary cautioned. "I don't have any kind of proof yet. I'm making inquiries; I need to do some interviews, try to find out what I can. Get enough evidence to start a police investigation."

"I'm not sure we want to go to the police."

Zachary hesitated, thinking about that. Someone in the public eye like Gordon would not necessarily want to be known as someone who had been cuckolded by medical technology. Even though there was clearly nothing he could have done to prevent someone from substituting his DNA for Gordon's in the lab, there might still be a stigma attached to not being the father of Bridget's twins.

And what about Bridget? She was all about appearances and reputation. It was very important for her to be seen as someone who was together and as close to perfect as a mortal could be. It had not been an easy decision for her to sacrifice her perfect figure for a pregnancy. Now she was in the position of having to decide whether to terminate that pregnancy. If her friends and worshipers found out that she had been pregnant by someone other than Gordon, that she was at the center of some fertility clinic scandal, what would that do to her?

So what was the goal?

"How far do you want me to go, then?" Zachary asked, feeling his way through the conversation. "If you do not want this guy prosecuted because of the possible fallout for you and Bridget, what is your preferred outcome?"

"I want to know who did this," Gordon said firmly. He cleared his throat, and there was a period of silence as he considered. "I realize that you will not be in a position to be able to prove that this man you are investigating was the culprit, but I want to get as close as possible. And then I want to make sure that he can never do something like this again. I want him fired and blackballed from the industry. I'll do whatever it takes to make sure that happens."

Zachary wasn't sure what exactly that would involve, but he was confident that Gordon could do it. He was a powerful man with plenty of resources. He could talk to prominent doctors and lawyers and somehow find a way to prevent McLachlan from ever getting a job where he had access to genetic materials and embryos again. If Gordon put out the word, Zachary was sure he could make it happen.

"Okay. So here's what I'm going to do. I'm going to talk to McLachlan's ex-wife and previous coworkers in Minnesota. I'm going to find out what I can about what happened at his previous clinic and if there was anything going on at the hospital before that. And I'll do what I can to find out whether he has any Huntington's Disease in his family. I've already got a researcher working on it."

"McLachlan?" Gordon repeated. "Is that his name?"

"Er, yes." Zachary realized he shouldn't have let that detail slip out. He should have kept his mouth shut until he knew more. "But so far, there is no proof that he's done anything illegal or unethical. He's just the best candidate at the moment. If I find out that he was involved in something similar previously, and if he has Huntington's in his family, then I think that's as close as we can come to establishing his guilt, short of a DNA test."

"That sounds reasonable," Gordon agreed. "And if you find there isn't anything there…"

"Then we look elsewhere. He's not the only one on our list. There are several others to look at."

"How long will this take?"

"I'm not sure. A couple of days to do interviews. Everyone I need to see won't be available the same day. Travel time. Maybe wait for some courthouse searches to come in."

Zachary couldn't see that it mattered how long it took. His investigation would not intersect with Bridget's decision to terminate the pregnancy. She would make that decision without knowing who the sperm donor was. He didn't know if she even understood that the positive Huntington's Disease meant that Gordon was not the father of the babies. Or alternatively, that she was not the mother.

"Will you let me know?" Gordon asked. "As soon as you can. I want to know if this guy is the one."

Zachary shifted uncomfortably. Gordon had every right to have animosity toward whoever had perpetrated the fraud, but Zachary had not expected the undercurrent of fury in Gordon's tone.

"Of course," he agreed. "I'll let you know as soon as I know anything."

22

As much as Zachary liked highway driving, he could not drive from Vermont to Minnesota for the investigation. Especially not with Gordon pressing for answers as soon as possible. Gordon had quickly approved his purchase of plane tickets the next day so that Zachary could get right to it.

Zachary picked up his emails from Heather and assembled what information he had on McLachlan's ex-wife, coworkers, and family in Minnesota and started making phone calls. He was as vague as he could be about his purposes for talking to them, trying to make it sound like a routine credit check or something of that nature. Of course, people knew that credit checks didn't involve face-to-face conversations with the lender, but Zachary did his best to make it sound dull and routine, nothing to get alarmed about. He cautioned them against calling McLachlan, making it sound like he wouldn't get whatever financing he was looking for if they contacted him directly.

They waffled and asked questions but, eventually, he managed to get several interviews lined up so he'd be able to get to work as soon as his wheels hit the ground. Others he would drop in on and hope that he could get a few minutes to talk to them.

He had hoped to begin with Forest McLachlan's ex-wife, but she had been harder to pin down than some of his former coworkers, so he would have to catch her later in the day. The fertility clinic McLachlan had worked at before Westlake had new management, and most of the old staff had been turned over, but Heather had managed to track people down at home or their new places of employment. The first person Zachary had an appointment with was Dr. Shane Patton. They met at a coffee shop a block away from Dr. Patton's new job, a large lab that did various kinds of testing that Zachary had never heard of before and would probably never need. He was a young man, his round cheeks giving him a baby-face that probably charmed the girls but also made people doubt whether he could be a real doctor.

"So, what exactly do you do?" Zachary asked him as they sat down with their cups of coffee.

"I do lab tests. There aren't as many openings for physicians as you might think. Yes, people are always complaining that there aren't enough doctors to go around, but there aren't many openings, either. Someone has to pay the doctors. We can't work for free."

Zachary nodded. Dr. Patton was, he thought, starting on the offensive, tired of people asking how good a doctor he could be when he was so young and didn't work at a doctor's office.

"And what do *you* do?" Dr. Patton returned. "I wasn't actually sure when I got off of the phone what it is that you were after. Something about Forest McLachlan, but I couldn't figure out what."

"To tell the truth, I'm a private investigator. I didn't want to say too much on the phone because this is a very confidential matter."

"A private investigator. For Forest?"

"No, for someone that Forest crossed paths with. I'm looking into the possibility that he was involved in an… unethical transaction." Zachary couched his explanation in more vague terms. Dr. Patton might think that it was a pyramid scheme, porn, gambling, or whatever he liked. He didn't need to know that it was something directly related to the work that the two of them had done at the fertility clinic.

"Unethical?" Dr. Patton said it in a hesitant tone. Like he might have misunderstood. He didn't say "Forest?" in a shocked tone, as if he would never believe that McLachlan had been involved in something shady. He was concerned with the word unethical and what it might involve.

"Yes. And I'm just talking to you for background. You used to work with him, didn't you?"

"Yeah, sure. We worked together at Sandhills Clinic. That was a couple of years back. I don't know what it could have to do with anything that's going on now."

"No, I didn't say that it did. But I need to look into Mr. McLachlan's background to satisfy all of the parties involved. It won't take long. A few questions and I'll be done here."

"Dr. McLachlan."

"Oh, sorry. Dr. McLachlan." Zachary noted with interest that Patton had corrected him. Then, as far as Patton was concerned, McLachlan was still a doctor in good standing.

"So." Zachary pulled out his notepad and flipped to a new page. "What can you tell me about him?"

"Well, I don't know what you're looking for. Nice enough guy. Got along with people. Decent at his job."

Pretty uninspiring compliments.

"Were the two of you friends?"

"Friends... no. We were friendly. We talked, you know, exchanged small talk over the coffee. Talked about sports the night before or coming up. Asked after each other's families." He shrugged. "Just... passing acquaintances, really. We wouldn't have been friends if we hadn't worked together. Never would have run into each other anywhere else."

"And he got along with the other doctors and staff that he worked with."

"Sure. Yeah."

"No conflicts there? No one who didn't like him? He didn't make any waves?"

"Conflicts?" Again, Patton repeated Zachary's inquiry and shook his head. "Who would he have conflicts with? I guess it's a high-stress environment in some ways. You have to follow exacting procedures; make sure you do everything right. Don't drop Mrs. Watson's petri dish." He gave a short laugh, inviting Zachary to share the joke with him. "But it wasn't like we were competitors, or fighting over anything. No one knew anyone socially. We just worked together."

"And he was good at what he did? He wasn't the one who dropped Mrs. Watson's petri dish?"

"That was just a joke. There was no Mrs. Watson. It's just a thing. You're dealing with... a very precious commodity. Arguably the most valuable thing in the world to our patients. And it's a very fragile one. You can't make an omelet without breaking some eggs, but when you're working in fertility treatments, you have to be very, very careful not to make any mistakes."

"I would imagine so. Did Mr. McLachlan have a specialty?"

"Dr. McLachlan."

"Right."

"No… none of us specialized. I mean, the younger doctors, we were just there to do the lab work, not to interface with the patients. That was for the gray hairs. They give people a sense of… wisdom and competence. Never mind that not one of them could probably do ICSI themselves. They had the social skills it took to deal with fussy, rich old ladies."

Ouch. Zachary had to school his expression not to give himself away. Dr. Patton was young, but he wasn't that much younger than most of the women who came into the clinic would be. But he made them sound ancient and batty.

"It sounds like you found it a frustrating place to work. You felt like… you were being held back?"

"Yeah. That's exactly it. We could have done so much more than we were doing if they'd just let us. But they only wanted us dealing with the technical stuff, and not to have a personal relationship with the patients. Which really means they didn't want to pay us for the patient-interface work. Keep us doing routine stuff in the lab while they were making the big bucks for consultation."

"Was there a big rift between the older doctors and the younger ones, then? Was it a two-class system? Or were there… a range of skills, and you just felt like yours weren't being utilized?"

"A lot of us younger guys felt like that. You go to school for a billion years, and then you think you're going to make a ton of money and live like a king. And then you find out… you have all of these debts to pay off, and you're basically earning minimum wage. I mean, there is hardly enough left over to eat. And you have to work for another ten years to advance and feel like you're getting anywhere, moving up the ladder. It's a tough economy out there. They don't pay you any more than they have to."

"Yeah. That must be really difficult."

"It is." Patton nodded eagerly, glad Zachary understood. "It's really hard to get ahead."

"And how was Dr. McLachlan handling that? Was he doing any better at advancement than you were?"

"He was trying. You gotta give the guy points for effort. He made coffee for the partners, chatted them up, asked them about their golf scores. Offered to help with procedures. Made a nuisance of himself, but in a good way. Trying to get anyone to take a chance on him."

"And you thought he was just being fake?"

"No. He wasn't fake. Who can blame him for trying to do the same thing as the rest of us? Why shouldn't he?"

"Anything about him ever hit you the wrong way? Like you thought… there was something wrong, or he was doing something he shouldn't?"

"No, nothing like that," Patton cocked his head. "I don't know what you're talking about."

Zachary figured he had elicited all of the up-front information that he was going to get. Bland, inoffensive stuff about McLachlan. It was time to turn the screws and see how Patton reacted.

"There was some trouble when the two of you were at Sandhills Clinic?"

Patton looked away, his eyes hooded. He sipped his coffee, looking like he wasn't surprised by what Zachary had said. He had been hoping, up until then, that it was just an innocent interview. McLachlan needed a mortgage or other kind of loan. A work reference, maybe.

"Trouble? I don't know what you're talking about."

"You really think that I would believe that? Of course you know what I'm talking about. There was a big to-do."

"Nah. Maybe there was a write-up or two in the paper on a slow news day. But it didn't mean anything. It wasn't the big deal that you think it was from reading what the shock-jocks had to write."

"So what was it, then?"

"Just… some procedural stuff. Some women with sour grapes. What you do in a place like that is very emotional. People get overwrought. When things don't work out the way they think they should, they get upset and look for someone to blame. They lay frivolous charges. It's nothing new. Been happening in America for years. You don't like your life? Sue someone. It's not your fault. You don't take responsibility for it."

"What were they suing for?"

Patton studied Zachary. "You know what it was all about. Don't bother trying to snow me. But there was nothing there. And they proved it in the end. There weren't any sanctions. No one got fired. And those women eventually faded into the woodwork. There wasn't any cash prize for suing the clinic. No free money."

"There were claims that mistakes were made. Samples mixed up. Implantations done when there wasn't anything to implant. Sleight of hand."

"And how would they know that?" Patton shook his head in disbelief. "How would any woman know whether we implanted an embryo or just squirted a syringe of growth medium? It isn't like we're transplanting fetuses that have been raised in chambers. It isn't anything you can see. And even if you do everything right, chances are, it still isn't going to take. You implant viable embryos, but for one reason or another, they just don't develop. What's miraculous is that they ever do. That we have this technology where we can make a baby outside the womb, and then put it back in, and it works. Do you know that science like that a hundred years ago would have been considered to be witchcraft? People don't stop and think about what it is that we're really doing."

"It is pretty amazing," Zachary encouraged.

"Women put off having babies until they're forty. They think that because they froze their eggs when they were twenty, that it's just a matter of squirting some sperm over it, and they're going to have a baby. The eggs were frozen, so they're still in perfect condition, right?" Patton shook his head. "No way, Jose. They don't last that long, even in the freezer. You wait ten years, and you're out of luck. They're not going to work. You ever seen freezer-burned meat? You know stuff still gets older and degrades even in a deep freeze."

"I never thought about it. You do hear about women who are just looking at getting pregnant at forty after their careers are firmly established."

"Yeah. And somehow the fact that their eggs have degraded over ten or twenty years is our fault. There must be incompetent people in your lab because my IVF didn't work the first time."

Zachary nodded sympathetically. "And... when it worked? What was this business about mixed-up samples? Do you think that ever happened?"

There hadn't been anything in the newspaper reports about mixed-up samples. That was Zachary's own fiction.

Patton looked at him, trying to decide what to say. He tapped a nail on the table, took a sip of his coffee, fidgeted with his earlobe. "Like I said, these rich old ladies… if anything doesn't go the way they expected, they start throwing around accusations. Do you know how much higher the risks of genetic damage are when you do IVF? People think that because we have this great technology, we can do miracles. Women want the embryos checked for specific problems. We want a baby without BRCA1. We don't want to take the chance that she will have a higher risk of breast cancer. So they want DNA tests done when the embryo has only gone through a few divisions. And we can do it, but there is a risk. Every time you touch that embryo, you could be doing damage. Fertilize it outside the womb, more risk. Do DNA testing to pick the embryo you want, more risk. Then people have a child who is blind or has cerebral palsy, and we're the bad guys. It's our fault. That doesn't run in my family, so how could I have a baby with that?"

"Does that happen?"

"IVF babies have a higher risk of being low birth weight or premature. They have a higher rate of cancer, blindness, cerebral palsy, autism, genitourinary malformations, heart malformations. You name it. There's a huge risk to having babies using technology like this."

"I've never heard that before."

Patton shrugged. "It's not like it's something that we advertise. Go ahead, store your eggs, or come to us if you're having conception problems, or if you want to make sure your child doesn't have a treatable cancer. Let's increase their risks of hepatoblastoma instead. That one kills children incredibly quickly. But who cares? You ask us, we'll give it to you. But don't blame us when things don't turn out the way you wanted."

"So these weren't cases of mixed-up samples. Just… mutations?"

"People don't like what they get, they sue. Your baby is darker or lighter skinned then you are? Must be a mix-up. Baby has blue eyes when both parents had brown? They must have used the wrong sperm. Baby has celiac disease? They couldn't have gotten that from the parents, so there must have been something nefarious going on at that clinic."

"Is that why you're not working there anymore? The lawsuits were just too stressful?"

Patton hesitated. He looked at Zachary, down at his coffee, out the window, thinking through what he wanted to say. "It's under new management now," he offered finally. "None of the old gang are there."

"You were all let go?"

"Eventually, yeah. There were a few waves, you know, a few sets of layoffs, and then once the new management was installed and they knew what they were doing, they brought in their own people and fired the last of the old staff."

"Was McLachlan let go in the first wave of layoffs?"

"Yes. It was one of those things, you know. Last in, first out."

"And you too?"

"Yeah. The younger people are always expendable. Easier for them to find new jobs. Yeah, we both were let go in the first set of layoffs."

"Well, I'm sorry for the rough time you had to go through. You must be a lot happier being out of that business."

"Yeah," Patton said after another pause. "Yeah, of course I am."

23

_____

Not everybody agreed with Patton's litany of complaints. The women especially seemed to have found Sandhills Clinic a warm and nurturing place to work. The focus on babies and motherhood and miracles seemed to touch them in a way that it didn't affect the men. They had found the stories in the news disturbing and stressful, but had nice things to say about the clinic itself.

But they didn't all have nice things to say about McLachlan.

Rose Turner had worked with McLachlan and didn't agree with what Patton had shared about him.

She pushed a few wild red curls back over her ear and scowled at Zachary. "I don't know what this has to do with anything. You need a character reference to give him a loan? Or what is this about?"

"I'm afraid I can't give you details about that. But I appreciate your cooperation."

"I'm not sure you're going to like what I have to say. Maybe you should just go on to the next person on your list."

"If you found Mr. McLachlan difficult to work with, or less than professional, I would like to hear about it."

Zachary noted with interest that unlike Patton, Rose didn't correct Zachary's use of mister instead of doctor.

"Less than professional. Yes, I would say that he was less than professional," Rose snapped. "The guy was always hitting on us. Other doctors, nurses, even patients. He would flirt with the women who came in for procedures. Like they wanted to be hit on by the doctor? That's not what people came to us for. It's just... gross. No one wanted to hear from him. That's why they tried to keep him and some of the others with... social skills problems... in the lab, where they were away from direct patient contact."

"He harassed you? And patients too?"

"Have you ever met a man who just didn't seem to understand when he was being offensive? Like you could tell him right to his face, and he would just laugh it off and say 'I didn't mean it that way.' And then turn around and do it again. He wasn't intentionally offensive. But he was... odious."

Zachary nodded understandingly. He could imagine what it would be like to be in a place like that, so focused on babies and reproduction, and to have a hound dog always making inappropriate comments, hitting on the female staff and patients, and generally making a nuisance of himself. It wouldn't make for a pleasant work atmosphere. They should have made a sexual harassment claim against him. Maybe they had. They could be notoriously difficult for a company to deal with.

"That couldn't have been easy to deal with. How were his skills? If you kept him in the lab, was he productive? Able to do his job?"

She shrugged and scowled. "It doesn't take that much skill. Honestly. If I ran you through it a couple of times, you could do it. Yes, he could do the job... though I wondered, sometimes..."

Zachary waited for her to finish, cocking his head slightly. Rose fussed with her hair some more, making up her mind whether she were going to say anything.

"There was some trouble," she said finally.

"At the clinic? What kind of trouble?"

Since she had brought it up, she didn't assume, as Patton had, that he had already read the news articles about it. She shifted in her seat and looked away from him. Probably reviewing how it would reflect on her, if it would get back to the clinic or someone else in the industry, maybe impact her future opportunities.

"I don't know if I should say anything. I mean... there's no proof."

"Proof of what?"

"There was some trouble," she repeated, starting over and trying to get the momentum to move forward. "There were accusations from a couple of sets of parents that there was something wrong with their babies. They didn't appear to be the right racial profile or had some disease or deformity that hadn't been seen in that family before…"

"So… what was happening? Were they paranoid? Or was there an issue?"

"I don't think they were just paranoid. Not with so many people coming forward and asking questions at the same time."

Zachary noted it was now 'many' instead of 'a couple.' "And was there any kind of investigation? I mean, a clinic like that must have all kinds of procedures in place to make sure that there aren't any mix-ups."

"Yes, of course." She answered a little too quickly and her eyes still avoided his. "There are procedures, security. Of course."

"So… nothing could have been happening? It was just a coincidence?"

"I don't think it was. I think that someone was screwing up fertilizations. Mixing up samples or intentionally sabotaging procedures."

"How could that happen?"

"On the 'accidental' end, maybe someone had dyslexia and was reading numbers wrong. Or was hungover or had poor eyesight. I mean, those numbers are pretty small. A mistake could be made if you were having trouble telling your sixes from your eights, or something like that."

"Was McLachlan dyslexic?"

"I wouldn't know. People get really good at hiding it. But mistakes were made. There were settlements. And then the clinic was sold, started up under new management to shake the reputation. A fresh start."

"So, there was something to it."

She studied the table, biting her lip. "Yes," she finally agreed.

"And you think it might have been McLachlan?"

"Not for sure. There were a few guys at the lab that I would have had questions about, if I was in charge. They were messing around… acting juvenile. You know, just not professional. Forest was just one of the possibilities."

"So you said that it could have been accidental, someone reading a number wrong. And what's the other option? You think that it could have been intentional?"

This was even harder for her. She cleared her throat a few times. Looked like she wanted to get up from her seat and pace around. He could understand the impulse. He didn't like to sit for long, especially when he found himself in the hot seat.

"You want to go outside?" he suggested. "Go for a walk while we talk about it?"

"Oh, no," she dismissed immediately. "I'm good."

He waited to see if she would fill in the details.

"Actually, yes," Rose said finally. "Let's go outside. Get a breath of fresh air."

Zachary nodded. They had already paid for their drinks, so they got up and left, wandering down the sidewalk. It was a beautiful day out. Zachary took in the sun and matched Rose's pace. She was a little taller than he was, her stride a little longer. She was anxious, so she walked fast. Zachary found the speed awkward. His walking pace was usually okay, but he hadn't quite reached the smooth, automatic stride that he had before his accident if he had to speed up. Hopefully, she would settle back to a slower pace once she got talking. Otherwise, he was afraid he was going to trip or have to tell her to slow it down.

"Do you think that someone was intentionally sabotaging samples?" Zachary pressed.

"I… that's one of the options, right? I wasn't in charge, I wasn't part of the investigation, so I couldn't tell you. But I didn't feel like it was something that someone could have been doing accidentally. I just had a gut feeling that… someone was mixing things up intentionally. For kicks? I don't know why someone would do that."

"I don't know why either," Zachary assured her. "I guess since we're not the kind of people who would do that, it's hard for us to understand someone who would. I really don't know. I guess sometimes it's ego. Seeing what they can get away with. Or it could be anger or revenge. Maybe he hit on one of those patients, and she rejected him, so he wanted to get back at her."

"Yeah." Rose nodded slowly. "I hadn't thought about that."

She was slowing to an easier walking pace.

"Did anyone talk to the… whatever you call the owners or managing partners? Someone higher up the food chain. Did anyone ever say that they had concerns about McLachlan or the other guys in the lab?"

"No, not as far as I know. We were all… you know, just trying to keep our jobs. No one threw anyone else under the bus. We hoped that it would just blow over. We didn't think that even if we stuck together, we would lose our jobs anyway."

"But that's what ended up happening when you got new management."

"Yeah. I guess it would have been smarter to make accusations, to try to get the person who was responsible fired. Then maybe the consequences wouldn't have been quite so dire. They'd be able to say 'we found the culprit and everything is good now,' instead of going further and turning over the whole staff."

"Maybe. Maybe enough damage had been done that they would have had to do that anyway. You don't know what would have happened if circumstances had been different."

"Yeah. I guess. Maybe everything would have happened the same way even if we'd all pointed fingers. I thought at the time that I was being loyal to my coworkers, that we were friends and had each other's backs. But now... I'm not friends with any of them anymore. Did I think that I would be? We were never really friends, so why would I protect any of them? Especially jerks like Forest. I'm sure he was probably one of them. Maybe he wasn't the one who messed up the fertilizations. But I bet he knew who did."

Zachary raised his brows. He juggled out his notebook and they stopped for a moment while he made a note to himself to check into that. Even if it hadn't been McLachlan, maybe he could point Zachary in the right direction. Maybe there was evidence somewhere still.

"I haven't been able to get appointments with any of the senior doctors. Did you know any of them?"

"Not well. As well as you know anyone you work with. Which is... pretty much not at all. You learn things like if they're married and have kids, get familiar with the way that they talk and how they like things to be done, but that's about it."

"Do you have any cell numbers that would still be in service? Personal email addresses?"

"No, nothing like that. I got rid of all of those contact details when I left there. I was pretty ticked. Didn't want ever to have to deal with any of those people again."

"I'm sorry. And here I am bringing it all up again."

"It's okay, actually. I feel like... I've never been able to really talk about it before, to process it. I was too busy staying quiet and protecting everyone else. It feels good to talk about it."

"Good. Can you give me the names of the others who worked with McLachlan and might be involved?"

Patton was one of them. Zachary noted a couple of other names that were new to him. Not people who had come up on their previous checks.

"Is there anything else? You said that there were settlements, so you felt that where there was smoke, there was fire?"

"Yeah. I don't think they would have paid anyone off if they'd been able to prove absolutely that there hadn't been any mishandling of genetic materials. Or that if there was, it was entirely accidental."

"Yeah. You're probably right. It wasn't just to make them go away?"

"No. I think they would have taken it to court if they were sure that there hadn't been any wrongdoing by anyone at Sandhills. They would have wanted to protect their good name. But they ended up not being able to do that."

2 4

Zachary met with McLachlan's ex-wife in her home, not a coffee shop or neutral location like his coworkers. Zachary wanted her to feel at home on her own ground. He wanted to give her a sense of control.

And he wanted to see what kind of place McLachlan had lived in, if they had lived there while they were married. Even if they hadn't, the ex-wife would have mementos. Pictures, maybe things he'd left behind. Things that would give Zachary a better sense of McLachlan and the kind of person he was. He was already getting a pretty good picture of McLachlan.

His wife was pretty. Blond, shoulder-length hair and a thin face. She appeared younger than McLachlan in the pictures Zachary had seen of him. But it was hard to tell sometimes.

She shook Zachary's hand, something that not a lot of women did. Her grip was dry and firm. She gave an image of calm competence. He didn't know what she did for a living, but he imagined that she was good at it and that her clients or customers were happy around her.

"Mrs. McLachlan, it's good to meet you."

"I don't go by McLachlan. I've gone back to Hubble. Don't know why I ever took his name to begin with. I never wanted to be just someone's wife."

"Ms. Hubble. Sorry."

"No, not a problem. You can call me Maureen. Forget about all of the mister and miz stuff."

"Okay. Maureen. And I'm Zachary, always."

"Come on in." She ushered Zachary into her living room. It wasn't a big, fancy house. Not like the mansions that the bigwig surgeons lived in. Instead, it was a little starter house like couples often got as they finished school and launched their careers. Neat, but small. It probably had all of the usual problems of dwellings in their income bracket. Knocking pipes, a leaky roof, windows that were not adequately sealed.

The living room was pleasantly furnished with a couch, loveseat, and easy chair covered with a do-it-yourself upholstery cover to make it match. The chair that Zachary sank into was comfortable enough. The room was clean, with bright sunlight filtering through the opaque blinds, pictures of Maureen and her family or friends on the walls, and some knickknacks here and there. Nothing that was readily identifiable as having belonged to McLachlan.

"This is very nice," Zachary said. "Did you move here after the divorce?"

"No. This is where we were living at the time. We still had another year on the lease, and I said that I would pay the lease and keep the place. Forest didn't want to pay for it, so he didn't object. Though I imagine he came to regret it later. It isn't so easy to get a nice place for a reasonable price these days."

Zachary nodded. "Yes, it's the same in Vermont. Seems like they cost more than they should."

"It's hard to make ends meet if you only have one income. Most people will try to find roommates to split the cost with if they're not half of a working couple. It's a tough economy."

"Very true. Have you seen Forest's place in Vermont?"

"I've seen some interior shots and his view out the window. On social media, you know. Not in person. I wouldn't have any reason to go out there and meet him in person."

"Sure. That makes sense."

"It's nice, but I think it's just a one-bedroom apartment. Not something he'd be able to start a family in."

Zachary glanced around the interior of the house Maureen had kept, estimating the square footage and the number of bedrooms. They had, Zachary figured, intended to start a family at some point.

"Do you have kids?"

"No." Maureen shook her head. "I figured once everything had settled down, we would be able to start. But things never worked out. I don't know if Forest ever intended to have a family, or if it was just convenient to have someone helping to put him through medical school. Pay any extra bills, have someone around to make meals and do the laundry. It was a pretty good deal for him."

"And when he finished school, you figured you would be able to move somewhere nicer and get started on having kids. Let him support you for a while."

She sighed. "It would have been nice, huh? But I don't think that was ever what he intended to do."

"He probably meant to, on some level. But things don't always work out the way we planned. Sometimes they're just... wishes, pie in the sky. Not something that we were ever going to put any effort into."

"Yeah. Maybe. We talked about it once, a long time ago. Seems like a long time ago now."

"You don't keep in contact with him anymore?"

"No. No reason to. Best we just go our separate directions."

"Can you tell me what happened here? When the trouble started at the clinic?"

"Hmm." Maureen settled back into her seat on the sofa. "I didn't know, at first, that anything was going on. He was irritable. Angry, sometimes, for no reason I could tell."

"Did he eventually tell you why?"

"Eventually it was all coming out, and he had to tell me before it hit the news. Or, he wanted to tell me before it hit the news. It was the right thing to do, but I don't think it was very easy for him."

"What did he say was happening?"

"He said it was just sour grapes. People whose pregnancies hadn't worked out the way they expected. When they go to a high-class place like Sandhills, they expect everything to be perfect. And things aren't ever perfect. If they have a miscarriage or the baby has defects, they blame the clinic. Even though that could have happened anywhere. It could happen with a natural pregnancy. But they have to have someone to blame it on."

"I guess that happens. People want to be able to explain why something happened. They want a reason."

"Yeah. I never tried to get pregnant, so I can't say what it would be like not to be able to get pregnant."

Zachary nodded. "So he didn't tell you that anything had actually gone wrong at the clinic? He said it was just people complaining?"

"Yes, to start with. As it went on… it became obvious that something was going on. It didn't just go away, you know?"

"I understand that there were settlements were made."

Maureen shrugged. "That doesn't mean anything. It might just be money to keep people quiet, to keep them from saying something in media, ruining the clinic's reputation."

"I'm sure there was some of that as well. But some of the others that worked at the clinic that I have talked to figured that it wasn't just smoke."

"Did you want a drink? I didn't offer you anything." Maureen got up and walked toward the kitchen. "Coffee? Tea? Wine?"

"Just water, if that's okay."

"Sure, yeah."

She returned with a coffee cup and a glass of water. Zachary took the glass from her and sipped the lukewarm tap water.

Maureen sat down. "So what did you need to know about Forest? I'm not really clear on what this is all about."

"I guess you know that when he left Minnesota, he started working at another fertility clinic in Vermont."

"Yes, I know he said that."

"My client's wife is one of the patients at the clinic. There have been some questions."

She pressed her lips together. "What kind of questions?"

"Prenatal testing shows that the baby has a genetic disease that neither of the parents has."

"Some of them can skip a generation or two."

"Apparently, this isn't one of them."

"But that doesn't necessarily mean that someone at the clinic made a mistake." Maureen clamped her mouth shut, then reconsidered. "Okay, it probably does. I don't… I don't like to hear that. I don't like to think about Forest or one of the other doctors at the clinic screwing up samples and making a mistake like that. That's just a parent's worst nightmare, right? Do you have kids?"

"No, not yet."

"I can't imagine finding out something like that about my kid, especially before he was even born. It would be terrifying. And you would be so angry, right? Someone screwing things up like that?"

Zachary nodded. "It's a violation. A betrayal. Especially if..."

She sipped her coffee, looking over the brim at him. She didn't prompt him to continue. As she had said, she didn't like to talk about it or think about it.

"Especially if someone did it intentionally," Zachary told her.

"Intentionally? No one is saying that. Forest wouldn't do that. Who would do something like that?"

"What is Forest like as a person? How did you get along, when the marriage was going well?"

"Oh, I don't know. He was an interesting guy. Very smart, very... self-centered in an attractive way. Confident in himself, you know? That can be very attractive in a man. Women like someone strong and confident in himself."

Zachary wouldn't know. He had never been that kind of person.

"It's nice to know that you can depend on someone," he suggested.

"Yes, it is. I liked it, felt safe with him. He knew he was going to succeed, so I felt like things would go well for us. I believed him."

"But things didn't work out the way you expected."

"No. He kept saying that he was doing great at this or that, that he was the best one in his class, or the clinic, or whatever, and he was going to work himself to the top. He was going to be one of the most prominent fertility doctors in America. I just had to believe that and to wait for that to happen."

"That *is* pretty confident."

"Yeah, and after a while, I got tired of it. He kept bragging himself up, and whenever anything went wrong or didn't turn out the way he expected it to, it was someone else's fault. For not recognizing his genius, or because they were jealous and pulled him down, whatever. The predictions of grandeur grew and grew, but he didn't advance. He was still basically a tech at the clinic. Not even dealing with patients most of the time. Not making enough money to make his loan payments. So here I was, still carrying him, and he was apparently the most brilliant doctor in the country."

Zachary wondered if this was an early warning sign of Huntington's. The literature that he had looked at talked about forgetfulness, mood swings, aggression, and confusion. Were McLachlan's mistakes just a symptom of his disease?

"And after a while, I just couldn't take it anymore. All of the bragging and whining about how everyone else was holding him back. The lack of progress, and worrying about whether he was even going to be able to keep his job."

"Did they fire him, or did he quit and go to Vermont?"

"He was... let go during the management change. They didn't call it firing. So he didn't have that on his employment record."

"He didn't put his Sandhills job on his resume."

"I guess... that makes sense. The way things ended up there, I can see why he wouldn't want people to associate him with it." She looked at Zachary, narrowing her eyes. "It wasn't him, though. No one ever proved that he did anything wrong."

"But that doesn't mean he didn't. Especially where this has happened at his new clinic... it's suspicious, don't you think?"

"I think I would know. If he was making mistakes like that at work, I would have known that there was something wrong. He would act differently. Guilty. Upset. Angry. Something."

"He might. Or he might hide it. Or maybe those things he was saying about everyone else blocking him and what he would do if they would just let him be brilliant *was* talking to you about the mistakes he had made or the things he had done to someone else."

Maureen shook her head. Zachary looked for another segue. He wasn't going to get her to admit that he could have been involved—accidentally or intentionally—in the problems at the clinic. And she didn't need to. He didn't need that to make his case. There were more important things for him to find out.

"What are his family like? Were his parents still living? Did you meet them?"

"Yes. Both were still living, and he has a brother and a sister."

"His parents must be getting on in years," Zachary suggested.

Maureen raised her brows. "No, they're not that old. Fifties, I think."

"And they're in good health?"

"As far as I know. I think his dad has some diabetes, but his mom is doing okay. They're both doing okay, I mean."

"No dementia or anything like that."

"No. They're too young for that."

"Sometimes, it starts younger. What about his grandparents? What's his family history like?"

"I don't know what you're looking for."

"I'm just wondering about these grandiose opinions of himself. Whether they come from his upbringing, or maybe they're cultural or even genetic. You never know, do you? All kinds of things can affect your mood and... stability. Has he ever been treated for bipolar?"

"No, I don't think so. His parents had him in some therapy when he was younger, but I don't know what it was for. He talks about it like it was like, speech therapy or something, but it was when he was older. I don't really know and I never asked. I don't think... not bipolar or anything like that."

"And his dad? Everything has been good with him too?"

"Just diabetes. He was in the hospital a little while back. I didn't know what it was for."

Zachary thought back to the notes he had made about Huntington's Disease. He took out his notepad to refresh his memory.

"How about clumsiness? Problems walking or weird movements?"

She gave him a look. "What are you looking for?"

"Things run in families. If he has grandiose ideas about himself because of bipolar, then his dad might too. Or his mom. Someone else in his extended family."

"No, nothing like that. And what would that have to do with being clumsy? That's not part of bipolar."

"No, but it could be a symptom of another disease. There could be something to explain the behavior you saw. It might not have been by choice."

"I don't know. It got worse, but I think it was just the stress at the clinic. Not being promoted, and then the accusations going around about tampering with people's embryos. It wasn't a disease. He's working at this other clinic in Vermont, isn't he? He couldn't do that if he had some disease that made him quit working here."

"I don't know. Maybe for a while. But this client of mine... it looks like the whole cycle is going to start all over again."

Maureen leaned forward. "Don't do it. It was such a mess, and everyone ended up feeling attacked and unfairly done by. Just... tell your client to let it go. He got his baby and if it wasn't perfect… well, they never are, are they? He's going to have to suck it up and raise it just like anyone. And he can try again. At another clinic, if he thinks there's something wrong at this new Vermont clinic. But don't… don't make it a big thing like Sandhills was. That wasn't good for anyone."

"If you could change the way things had gone down, is that what you would do? Just make everyone look the other way at the clinic?"

"Everyone has to deal with risks when bringing a baby into the world. Whether they use IVF or other technology or just have them the old-fashioned way. There are always risks, and you take what you can get."

"Even if someone else has sabotaged it? If someone other than Forest swapped vials or fertilized the eggs with his own sperm, do you think they should just ignore it?"

"His own sperm?"

Zachary looked at her. "If the baby has a genetic disease that didn't come from either of the assumed parents, then it had to come from somewhere else. Maybe the technician who did the fertilization. Maybe it was just an internal mix-up, but in a lot of these cases—" That was, Zachary knew, an exaggeration, "—then it wasn't an accidental switch, it was the doctor using his own DNA for the fertilization process. When it was supposed to be donor sperm, or even the husband's sperm."

"Forest would never do that. That's horrible."

"You wouldn't like the idea of him fathering babies all over Minnesota and Vermont, would you? Even if he didn't have direct contact with the mothers? It's still not a nice idea."

"No. And he wouldn't do that. I could complain about a lot of things about Forest, but that isn't one of them. He didn't do that."

"He's brilliant. He's egotistical. He thinks that the babies would all turn out to be better if he was the father. They would all be as brilliant and exceptional as he is."

Maureen shook her head slowly, eyes wide.

But Zachary wondered. Forest McLachlan fit the pictures of the egotistical, self-centered doctor that Kenzie had sketched for him. A doctor who thought the world would be a better place if it were filled with more people just like him.

25

Zachary had already promised Mr. Peterson and Pat that he would be at dinner on the weekend when Pat's mother and sister were over for a visit. He finished up his interviews with that appointment in mind, and returned home in enough time that he could drive down Friday night to spend a quiet evening with Pat and Mr. Peterson, knowing that Saturday evening's dinner would be more stressful and he would have to put on his company manners.

Kenzie fussed a bit about whether he was jet-lagged, but it wasn't that long of a flight. He had slept okay at the hotel and he enjoyed the highway driving.

He called Gordon while he was on the road, and outlined to him the discoveries he had made. None of it was proof of wrongdoing on the part of Forest McLachlan. But it was strongly suggestive. He and Heather would delve as deep into McLachlan's family history as they could, looking for early deaths, dementia, aggression, and any unexplained mental impairments. If McLachlan had Huntington's in his family, they would find it.

"What if you don't find anything?" Gordon asked. "Is it back to the drawing board?"

"No, I don't think so. We have other suspects that we can look at, but I think our subject is probably the culprit. I talked to Kenzie about the genetics, and it is possible that someone who is not showing any symptoms or family history of Huntington's Disease could pass the expanded form of the gene on to his child. It's not common, but it is a possibility."

"Then he's the guy. Whether you find it in his family or not, he's the one."

"Probably, but we would need direct proof to have him charged. We can't just go on guesses and circumstances. It is possible that he didn't do anything wrong in Minnesota. Or that he didn't do anything wrong here. Or both. It could be pure coincidence that there were problems in both places. It could happen in the industry all the time, and we just don't hear about it."

"We would hear about it," Gordon insisted.

"They do everything they can to keep it quiet. Just like you did everything you could to keep that business at Chase Gold quiet so it wouldn't affect your bottom line."

There was silence on the line from Gordon.

"Gordon?"

"Yes, okay," Gordon agreed, his tone more clipped than usual, lacking its usual warmth. "They would do everything they could to keep it out of the media. Of course. But if it was happening too often, they wouldn't be able to keep it quiet, would they? It would still get out. You would have parents up in arms all over the country trying to find out who had screwed up and why the clinics couldn't put procedures into place to make sure it didn't happen again."

"Yes. I'm just saying; we don't know how often the clinics have to quash problems like this. It could be far more common than they would have us believe."

"Let me know what your researcher finds out. I want to know as soon as you do."

"I'll keep you updated."

"Thanks, Zachary."

Zachary pulled in front of Mr. Peterson's neat little bungalow and looked at it, feeling warm and happy to be there. He didn't get that feeling from a lot of things. But Mr. Peterson and Pat had been a constant in his life for a lot of years. The only people who had been there for him since he had been a teenager. He'd been through some bad times, and Mr. Peterson was always there, visiting him at the hospital, helping him with a tough problem, working through old memories that were painful to discuss. He'd been there for all of it. And Pat was always warm and welcoming, trying to tempt Zachary with a plate of cookies or the other homemaking hobbies he enjoyed. Neither fell into the stereotypical roles or affectations of gay men popularized by the media. Just two family men devoted to each other and their circle of friends.

Zachary got out of the car with his one packed bag, locked the car, tried the handle, and clicked the key fob a couple more times. He stood there looking at the locks, then up and down the street, looking for anything out of place or anyone watching him. He couldn't help feeling uneasy sometimes, knowing that the couple had previously been targeted because of Zachary's involvement in a case. He wanted them to be safe and needed to know that he wasn't bringing any more danger in their direction.

He clicked the key fob one more time and then forced himself to walk up the sidewalk to the house. He could see lights on in the living room and kitchen. As he got closer, he could see Mr. Peterson on the couch reading. His head went up as he saw the movement outside, and he motioned for Zachary to let himself in.

It made Zachary anxious to know that the door wasn't locked or the burglar alarm armed. He opened the door to let himself in.

"Zachary." Mr. Peterson laid aside his book and stood up, taking a couple of steps over to Zachary to give him a quick hug in greeting. "I wasn't sure what time you'd get here. How was the trip?"

"Good. Dry roads. No traffic problems."

"Glad to hear it. You want to put your bag in your room? Pat will be just a minute. He needed something at the store."

"Okay. Great." Zachary went to the guest room to put his bag down. He guessed that Pat's mother and sister would not be staying overnight. Or if they were, perhaps they would be at a hotel. There was a rollaway in the small bedroom Mr. Peterson used as an office, but that would still leave them one bed short. Zachary could take the rollaway and Pat's mother and sister could share the queen bed in the guest room, but since Lorne had told him to take his usual room, he assumed they had made other arrangements.

He stood in the bedroom for a moment, looking around for anything that had changed or was out of place, but everything seemed to be as it was the last time he had visited. He looked out the window but didn't see any unusual activity in the neighborhood.

Pat wouldn't have gone out and left the door unlocked and burglar alarm unarmed if he had thought that there was anything to be concerned about. And he was probably right. Zachary wasn't there because of a case this time. He wasn't investigating anything in town or anyone who had indicated any interest in Zachary, his background, or his family. It was just a regular visit. And meeting Pat's family.

He returned to the living room and sat down. "How has everything been? No problems?"

Mr. Peterson looked at him for a moment, not understanding. Then he shook his head.

"No, no security issues. Everything has been just fine. We'd let you know if there were any problems."

Zachary looked out the front window, then leaned back, relaxing his muscles. Once he got into the visit, his anxiety would ease. He was safe there. Lorne and Pat were safe.

"How is Pat?"

Since Pat was out, that made it a lot easier to talk about him and get a temperature reading from Mr. Peterson. Pat had been struggling since the murder of Jose. He had gone through a period of depression, but was, as far as Zachary knew, doing fairly well on an antidepressant prescription and occasional therapy sessions.

"He's doing pretty well. Very excited about you meeting his family. It's been a long time, you know, and now he's finally able to merge these two sides of his life together. The family he grew up in and... well, me. And you."

It was hard to believe that Pat's family had refused to have anything to do with him just because of his relationship with Mr. Peterson. Zachary knew there were people out there who were so against gay relationships that they would not associate with anyone who was in one. But Pat was such a warm and giving person that Zachary couldn't imagine him coming from a family like that. And he couldn't imagine how they had held his orientation against him for decades.

But Pat's father had passed away, and his mother and sister had finally decided that they wanted to get to know him again.

"What are they like? What was it like when you met them for the first time?"

"Well, you can imagine that it was awkward. It's one thing to decide that you'll start talking to your son or brother again. But it's another to take that step and meet the person you've hated all of those years. I suppose they thought that I was some kind of..." Mr. Peterson shook his head and searched for the words. "Some sort of devil that managed to tempt Pat away, to twist him into this relationship. It has been difficult for them to accept that he just happens to have a different orientation than they have."

Zachary smiled. He couldn't imagine Pat being anything else. And he couldn't picture Mr. Peterson as being some kind of incubus. In his sixties now, his fringe hair turned white and he had a bit of a paunch. He had always been a father figure to Zachary.

When Mr. Peterson had come out, he had lost his accreditation as a foster parent. Zachary hadn't been told at the time what was going on but, after Lorne was divorced and Zachary's social worker figured out that Zachary had still been visiting him, he had assumed that Mr. Peterson must be a pedophile and a predator. That had led to some interesting conversations.

Zachary had been banned from seeing him anymore. But Zachary had been fifteen or sixteen at the time, and he hadn't listened to anything he was told. It had been only a week later that he had taken his next roll of film over to Mr. Peterson's apartment to develop it in his darkroom. And he had met Pat for the first time.

He'd never felt threatened or uncomfortable around either one of them. If all foster parents could be like Mr. Peterson and Pat... maybe Zachary's teenage years wouldn't have been quite so difficult. He'd had too many issues for the Petersons to handle. Mrs. Peterson had insisted that he be removed from their family. And maybe she was right. Maybe they had not been the right family for Zachary. He hadn't been stable enough to be with any family for long.

"You're far away," Mr. Peterson observed.

Zachary shook off the memories. "I can't imagine anyone thinking about you like that," he said with a little laugh. "You and Pat have always been... well, just you and Pat. You were older than him, but you were never... You didn't force him or lure him into the relationship."

"Of course not," Mr. Peterson agreed. "I could never do anything like that. He's his own person, and if we hadn't been compatible, we would not have stayed together."

Zachary heard the garage door opening and then closing and, in a few minutes, the kitchen door opened and Pat entered carrying a couple of bags of groceries. He saw Zachary through the doorway and smiled.

"Zachary! You made it. I'm so glad you're here."

"Of course. I wouldn't miss it." He had, of course, missed it the first time Pat had asked him to meet them. But that had been Christmas. Zachary was never doing very well around Christmas. He hadn't been up to it then.

"It's so nice to be able to have my family... be part of my family again. My mom is very excited about meeting you."

Zachary's face got warm. He hadn't ever had a grandparent, and the thought of Pat's mom being excited to 'meet her grandchild' felt a little weird. Pat had been more of a father to him the past couple of decades than anyone but Mr. Peterson, and Zachary was happy to call him a foster father or stepfather, but it was strange to think of Pat's extended family being part of Zachary's family.

"I hope she's not disappointed." There was a tightness in his stomach that hadn't been there before. He wasn't exactly the cute baby bundle that most grandparents looked forward to seeing. He was about as different from a cute little baby as he could be.

"Zachary, I've talked so much about you. She's really looking forward to it. You don't need to feel like you have anything to prove or to measure up to. You're just family. I just want my family to meet each other. You're not expecting anything from them, are you?"

Zachary considered. He wasn't. He would take them however they were. Whether they were sharp and acid like Joss or warm and caring like Tyrrell or Mr. Peterson, it didn't really matter. He'd take them as they came. He knew that he wasn't getting a doting grandparent. He was just meeting the woman who had raised Pat. And Pat was a great guy.

"No. It will just be nice to meet them," he agreed.

"I've met some of your siblings now. There wasn't anything awkward about that, was there?"

"No." Pat was always the consummate host. He made everyone feel comfortable. Kenzie and Zachary's siblings had immediately felt at home with him. And Pat would make things comfortable when his family came. "No, it was really nice," he agreed.

"There you go." Pat put his bags on the kitchen counter. "I just have to get these put away. Have you had supper?"

"I grabbed something on the way."

"So, no," Pat discerned. "Granola bars or fries don't count."

Zachary scratched his jaw. "Well then… no, I guess I haven't," he admitted.

"That's what I thought. How are you ever going to put on weight if you don't eat at least three meals a day?"

"I've been gaining weight."

"A little," Pat admitted, looking at him critically. "But not enough. I could fatten you up a lot faster."

Mr. Peterson chuckled. "We're not going to cook him for Easter dinner."

Pat laughed. He moved around the kitchen, putting his groceries away, while at the same time pulling seemingly-random items out of the cupboards and fridge. Zachary watched him through the doorway. Watching Pat pull a meal together was like magic. Nothing like when Zachary put a burrito in the microwave or Kenzie boiled pasta on the stove, adding bottled sauce after it was drained.

"I know you're going to tell me that you're not very hungry…" Pat said.

"No. I don't really need anything."

"Yes, you do. Let me make you something nice."

Zachary went to bed with a full stomach despite himself. He felt stuffed. Pat's omelet, toast, and hash browns had been way too much for him. He'd done his best but hadn't made much of a dent in them. Pat was used to that and just laughed good-naturedly.

"You can have it for breakfast tomorrow."

The morning was the worst time for Zachary's nausea. He didn't plan on having a big, eggy breakfast in the morning.

He took a walk through the house to make sure that everything was in place and the burglar alarm was armed. Pat and Lorne headed off to sleep, and Zachary sat on his bed, checking his email and social media and waiting for his eyelids to get heavy enough that he could try to sleep.

26

The next day, he was up before Mr. Peterson and Pat, even though he'd gotten to bed several hours after them. He booted up his computer and worked on what he could until he heard the two men up and around.

He looked at the time on his system clock and decided that it wasn't too early to call Heather and see what she had been able to find out.

Just as his call rang through, his computer dinged and he saw an email come in from her. Heather answered the phone, laughing. "How did you know I was going to send that?"

"I just wanted to know how you were doing. I wasn't sure whether you would have anything yet."

"Well, I worked pretty late the last couple of nights."

Zachary double-clicked the attachment on the email she had sent and looked over the bolded headings. "So he does have some dementia in his family."

"Yes. Nothing that was ever identified as Huntington's Disease, though," Heather summarized. "Usually it says dementia or Alzheimer's. No requests for donations to Huntington's Disease research or anything like that. Sorry."

"That's okay. I didn't expect that we'd be quite that lucky. I'm happy that you managed to find something."

"Yeah. I don't know if it has ever actually been diagnosed."

"In some cases, it isn't, especially if it is later in life, or if they have a few generations where people die young before it hits. I guess some people get it when they're fifty, but some don't get it until they're seventy or eighty. And then… they just call it aging… or maybe Parkinson's."

"Yes. I think there was one in there that they said was Parkinson's."

"Okay. Well, that's really helpful. And you have his contact information in here." Zachary scanned through the information that Heather had sent him. "Okay. I'll talk to the client, and then see whether I can get ahold of McLachlan."

"Do you think you should contact him directly?" Heather asked worriedly. "He's not going to want to talk to a private investigator. He could get violent if you start digging into his family history and what's gone on at these clinics."

"I'll be careful. I'll approach him with some other story. Stroke his ego. Kenzie said that these doctors who have done this kind of thing in the past, you know, substituting their sperm in fertility treatments, they've got big egos, think that they are something special. I'll focus on that. Tell him that I've heard how wonderful he is or something. That my client noticed him at the fertility clinic and wanted me to reach out to him… for something. Advice."

"I don't know. It still seems like… I don't know; I would be worried about it."

"I'll be careful." Zachary had run afoul of enough other bad actors that he knew he needed to be careful. This time, it wouldn't turn out like it had before. And it wasn't like McLachlan was a serial killer. He was a doctor—someone who had sworn the Hippocratic Oath. Do no harm. The danger would not be in his acting violently toward Zachary, but in figuring out that the jig was up and running away.

"Make sure you are," Heather instructed him in her big-sister voice. "Do you need anything else from me?"

"No, I don't think so. I'll let you know if I need something, but I think this wraps it up pretty neatly. He's got to be the guy."

After Zachary was off the phone with Heather, Pat poked his head in.

"Morning, Zachary. Early bird as usual."

"Yeah. You know me. If I get a few hours in, I'm doing well."

Pat knew better than to suggest sleeping pills. He knew what had happened the last time Zachary had taken sleeping pills when he was there and they had interacted with his painkillers. Zachary had nearly ended up back in hospital when Pat and Lorne couldn't wake him up.

"You up for coffee and toast?" Pat inquired.

"Coffee sounds good," Zachary agreed. Toast would be pushing it. A few cups of coffee to get his day going, and he would have something to eat later in the day when he was feeling up to it.

Pat rolled his eyes. "I'll put the coffee on."

Zachary smiled. He listened to Pat clinking mugs and whatever else in the kitchen, and figured he had a few minutes before Pat and Lorne were ready for breakfast. He'd get in another call or two.

He tried Gordon first. The first call went to voicemail. Zachary switched over to his text messaging app and scrolled through to find Gordon's number. He was probably in some big high-powered meeting at Chase Gold. When the markets closed in Japan. Or opened. Or whatever they did.

He shot off a quick text to Gordon, just letting him know that Heather's research seemed to confirm that the employee they suspected might have Huntington's Disease in his family. So Zachary would contact him and, if possible, get the police involved. Zachary wasn't sure what the charges would be. What did you charge someone with who substituted his own sperm for someone else's in an IVF procedure? Wrongful birth? Fraud? Sabotage? He wasn't sure what statute it would fall under.

There was a quick text back from Gordon indicating that he understood and would follow up with Zachary when he was able.

Zachary put his phone down, filed the email from Heather on his client file in cloud storage, then got up off of the bed and stretched. He was dressed for the day, but hadn't spent enough time in the bathroom, not wanting to wake the other men up. He needed to shave if he was going to be shown off to extended family at dinnertime. And probably shower and wash his hair too. He never did much with his hair; just kept it buzz-cut short so that he didn't have to fuss.

When he returned from his shave, he saw that his phone screen was lit up as a call came through. He dove for it and saw Gordon's profile on the screen. He swiped the call.

"Hi, Gordon?" He wasn't sure he had caught it in time. It might have been ringing for a while before he had seen it.

There was silence for a moment. Zachary pulled the phone away from his face and reached out to tap the number to call it back. But he could see that the call was still live.

"Gordon?"

"Not Gordon," came the sharp retort.

Zachary's blood froze in his veins. *Bridget?*

In a split-second, he realized that he must have called Gordon's home number instead of his work number. There was a stabbing pain in his chest. He couldn't breathe.

He had called Gordon's home number, which was also Bridget's number, and she thought that he was stalking her.

A stupid mistake. As a PI, he was supposed to know a thing or two about stealth and not giving the game away when one spouse was investigating the other.

He swallowed, trying to think of what to say. Or should he just hang up and let Gordon try to explain it or to calm her down later? He gasped, finding it hard to breathe.

It was just anxiety. He was used to feeling that way when confronted by Bridget. It would pass. But he didn't know what to say or do.

"Why are you calling me?" Bridget demanded. "You know you aren't supposed to have any contact with me."

"It must have been a pocket dial," Zachary said, his voice strangled, sounding like a thirteen-year-old whose voice hadn't changed yet. "I didn't mean to…"

"I didn't mean to," she mocked. "You shouldn't even have my number in your phone. You shouldn't be able to pocket dial me."

"I didn't have it down as your number; it was on Gordon's… from when I was doing the investigation at Chase Gold. I'm sorry. I'm not even in town; I'm down at Mr. Peterson's. It was unintentional."

"You've always got an excuse. What makes you think I would believe anything that comes out of your mouth?"

"Bridget…"

Zachary could see Mr. Peterson walking down the hallway, past his partly-open doorway. Mr. Peterson stopped where he was and turned toward Zachary. He mouthed the name. *Bridget?*

Zachary made a frustrated motion that tried to express to Mr. Peterson that he hadn't called Bridget and was trying to get off of the phone with her. He didn't want to have to explain why he was on the phone with his ex-wife. Mr. Peterson knew all—or at least most—of the gory details of Zachary's life with Bridget, and all of the ugly stuff that had happened since they had broken up.

Of course, there were still things that Lorne didn't know, but he knew how it had torn Zachary up, how he hadn't been able to let her go, and about all of the ups and downs of trying to get over her since. He knew that Zachary shouldn't be on the phone with Bridget now.

"You know what? Enough is enough. I'm going to get a restraining order. Do you understand me? I'm going to make your life a living hell! You keep calling me. Following me around. Coming into the house when I'm not here! You can spend the rest of your life inside a jail cell. They can keep you there until you finally figure out that I don't want anything else to do with you. You need to leave me alone!"

"Yes, yes. I'm sorry. I didn't mean to call you. Ask Gordon. It was just because of the case at Chase Gold. You know. The girl who died. The intern."

Going to the house when Bridget was not there? He had never done that. Not since she had kicked him out. He'd never fallen that low.

"I know what case you're talking about, but that is over. You don't need to talk to him about that anymore. That's just an excuse to call me and think you can get away with it. But you're not. You're *not getting away with it!*"

Her last words were a shriek of rage. Zachary pulled the phone away from his ear, wincing at the volume and pitch. He tapped the button to end the call. Then he sat there, looking at the blank face of the phone.

He'd hung up on Bridget.

There was nothing else he could have done, of course. But he'd never thought that he would choose to hang up on her. He would always keep her on the phone for as long as he could, just to hear her voice. Even if she were criticizing him, he would rather hear her voice than to think that she was gone from his life for good. That maybe she had forgotten about him altogether. That was what he couldn't handle.

Nothing happened at first. Bridget was probably just as shocked that he would hang up on her as he was. Then his phone lit up again with an incoming call. Again, Gordon's profile. But Zachary couldn't tell whether it was Bridget calling from the house phone or Gordon calling him back from his work phone or cell phone after his meeting ended. Zachary looked at it and didn't answer.

After a long time, the call went to voicemail. Zachary stared down at the dimmed screen, wondering whether Bridget or Gordon would leave him a message.

A text message popped up. Bridget's name. The message didn't come up on his lock screen, but he saw her name and knew that she was the one who had called him back. And now she was texting him. And he probably didn't want to read whatever she had sent him in text. Or maybe she had even sent a voice message or a video message via text. So that she could continue yelling at him.

He swallowed and didn't unlock the screen.

The phone rang again.

He didn't answer it.

Another text notification.

And his text notifications would keep buzzing even if she didn't text him anymore, because he had it set to remind him indefinitely, so that he wouldn't miss it when someone texted him.

Another phone call.

Zachary waited for it to go to voicemail. He swiped to unlock the phone and used his fingerprint to get past the security screen. He went into his notifications and turned off the repeating notifications for text messages.

Without reading the texts from Bridget, he locked the screen again, and put the phone down on the bed, looking at it like it was a live snake. Waiting for it to strike.

It didn't ring again.

Zachary looked up at his door. Mr. Peterson was no longer there. He had moved on, but would certainly want to know why Zachary was talking to Bridget again. Especially in that pleading tone of voice.

27

He tried to breathe until he was calm. It wasn't working. His chest still hurt and he couldn't get enough oxygen. It wasn't a full-blown meltdown, but he still couldn't get his breathing under control.

He left his phone on the bed. If Bridget were going to call or text him any more, he didn't want to see it. He needed to get some distance.

Zachary walked out to the kitchen, knowing that he was going to walk in on Pat and Mr. Peterson discussing him or at least casting glances in his direction while they tried to figure out what was going on. He staggered to the table and sat down heavily.

"You look terrible," Mr. Peterson commented.

Pat said nothing, but slid a mug of coffee across the table to him. Zachary took a couple of sips of the boiling-hot coffee. It probably stripped off the first two layers of skin, but he hoped that it would calm him down and bring him back to the present.

It was a struggle to hold back tears. Not from the hot coffee, but from the memories of Bridget. How close they had been at the beginning. How thoughtful and nurturing she had been. And how that had all dissolved in the two years of their marriage, until none of it remained. But his feelings for her endured, and he didn't know how to wipe them out. Even being in another relationship, he didn't know how to erase his feelings for Bridget.

He took a couple more big gulps of coffee.

"That's going to burn a hole right through your stomach," Pat said, shaking his head. "Slow down. Are you okay?"

Zachary wasn't okay. How could he be okay when Bridget was again on the warpath and he was trying to solve the problem that she didn't even know they had?

He wanted to fix everything, just like she had tried to fix him. He wanted to fix the situation with the babies. But he couldn't. No matter what he did to help bring charges against McLachlan, it wasn't going to change their genes. And Bridget was still going to be in pain over the choice that she had to make. Either bring two babies into the world who were not Gordon's and were going to eventually get Huntington's Disease, or terminate them. It wasn't fair that she should have to make that decision.

The thought that she faced a painful decision like that helped to contain his tears. What was *his* problem? He was upset that she thought he had called her. That didn't compare in any way to the decision that she was going to have to make.

He wouldn't want to be in Bridget's shoes for anything.

He took a deep breath and tried to blow it out slowly. All the way until his lungs were empty. Or as empty as he could make them. He took another breath in. He swallowed and looked at Mr. Peterson.

"Bridget?" Mr. Peterson said.

"Yeah… well… that was a mistake."

"I would guess so. Why were you on the phone with Bridget?" Mr. Peterson put his hands up, stopping Zachary from answering. "Not that it's any of my business. Of course you can call whoever you want. I'm just… concerned. Is there something going on that you want to tell me about?"

Zachary took one more breath, his heart still thumping hard in his chest. "I meant to call her husband. Accidentally called the home number instead of his office."

"Ouch." Mr. Peterson winced.

"Yeah. So she thinks I was trying to call her. I told her I just pocket-dialed, but she doesn't believe me." Zachary shrugged. "Of course not. Why would she?"

"Why would you be calling her? That's not exactly covert stalking behavior."

"No. I don't know. She's just upset to see my number; she's not thinking about whether it is logical for me to call her." Zachary shrugged and shook his head. "And maybe… if I was having problems… maybe I would call her even though I know better."

"Well, there isn't anything you can do other than just telling her what you did," Pat said calmly. "Whether she chooses to believe it, or not believe it, that's her own choice."

"She said she's going to get a restraining order."

"She's threatened that before," Mr. Peterson pointed out. "So far, she hasn't."

"No… but she'll be able to prove that I called her."

"A phone call, especially a pocket dial, doesn't exactly get you a restraining order. It isn't evidence that you are stalking or threatening her."

"She could say it was, though. She knows plenty of the cops at the police station. She could get someone to help her out."

"You have friends there too."

"Who would listen to me over her? I doubt it. I'm the one with emotional problems. People love Bridget."

"You'll get through this, Zachary," Mr. Peterson told him calmly. "You're doing the right thing. You're disengaging from her and not trying to convince her of anything. She's not going to believe it, and you'll just get her more wound up by trying."

Zachary nodded. He took a slower sip of coffee, trying to relax and enjoy it.

Bridget could choose to believe whatever she wanted to. She was going through a very difficult time, so of course she was even more emotional than usual. She had every right to be upset, but that didn't mean he had to be.

It was difficult to go on as though nothing had happened. Zachary finished his coffee with Mr. Peterson and Pat, trying to pace himself by how much was left in their mugs. They had toast too, but he wasn't ready for solid food. When everyone had drained their cups, they went their different directions.

Zachary went back to the guest room and looked at his phone. It was no longer lit up with incoming phone calls. So Bridget had, hopefully, given up. Maybe she had called Gordon to complain about Zachary calling her when he wouldn't take any more of her calls. If that were the case, he might be facing Gordon's anger too, and he was a powerful man. He wouldn't be happy about Zachary calling Bridget and then admitting that he had meant to call Gordon. He would have to tell her what Zachary was investigating or make up a lie. Either way, Bridget wasn't going to be happy about it. She would want to know why Gordon had hired Zachary instead of another investigator. One who didn't have a history with Bridget.

Which was a really good question. Why had Gordon hired him?

It was probably because Gordon knew that Zachary would do whatever he could to help. He would go the extra mile to come up with a solution or to figure out what had happened. Another investigator wouldn't do that. He'd do the basics and, even if Gordon offered to pay extra, they wouldn't go much beyond that. But Zachary would. Because he would do anything for Bridget, even if it were to his detriment.

He picked up his phone and glanced at the lock screen. He didn't really want to know how many times Bridget had called or sent him a text message. Her name and Gordon's were interspersed on the screen, so either she had called him from both her cell phone and the house number that was listed under Gordon's name, or Gordon had tried to reach him as well.

But it was probably best to let the storm blow over. Give Bridget some time to cool down. And the same for Gordon. He was usually even-tempered and patient with Bridget's tantrums. But it would be a good idea to make sure he'd had plenty of time to cool off after learning of Zachary's mistake.

He didn't listen to his voicemails or read his text messages. He touched his computer keyboard to wake up the laptop, and checked the contact details for McLachlan again. He dialed the number that he assumed was a cell phone. There was no answer and he ended up in a voicemail box with the default robotic message. He hesitated whether to leave a message, and then ended up doing it at the last moment, rushing it but hopefully still sounding coherent.

He tried the Westlake clinic number and asked for McLachlan. The receptionist sounded surprised to have someone ask after him. Probably friends would call his cell, and clients wouldn't ask for him at all, since he was a lab worker and not their primary contact.

"May I ask who is calling?"

"It's personal. I just couldn't get him on cell, so I thought I would try him there."

"Well…" The receptionist hesitated. Zachary waited for her to tell him that they weren't allowed to take personal calls or something to that effect. "I actually don't know… Forest isn't in the office today."

"Oh, of course. I suppose it's a weekend, so he wouldn't be, would he?"

"He does work some weekends. We are still open and can be pretty busy on weekends, since that's the only time some patients can get off work."

"But he's not scheduled to be in today?"

"He's not in," the woman told him.

Zachary considered her answer. She hadn't answered whether McLachlan was supposed to be in, just that he wasn't. Was she avoiding the issue?

"Was he supposed to be in today?"

"I really can't tell you about staff schedules. He isn't in the office today. Is there anything else I can help you with?"

"No… that's fine. You don't think there's something wrong, do you?"

She didn't deny it or hang up on him. Zachary sensed she was warring with whether to obey the office policies and keep staff confidentiality or to confide in him as a personal friend of McLachlan's.

"He doesn't normally just not show up for his shift, does he?" Zachary guessed.

"No, I don't think that's ever happened before."

"Have you tried reaching him? I suppose you just keep getting his voice-mail, like I do."

"Yes. I've left a message, but I don't know whether to think…"

"That there's something wrong or that he's just hungover or something?"

"He could be sick with the flu and just can't get to the phone. It might be nothing at all."

"But he hasn't done this before."

"No."

Had someone called McLachlan and told him about Zachary's inquiries? He'd tried to ensure that each of the people he had interviewed understood that they were not to call McLachlan to tell him anything about the inter-views but, of course, people didn't always listen. If they thought that it was important for McLachlan to hear something, or they wanted to apologize for something they had said that might ruin his chances at getting some kind of financing, they might have called anyway. And if McLachlan knew that someone was investigating both in Vermont and in Minnesota… he would run. He wouldn't wait around to see if he would get put in jail this time. He'd been lucky once, but he couldn't count on Westlake Clinic treating him the same way as Sandhills had.

"I'm a little concerned," Zachary said. "Maybe I should go to his place and just make sure everything is okay."

"Would you?" The woman sounded relieved. Clearly, she could not leave her station to see what was going on. And there wasn't anyone else she could send. Especially if McLachlan had left them short-staffed for the weekend.

"Is this the address that you have?" Zachary asked. "I know he was looking at a new place, but he hasn't moved yet, has he?" He read the address off for her.

"Yes. He's still there. That's right."

"Okay. I'll pop over and see if everything is all right."

She thanked him warmly, and Zachary hung up.

The question was, should he really go see whether McLachlan was all right?

It would mean a two-hour drive to his apartment, just to find out that he had slept in or had rabbited, and then two hours back. He needed to be back in time for dinner. That left him with enough time to spend a couple of hours looking for or talking to McLachlan. It seemed like enough time, but he didn't want to risk being late for dinner.

2 8

Zachary couldn't spend long deciding what to do, or he would run out of time. He grabbed his notepad and the few things he needed and headed for the door.

"Out for a walk?" Mr. Peterson asked pleasantly.

"Uh… a drive. I need to go check out a suspect. I'll be a while. But I'm going to be back for dinner. You can tell Pat I'll be back for sure."

"What's that?" Pat came out of the kitchen.

"I was just telling Mr.—Lorne that I have to go out. To deal with a case. I'll be back, though. I'll be here for your dinner."

"Okay," Pat agreed, raising his eyebrows. His voice was a little higher than usual, as if he didn't quite believe Zachary.

"I'm not going to miss it. I know it means a lot to you. But I don't want to leave this for another day. If this suspect has run, I can't let the trail go cold."

"Who? Where would he run?"

Zachary looked toward the door. "I'll tell you about it later. It will take some time. I want to get on my way as soon as I can."

Pat nodded. Zachary looked toward Mr. Peterson, seeing what he would say.

"This is important," Mr. Peterson said quietly.

"I know. And I'll be here."

The two of them nodded. Zachary felt a heavy weight in his stomach. They didn't believe him. They thought he was just going to take off and forget about the family dinner. That it wasn't important to him or that he didn't understand it was important to them. Zachary didn't know what else to say. Words weren't going to convince them. He was just going to have to show them with his actions.

But he couldn't leave it another day. If McLachlan had rabbited, Zachary needed to pick up his trail as soon as he could. He could do that and get back in time for the dinner. He wasn't going to forget or take too long. He had the time to deal with it.

He tried to smile at the couple, gave a nod, and went out the door. They would see. He would be back and there wouldn't be any problems.

He *might* have broken the speed limit a little more than usual on his way back to the city. He was usually careful not to pass too many other cars, not to be obviously going any faster than the flow of traffic. Then no police would single him out as being reckless or speeding more than anyone else, and they would not pull him over.

This time, he wasn't as careful. He didn't want to get pulled over for speeding, but he also wanted to get to McLachlan as quickly as possible so that he could be finished and back to Mr. Peterson's in plenty of time to meet Pat's family.

Luckily, he wasn't pulled over. He made it to the apartment he had confirmed was McLachlan's current address without a hitch. In the glassed-in alcove, he pressed the button beside the name McLachlan and waited impatiently.

There was no answering tone. He pushed it again.

Maybe the button wasn't even working. The building was a little run down, there were discarded flyers on the floor of the lobby area. Maybe the buttons didn't even work.

He pushed several other buzzers in a row, hoping that someone would simply ring him in.

There were a couple of irritated answers. Zachary covered his mouth and talked in a muffled voice that would be impossible for them to understand. He repeated the process a couple more times when they asked questions and, eventually, one of them hit the door release, figuring he had a good reason to be there and not wanting to try to figure out who he was or what he was saying. Zachary pulled the door open and took the elevator up to the fourth floor. He found McLachlan's door and knocked. To begin with, just a normal knock. Like any friend or deliveryman might make. When that didn't get a response, he hammered on it more loudly. Maybe McLachlan was sick in his bedroom or the bathroom and couldn't hear very well. Zachary pasted his ear to the door and listened for any activity within the apartment. There was nothing. One of the doors down the hall opened, and Zachary pulled back quickly. He smiled at the wild-haired man who had opened the door.

"Is Forest around?" he asked cheerfully. "He said one o'clock." Zachary pulled out his phone and looked at it pointedly. "He said he was going to be here. Have you seen him around today?"

The man started to pull back from the door, not wanting to be pulled into a conversation. He shook his head, backing up and preparing to close the door.

"He didn't leave, did he?" Zachary pressed. "I know he was thinking about moving, but he didn't yet, right? I mean, I got the right apartment, didn't I?"

The wild-haired man's eyes went back and forth. He shook his head again. "He didn't move. I haven't seen him since last night."

"He was here last night?" Zachary hammered on the door again. "What, is he hung over?"

"He went out. I didn't see or hear him come back." The neighbor hesitated, his hand still on the door to make a quick retreat. "He had a bag with him. I thought maybe... he was going away for the weekend."

Zachary's heart sank. He'd run. McLachlan had run. He swore aloud. "Where did he go? Did he say where he was headed? He wasn't going back to Minnesota to see his family, was he? I'm really screwed if he's gone all the way back home."

"He didn't tell me where he was going. I don't know him. He had a bag, that's all I know. It looked like he was going somewhere."

"You don't know him?" Zachary pressed. "He was a good guy, you never went for drinks? Picked up each other's mail? I thought he was a pretty good neighbor."

"He was okay," the man said, holding his hand up to stop Zachary. "I just didn't know him very well. We didn't talk a lot. Just said hello in the hallways. I don't know anything about his family or where he might have been going."

"Well, if you see him, would you let him know I was by?" Zachary didn't use one of his business cards, but tore a sheet out of his notepad and wrote his name and phone number on it. "I was really hoping to talk to him today. If he shows up... would you...?"

"Why don't you call him?" the man asked suspiciously.

"I have. He's not picking up his phone. It just keeps going to voicemail."

The neighbor's body language shifted slightly, his head tipping in the direction of McLachlan's apartment, a slight frown crossing his face.

Zachary swallowed. He woke up his phone and selected McLachlan's number from his recent calls list. As they both stood there, waiting, a cell phone started to trill from inside the apartment.

"He's home," Zachary pointed out.

The neighbor frowned, nodding slowly and looking at the closed door.

"I haven't heard him, though. He was getting his bags packed. I went out for dinner. I never saw him again after that. Why would he pack his bags if he was just going to stay home?"

"His bags?" Zachary focused on this. "You said he had a bag. Now it's more than one bag? How many?"

"I don't know." The neighbor shook his head. "Maybe... three. A couple of suitcases and a duffel. Just... he looked like he was going on vacation."

"Three pieces for the weekend? He must have planned to be away for longer than that."

"I don't know. I didn't ask where he was going or for how long. I just said 'going on a trip?' And... he said yes. Maybe he's going to Hawaii for a week. I wouldn't know."

"I don't think he's going to Hawaii," Zachary said. The apartment building didn't look like it rented to people who would be able to afford a week in Hawaii. Even with a job as a lab tech, Zachary suspected McLachlan probably barely made the rent. He wouldn't have money to be throwing around on extended vacations. If he was packing three pieces of luggage, he was leaving. For good.

But why was his cell phone in the apartment? Was he still there? Ignoring them and planning to leave covertly once there was no one around? Or maybe he had left his cell phone there so that his new location couldn't be traced. Once he got to his destination, he could pick up a burner phone. There would be nothing to connect him with Westlake or Vermont.

Zachary looked at the closed door again and swore once more. "You don't have the key, do you? Did he give you the key to give back to the super? Or maybe you have his key in case he needed something done while he was on vacation? Take in the newspaper or feed the cat?"

"He doesn't have a cat. And I don't have a copy of his key. We're not supposed to make copies or give them to anyone."

Zachary knocked on the door again. "Forest! Forest, are you in there? I need to talk to you!" He waited for a few beats. "Is everything okay? Do you need help?"

The dread was spreading up from the pit of his stomach to his chest, strangling his breathing. He told himself again that McLachlan had left his phone behind deliberately so that no one could track him. It was too easy for someone to track a phone's location. If he thought that Zachary had figured out what was going on and tried to have him arrested, he wouldn't want the authorities to find him.

Zachary scratched his jaw.

One of those PIs on TV would just pick the lock or kick in the door. It looked pretty flimsy. But Zachary had never kicked down a door in his life, and he wasn't about to try to explain to the police why he had done so.

The call he had made to McLachlan's phone had gone to voicemail. Zachary sighed and dialed the police.

He didn't try 9-1-1. A missing suspect wasn't quite an emergency, even if his place of business were wondering where he had gone. He could still just be out on the town or taking a weekend holiday even though he was supposed to be working. People did that kind of thing all the time. Sometimes even disappeared for several days at a time and then showed up at work as if nothing had happened, expecting to have their jobs still and not understanding why everyone was so pissed off.

He tried Mario's number, but he wasn't at his office, and instead, Zachary got Waverly, who wasn't nearly as easy to deal with as Mario. Mario must have gotten the day off. Or wasn't on until later in the day.

"Waverly. This is Zachary Goldman."

"Goldman," Waverly snorted. "What's your problem this time, Goldman?"

"I need a welfare check."

"And you think we're at your beck and call? Call it in at the non-emergency number like you're supposed to."

"I can do that… I just thought… well, this guy might have had something to do with a fraud perpetrated on Gordon Drake. Do you know Gordon Drake…?"

Gordon was well-known. A wealthy man with good political connections. He probably gave to the police relief fund and all of those other good things. Keeping the wheels greased for when he needed any favors.

"Gordon Drake," Waverly repeated, and this time he had toned down the contempt in his voice. "The investment banker?"

"Yes, that's him. I can have him call it in to the main number if you want. I just thought we could be a little more discreet and send someone over… maybe put a little priority on it."

Waverly cleared his throat. Even knowing who Gordon was, he probably didn't have the discretion to make that decision himself. "Exactly who is this? What's going on?"

"The guy's name is Forest McLachlan. He's a doctor, a lab tech. He didn't show up at work today and his office is worried about him. I'm over at his apartment, and he's not answering, but his phone is ringing inside."

"Well, he's home, then, and just doesn't want to have to deal with you. Can't say I blame the guy. I wouldn't want any private dick looking over my shoulder either. We're not in the habit of using police resources just to go after people who didn't feel like going into work today."

"I think it's more than that. I'm worried that something might have happened to him."

"I thought he was a suspect. Something about a fraud."

"Yes. Gordon isn't going to be happy if we let him slip through our fingers. If McLachlan has left town…"

"But you don't think he's left town. You think he's hiding in his apartment and you want the police to roust him for you."

"Do you want to talk to his neighbor? He's concerned too…" Zachary met the neighbor's eyes. The man shook his head and backed away, but still didn't shut his door, his eyes wide and interested in Zachary's phone call. Clearly, things like this didn't happen every day. It was a spectacle.

"What neighbor?"

"The guy in the apartment next door is worried that something might have happened to him too. He thought that he had left, but with the cell phone ringing in the apartment... Anything could have happened to the guy. He could have slipped and hit his head. You don't know. Don't you think it is a little suspicious that he isn't answering any calls from work or from anyone else? But he hasn't turned off his ringer?"

Waverly considered this for a moment. If someone wasn't going to answer their phone, why would he just let it keep ringing and ringing. Especially when he knew Zachary was right outside his door. He would at least turn off the ringer. Reject the call. Turn off the phone. People didn't like to hear their phones ringing endlessly.

"Fine," Waverly huffed finally. "I'll see if we can spare a couple of officers for a welfare check. But if this is some wild goose chase..."

"I have no idea where McLachlan is. I swear to that. I don't know whether everything is okay or not."

"Give me the information you have."

Zachary gave him the address, McLachlan's phone number, the number of the clinic if he wanted to check in with them, and McLachlan's full name.

"And you want to explain to me how this is connected to Gordon Drake?"

"I don't want to go into details over the phone with people listening in. Gordon wouldn't want his personal business spread all over town."

Waverly grumbled under his breath, but didn't push it. "You might be waiting a while. I don't know how long it will take to free up a unit to send over there."

"I'll hang out here."

29

It didn't take very long for a couple of police officers to arrive. It must have been a quiet day. Or else Waverly had been more concerned about it than he had given Zachary reason to believe. They stopped to talk to Zachary for a moment before knocking on McLachlan's door.

Zachary explained again about McLachlan not showing up for work and about how his phone was ringing inside the apartment but he wasn't answering.

"You want to call it again?" the cop who had introduced himself as Louden suggested.

Zachary nodded and tapped the number again. Once more, they could hear McLachlan's phone ringing on the other side of the door.

The cop banged on the door. "Mr. McLachlan? Police welfare check. If you are there, please come to the door."

There was no answer. Louden banged some more. "If you're in there, you need to answer the door, or we are going to have to force it."

The neighbor was still hanging around watching and a few other doors had opened. People stared, wide-eyed, at the police standing outside of McLachlan's door.

"Does anybody know where he might have gone?" Conners, the other officer, questioned, aimed at the various neighbors. "Did he leave travel plans with anyone? A key?"

They shook their heads, looking at each other.

"Is there an onsite manager? Someone in the building with a master key?"

"Downstairs," a woman offered. "He has an office on the second floor."

"Would you mind seeing if he can come up with a key?"

She looked like she would have preferred to watch him break the door down, but eventually nodded. "Okay, sure."

They waited while she took the elevator down to find the manager. Louden knocked a few more times, just to be doing something. Eventually, the elevator dinged and the neighbor returned with a man with black, greasy hair and stained coveralls.

"I have other work to do," he grumbled as if the police regularly harassed him and forced him to abandon important work projects.

"If you could just open Mr. McLachlan's apartment, it would be very helpful for us. We would like to make sure he's okay."

"Why wouldn't he be?" The manager looked at Zachary, and then back at the police officers while he went to McLachlan's door and jingled through his keychain to find the right key.

No one gave him any explanation as to why McLachlan might not be okay. They just waited for him to open the door and, eventually, he inserted a key and turned it. Louden didn't let him open the door, but motioned him back. He also gave Zachary a stern look.

"You are to stay out here. We are not in the habit of letting civilians into a private residence, whatever you might have seen on TV."

"I'll stay here," Zachary agreed.

He didn't want to contaminate the scene if there were any evidence of McLachlan's wrongdoing or where he had gone. The police would be taking over that part of the investigation. If there were anything to investigate.

The police opened the door far enough to slip into the apartment and closed it again behind them. Zachary could hear them calling ahead to advise McLachlan, if he was still home, that they were coming in. It was a few minutes before they came back to the door.

"No one home," Louden told Zachary.

"Does it look like he's run? I don't know if Waverly told you I've been investigating him for Gordon Drake."

They exchanged looks. "There's one packed bag in here," Louden told

Zachary finally. "And the phone. I don't see why he would leave them behind. If he ran, why wouldn't he take all of his bags?"

"One of the neighbors said that he had several bags packed. The neighbor left while he was getting ready to go, and thought that he had gone away for the weekend because he didn't see any more of him."

"We'll check to see if his car is in the parking lot. But it doesn't make much sense that he would pack his bags and then leave this one here."

Zachary checked the time on his phone to make sure that he was still well within the time he would need to get back to Mr. Peterson's for dinner.

"Maybe… he was interrupted."

"But then he would be here. Wouldn't he?"

"There's no sign… that something happened to him?"

"No blood, no signs of violence. Just looks like he left of his own accord."

Zachary shifted uneasily, thinking about it. His mind went unwillingly to Gordon. He'd had his suspicions about Gordon when he'd investigated Chase Gold. He remembered his worries that Gordon might have been involved in Lauren Barclay's death. Daniel's assertion that Gordon was a psychopath. The little things that had niggled at Zachary, making him wonder if Gordon was all he appeared to be, or if it was all just a mask hiding something far more sinister underneath.

Gordon knew that Zachary had been investigating McLachlan and thought that he was the one who had swapped Gordon's sperm for his own. For a man like Gordon, so powerful and used to having things done his way, it would be a terrible blow to find out that another man had fathered Bridget's children. Had he decided to speed up the timeline and not wait for Zachary to finish his investigation? Had he been sure enough that the culprit was McLachlan that he had gone ahead and taken things into his own hands?

McLachlan had been ready to run. He had been preparing to go. But something had prevented him from taking that last bag and phone. Zachary hoped that he'd just left them behind in error. Maybe he had been distracted or interrupted and decided to just go without them. He was out there on the road somewhere. Maybe they would be able to track him down and maybe not. But he was still okay.

He didn't want to think that McLachlan might be in the trunk of his car at the bottom of a nearby lake.

Eventually, Zachary had to leave. There were no answers to be found at McLachlan's apartment. The manager locked it back up. The officers would report what they had found and would wait to see if McLachlan appeared somewhere or if he was a missing person. There was nothing to be done until they found out more. Maybe he had gone back to Minnesota to see his family. Maybe he had just struck out for Arizona or Mexico or somewhere else he could start over again with a new name and identity.

But it was getting late and Zachary didn't want to take the chance of being tardy for Pat's dinner. He got back into his car and made the journey back to Pat and Lorne's house.

He got a broad grin from Mr. Peterson when he stepped in the door. "You made it!"

Zachary looked at the time on his phone. "Plenty of time for a shower and shave," he suggested.

"Yes. All yours. Thank you, Zachary. I just wanted… I know how much Pat has been looking forward to introducing you to his family. It's important for him to… be able to bring both parts of his life back together into one integrated whole. To… be himself, one hundred percent, and not have to be different things for different people."

Zachary nodded slowly. There had always been that rift in Pat's life. He didn't make a big deal of it. He seemed happy most of the time and rarely referred to his family, but Zachary knew that he had been hoping to reunite with his family one day. And now that he had… to merge the two lives into one.

"I'd better get ready." He touched Mr. Peterson on the arm and walked past him to get himself ready for the dinner.

Zachary paced around the house restlessly, waiting for Pat's family to arrive so that he could get through the initial awkward stages of introduction and conversation. The house was tidier than usual, with reading materials and projects put away, and all decor carefully reviewed and adjusted. Pat was in his glory in the kitchen.

He had made several varieties of ravioli and the sweet and spicy scent filled the air. Some spring potatoes and vegetables rounded the meal out, and there were a couple of bottles of wine to choose from.

On one hand, Zachary was anxious about meeting Pat's family, but the other part of his brain was occupied with trying to unwind the problem of Forest McLachlan. Where had he gone? Had he been warned of the investigation and fled? Or had he been taken against his will? He was comforted by the fact that there was no blood or sign of violence at the man's apartment, but the phone and packed bag were out of place. They didn't fit with the idea that McLachlan had just left of his own accord.

The police would probably reach out to his friends and family, see whether anyone knew where he was or if they had any concerns. But what if no one knew anything and the trail got cold? What if the BOLO on his car never turned anything up?

Was it possible that Gordon had been involved in Forest's disappearance?

As things stood, Zachary wasn't about to call Gordon again. His client had still not returned his text message from that morning but, considering what he might have to say about Zachary's unfortunate call to the house, Zachary figured he could use some time to cool down before they spoke.

There was nothing more Zachary could do for Gordon that evening. The case was, more than likely, closed. Gordon had all of the information that it would be possible to gather for him.

3 0

"I think they're here," Lorne called out, peering out the window of the living room. "Yes, that's them. Pat!"

Pat hurried out of the kitchen, wiping damp hands on the towel over his shoulder. He smoothed his already-perfect hair and raised eyebrows at Zachary.

"This is it!"

Zachary swallowed and nodded.

"You don't need to look like I'm throwing you to the lions," Pat said with a grin. "Really, they're not going to eat you."

He walked to the door and threw it open to greet his family.

He ushered an older woman into the house. While Zachary knew she must be in at least her seventies, she didn't look it. She had black hair and pink cheeks and not very many wrinkles. She stood up straight, her full height about even with Zachary's.

Patrick's sister was a younger, softer, taller version of her mother. Her hair was a little lighter, but Zachary suspected they probably were both dye jobs. Pat himself was starting to go gray, his appearance at odds with the way Zachary still pictured him when they were apart, as the broad-shouldered, athletic-looking man in his mid-thirties that he had been when they had first met. Not a lot about him had changed in his appearance, aside from the graying temples and some fine lines around his eyes and mouth.

After hugging both women, Pat ushered them over to meet Zachary.

"Zachary, I'd like to introduce Gretta and Suzanne Parker, my mom and sister. Mom, Suzie: Zachary Goldman."

"A pleasure to meet you," Gretta said immediately, holding out a hand to shake Zachary's. He took her firm, dry hand, and hoped that his was not too clammy by comparison. He turned to shake Suzanne's hand as well, but she put her arms around him and pulled him in for a hug.

"No need for formalities!" she insisted. "You're family, right?"

Zachary was startled, but submitted to the hug and stepped back slightly when she released him. He smiled at her.

"Yes. Family," he agreed.

"Let me have a look at my grandson," Gretta said, giving Suzanne a little nudge to the side. She gazed into Zachary's face, her eyes sharp, but not critical. "There's not much of a family resemblance, is there?" she cracked.

Everyone laughed. Zachary shook his head. "Afraid not. It's very nice to meet you."

"Well, it probably should not have taken this long," Gretta admitted. She gave a little sigh and looked up at her son. "We lost a lot of years, and I have no one to blame but myself for that."

"And Dad," Suzanne reminded her.

"I should have stood up to him. Should have said that I just wasn't putting up with that nonsense. But… I thought…" She looked at Pat again, apologetic. "Well, twenty years ago, we had some very different views on homosexuality. There were a lot of proponents for tough love, conversion therapy, keeping gays out of the churches, that kind of thing. We were told that if we made our position clear and refused to associate with Patrick as long as he was 'acting out,' that he would come to see the errors of his ways."

Pat shook his head ruefully. "I did want to see you," he told her firmly. "But… I had to be who I am."

"We heard about families that it had worked for," Gretta said. "They just held out for a few months… or a couple of years… and eventually, their wayward child came back again. Settled down, got married, had babies."

"And were miserable," Pat said. "I knew a lot of gay men and women who died, too. They couldn't bear being cut off from their families, but they couldn't be what society expected them to be. They couldn't live with the pain."

Gretta's mouth turned downward in a deep frown. Zachary didn't know if he would have had the courage to say something like that to her. To point out how much pain their decision had caused Pat over the years.

"Let's sit down," Mr. Peterson suggested, motioning to the living room.

"Actually, if you want to go straight to the table, everything is ready to go," Pat announced. He pulled the towel off of his shoulder, smiling. "Lorne, you get everyone settled and I'll bring out the food."

The painful moment put behind them, everyone cheered up and moved to the table, excited to dig into the ravioli that smelled so heavenly.

"Did you teach him to cook?" Zachary asked Gretta. "He really has a talent for it."

"Only the basics. I wanted my kids to be able to look after themselves. The rest he's taught himself. My mother was an excellent cook. Maybe he got it from her."

"I remember cooking with Bubba," Pat said, bringing a covered dish to the table. "She made such good food!"

"She did," Gretta agreed. Suzanne nodded.

They got settled around the table, Zachary sitting with Mr. Peterson on his right so that he had an anchor among the unfamiliar faces. There was some light chatter as Pat finished bringing the various dishes to the dining room table. They all exclaimed over each dish as it was uncovered and passed around.

"Now, you know you don't have to cook fancy every time we come," Gretta said sternly. "We can eat sandwiches or macaroni or a frozen pizza. It's the company we want; you don't have to spend hours in the kitchen for us."

"Not that we don't like this," Suzanne inserted.

"Of course, we love this. Who wouldn't?" Gretta agreed. "But you don't have to do something special every time. And sometime, you can come home and I will cook for you. Or not cook for you. Depending on how I feel."

Zachary could see where Pat got his down-to-earth nature. He'd always made Zachary feel comfortable and at home, no matter what Zachary threw at him.

"I enjoy cooking. It relaxes me. And this meal is special, because it's the first time that you and Zachary have met."

"Yes," Gretta agreed. "Just don't feel like you've set a precedent that you have to follow every time. So far, we've only had special occasions, but at some point, we'll want to have just casual visits too."

Zachary knew he had put too much of the intoxicating food on his plate. He'd never be able to eat it all. But he didn't want to look like he didn't appreciate it, either. If everybody else had full plates and he only had a couple of spoonfuls of food, they might think that he didn't appreciate the work that Pat had done or that he was a picky eater.

Mr. Peterson glanced at his plate and raised an eyebrow, fully aware that Zachary would never eat that much.

"Patrick said that you're a private detective," Gretta said, looking across the table at Zachary and taking a bite of pasta.

"Yes," Zachary agreed. "But don't think that it's the romanticized job that you see on TV. It isn't anything like that."

"I don't imagine so!" Gretta agreed. "I've always thought those shows were pretty unbelievable. But they are entertaining. So what kind of a private detective are you? What sorts of files do you get?"

"A variety," Zachary said with a shrug. He took a small bite of the cheese ravioli, which melted in his mouth. "Mmm," he looked over at Pat, "this is wonderful." Then back to Gretta. "I don't do a lot of high-profile cases. Mostly small stuff. Surveilling spouses or employees. Doing accident scene reconstruction. Skip tracing. Those are the bread and butter, jobs that will always be around."

"But you have done some murders and others that have made it into the media. I've seen some of the coverage. And you helped with that poor boy that Patrick knew."

"Yes." Zachary glanced over at Pat, not wanting to make him feel bad about what had happened to Jose. "I have done a few of those cases."

"What are you working on right now? Anything interesting?"

Zachary thought about his workload. "Mostly the routine stuff. One of my sisters is helping out now with some of the research and skip tracing. I've been working on one case—just wrapping it up, really—that involves paternity issues."

"A cheating spouse?"

"That's the way that it looked at the start. But it looks like it might have been fraudulently committed by one of the workers at the fertility clinic they used."

"Really!" Gretta shook her head. "That's terrible! How could something like that happen? Don't they have safeguards?"

"Not that will stop men from using their own sperm or mixing their own into a sample. Their security is all against outside parties, and all of their protocols inside are to prevent accidental mix-ups. Not intentional contamination. How would you stop something like that?"

"Well…" Gretta's forehead creased, "there has to be a way."

"If someone is really intent on it, I'm not sure there is anything they could do to stop them."

"They must do the fertilization in a controlled environment. They search people as they come in… keep surveillance cameras on them… film the whole process…"

"Pretty hard to keep eyes on people every second, even with surveillance cameras. What is going on below the tables? What about sleight of hand while fertilizing a sample? You have to assume people are honest and not trying to game the system."

Gretta wrinkled her nose. "How disgusting. Well. I'm never going to one of those places."

Suzanne and Pat burst out laughing. Zachary wasn't sure how to respond to Gretta's declaration. Of course as a seventy-something she had no need for a fertility clinic.

Gretta gave Zachary a small smile, letting him know that she was only joking.

"Well, I agree," Zachary agreed. "I don't think that would be a good idea."

"Would you? With what you know now?"

Zachary considered the question. "Well… if it was the only way to conceive. I guess I would. Bridget—my ex-wife—she had to have her eggs frozen before she had treatment for her cancer. So there wasn't really any other option."

"Then adopt," Suzanne put in. "There are a lot of kids out there who would give anything for a family."

Pat looked over at Zachary for his reaction. The angle he held his head at told Zachary that he was ready to step in and shut down the conversation if he thought it was bothering Zachary.

Zachary swallowed and shrugged. "Most of the kids in foster care are not infants, which is what people want. There are fewer and fewer babies available for adoption all the time, because of improved birth control, abortion being available, and people waiting until they are older to start families."

"How selfish is it to only take an infant when there are so many other kids in care?" Suzanne looked at Mr. Peterson. "You were a foster parent for a while, right? So you saw what it was like. How much love those kids need."

Mr. Peterson looked at Zachary.

Zachary nodded at him.

"I saw kids with very high needs in foster care," Mr. Peterson said. "Most of them were not free for adoption and a regular family would not have been able to deal with their needs."

"But there must still be a lot who could go to forever families. Take the pressure off the system. Give people the children they want but can't have."

Mr. Peterson took a few bites of his dinner, not answering.

"Like Zachary," Gretta said. "You were one of the Petersons' foster kids, and you kept in touch with him all this time. You would have been adopted if you could have, wouldn't you?"

Zachary shook his head. "I wanted to go back to my biological family, I wasn't interested in adoption. I was ten when I went into foster care, too old for adoption. And family groups... you hear about people adopting whole families sometimes on TV, but it's so rare... that's why it's news."

Zachary toyed with his vegetables, looking for something to do with his hands so that he didn't have to look at Gretta or Suzanne.

"Even if everything had lined up... I couldn't have managed in a family. I was in institutional care a lot of the time. Group homes, therapeutic settings, care centers. I was too..." He looked at Lorne, trying to find the words.

"Zachary came to us from a very traumatic background," Mr. Peterson explained. "He had some very difficult issues to work through. We were not able to keep him, and we had all of the necessary training. A couple who didn't have experience dealing with high-needs, traumatized kids... the kind of family who is looking to start a new family together... things would not have turned out well."

Gretta focused on her meal. Suzanne darted glances at Zachary, wondering about him and his background. Zachary didn't know how much

Pat and Mr. Peterson had previously told them about him. Probably not enough for them to understand what he was talking about.

"I still have a lot of issues," he explained. "I'm on medications and regular therapy. And I still have cycles of severe depression, panic attacks, flashbacks. PTSD."

"You look so normal," Suzanne observed.

Zachary rolled his eyes, not sure how to answer that one.

"Having people adopt from the system is not a reasonable replacement for reproductive technology," Pat said. "Some adoptions from foster care turn out great. But it has a very high failure rate. Zachary did well to be able to carve out his niche and find a way to earn a living and stay on the right side of the law. A lot of foster kids end up homeless, addicts, unqualified or unable to find work, or in prison. It's not a perfect system."

"So what is your client going to do now that they know what happened?" Gretta asked, returning to the original topic. "Are they going to sue him? Make him pay child support or something? Is there such as thing as a wrongful birth suit?"

"I suspect they're going to terminate the pregnancy. That was the original suggestion. My client was hoping to avoid it. Not sure she'll ever agree to get pregnant again, and he would like to have a child with her."

"Tough luck for him," Suzanne said unsympathetically.

Zachary tried to swallow the lump in his throat. He hated to think of Bridget terminating her pregnancy. She had never wanted his children, but he had longed for hers. But biology worked against Zachary. He couldn't take on pregnancy, labor, and nursing a baby. He could help to care for a child once it was born, but he couldn't step in and take the rest of the burden away from Bridget. And she hadn't ever considered adoption either.

And now, it was going to be her choice not to have them with Gordon either.

On the one hand, Zachary felt a little vindicated. At least that was one way that Gordon was not better than he was. He had thought that Gordon would step in and become the father that Zachary had always wanted to be. But Gordon couldn't. As successful as he was, as competent in everything, he could not control that.

"How did they find out the baby was not his if it hasn't even been born yet?" Pat asked, cocking his head slightly. "I was thinking it was something in the baby's physical features that had tipped them off. Wrong color of skin or eyes."

Zachary shook his head. "They did prenatal genetic testing to make sure that everything was okay… and found out that the baby had a genetic disease that isn't in either of their families."

"Oh." Pat nodded his understanding. "Yeah, I guess that would do it."

"I have a friend who has that breast cancer gene," Suzanne said. "She's so paranoid about passing it on to her children, she was having IVF and they were testing each embryo for the gene, so that she would only have children without it."

"She had breast cancer?" Gretta asked.

"No. Just the gene that predicts that she has an eighty percent chance of getting it, or something like that. I don't even know the percentages."

"She didn't have any symptoms? They screen for breast cancer so they can catch it right away."

"No, Mom," Suzanne said with exaggerated patience. "She didn't have cancer. She didn't have any symptoms. It probably won't develop until later in life. She won't have symptoms until then."

Zachary remembered what Patton had said about the dangers of reproductive technology, the birth defects and other problems it could cause. He wondered whether Suzanne's friend had been told that. Screen for a known danger like the BRCA1 gene and end up with a child with a hundred times higher chance of getting hepatoblastoma or another fast-growing childhood cancer. Or blindness. Or CP.

If Bridget chose to raise the babies, she would never have to worry about getting Huntington's herself, but she would have to watch her children growing up, knowing that one day they were going to develop it.

She would see one of her daughters starting to develop more erratic, irrational behavior. Maybe get violent. She would know what was happening because they had done the testing. But they wouldn't be able to do anything to stop the progression of the disease.

3 1

Something suddenly clicked into place.

Zachary's brain clicked into high gear as he suddenly saw every-thing from a different angle. His ADHD brain started spinning through all the possibilities.

"Zachary?"

He didn't move. He didn't want anything to interrupt the moment of clarity.

They'd been wrong about everything.

Everything.

Zachary heard his fork fall from his hand with a clatter.

He pushed back his chair, murmuring an apology.

"Zachary? Is everything okay? What is it?"

He groped his way to his room and picked up the notepad he'd left on the bed. He started writing it all down. His hand couldn't keep up with his thoughts, and he knew he wasn't getting all of the missing pieces written down, but he persevered, trying to wring it all out of his brain and come up with a clear picture.

He didn't know how much time had passed when Mr. Peterson came into the bedroom.

"Hey, Zach. Are you okay? What's going on?"

Zachary blinked at him. "I just figured it out. I can't believe I didn't see it before."

"See what?"

"We were wrong about everything, start to finish. We started with the wrong premise."

"Uh… we're going to take the ladies out for ice cream. Do you want to come along? Or do you want me to pick something up for you?"

"No. I need to make a plan. Figure out what to do next."

"Ice cream. Do you want some?" Lorne persisted.

Kenzie had found that ice cream was something that Zachary could usually manage, even when he was nauseated and didn't have an appetite. And his doctor approved of a fatty, sugary treat to help him with his weight gain.

"I don't know. I guess if you see something that I would like."

"Chocolate? Maple Walnut? Do you have a favorite?"

"Anything." Zachary flipped through the pages of his notepad. "Cherry Jubilee. Kenzie likes the blue ones. Raspberry. Bubble Gum."

"Kenzie isn't here."

"Right." Zachary stared at the pages. How had he not seen it before?

It seemed like they were only gone for a few minutes and then they were back again. Mr. Peterson brought back a pint of Cherry Jubilee ice cream and put a scoop in a dessert bowl for Zachary but, by the time he paid any attention to it, it was just a puddle of sweet, cherry-spotted goo.

"Do you need anything?" Mr. Peterson asked before heading to bed.

Zachary realized that the house had been quiet for some time. He rubbed his head.

"Did I… did I screw everything up with Pat's family? I left right in the middle of dinner, didn't I? I'm sorry."

"It's fine. They wanted to meet you, and they got their opportunity. They understood that you were working a case. Sometimes inspiration strikes at the most inconvenient moment."

"Thanks. I really didn't mean to leave you all in the lurch like that."

"Do you want something to eat? You didn't finish your supper." Mr. Peterson smiled. "Not that I expected you to eat everything that you dished up! But I think you only had about three bites, and it doesn't look like you made a dent in that ice cream."

"Yeah… I'll have some tomorrow before I leave. Is Pat still up? I should tell him that I enjoyed everything… meeting his family and the dinner…"

"He was pretty wiped out after everything he did the last few days to get ready. He took a pill and headed to bed a while ago."

"Oh. I'll talk to him tomorrow, then. Was he upset?"

"No. It's fine. Talk to him in the morning."

"Okay. Don't let me forget."

"I'll remind you tomorrow, then. Are you going to stay around tomorrow?"

"I might need to go. I have to follow up on this lead."

"Will it wait one more day?"

"I suppose." Zachary considered. Gordon hadn't called him back. The police were not likely to find anything out about McLachlan. If Bridget made her decision that night or the next day, Zachary couldn't do anything about it.

"Then maybe you should take a day off. You worked most of today. Give your body and brain a break. You'll be more productive on Monday."

"Maybe."

"Do you need anything before I hit the sack? You look like you have a headache."

Zachary continued to knead his forehead with his knuckles. "Yeah… I guess I do."

"Your body's way of telling you you've had enough. You want a Tylenol?"

Zachary hesitated. He usually just tried to 'tough out' his headaches. He didn't like to take anything he didn't have to. With the meds he was taking regularly, interactions were always a danger, and he didn't know when his body chemistry might change and he would have a bad reaction he hadn't had before. Or something would stop working. It was best not to mess with the delicately balanced system.

"I guess… just one Tylenol, yeah," he agreed finally.

Mr. Peterson nodded. "I'll get you one."

One precaution that he and Pat had taken was to keep all medications in their bedroom rather than in the bathroom, so that when Zachary was in the darkest depths of depression, it wouldn't be right there in front of him. One less thing to worry about.

Lorne returned with a pill and a glass of water. He watched Zachary take it. "And you've got everything else you need?"

"Yeah. I'm not taking anything else before bed."

The older man nodded. "Good. All right. I'll see you in the morning. Try to get some sleep."

Like Zachary, Mr. Peterson knew that with Zachary's brain spinning through all of the possibilities, he wasn't likely to get more than an hour or two of restless sleep.

It wasn't easy to do as Mr. Peterson had suggested and just take a day off. He wanted to be following up on the new leads. It would wait, but waiting was excruciating.

But Zachary felt like he owed it to Pat to stay and be sociable for another day. To talk to him about his mom and sister and how interesting they had been. He raved about how good the food had been, and had a little of the Cherry Jubilee ice cream for breakfast.

"So… what did you figure out?" Pat asked as he sat back in his chair, sipping his coffee. "Was it on the case that you were talking about?"

"Yeah, it is. I can't talk about any details, but I just realized that I'd been looking at everything the wrong way. I know better than to make assumptions, but you always do… there are always things that you have to assume or take for granted as being true when you start on a case."

"It's pretty hard to challenge every fact," Pat suggested.

"Yes. But I know that clients don't always tell the truth. They keep things back. They have secrets that they don't want you to know about."

"And you think that your client in this case lied to you?"

"They usually do… even if they don't know that they are."

"That sounds very complicated. How are you supposed to solve a case when they lie to you? Especially if *they* don't know they're lying?"

Zachary thought back to his last big case. Ben Burton. He had told Zachary repeatedly that he didn't have any siblings and that he didn't remember what had happened to him as a child. But Zachary had known that those were lies. He had been able to tell by Burton's body language, even if he hadn't known it himself.

"Sometimes you can figure it out by what they say or don't say, by facial expression or body language, the way they react to something. And sometimes… nothing fits until you figure out what the lie was."

Mr. Peterson had been sitting quietly, listening to them. Zachary thought that Pat needed his personal attention, and Mr. Peterson realized that. He was always so perceptive about his partner's emotional state.

"Zachary… this case…"

"Yeah?"

"You're not working for Bridget's husband again, are you?"

Zachary supposed he'd given that away when he called Gordon's home number by mistake and Lorne had overheard him talking with Bridget.

"Well… I can't really tell you who I'm working for."

Mr. Peterson pondered on this, taking another sip of his coffee.

"Do you really think that you should be working this case? Doesn't it… hit a little too close to home?"

Zachary cleared his throat and took another small spoonful of Cherry Jubilee. "It's, uh… had its moments."

"You probably shouldn't have taken it. Don't you have to recuse yourself if you have a personal bias?"

Zachary laughed. "No. I'm not a judge or even a cop. Gordon—if I was working for Gordon—he already knows my… personal bias."

"He shouldn't have come to you. Really. It wasn't a good idea."

"Maybe not," Zachary admitted. "I wasn't sure about taking it. It took some talking me into it. But he knows I'm the best man for the job."

"I'm not sure that's true. You don't have any objectivity."

And that had ended up being his big mistake. Maybe if it hadn't been a case involving Bridget and Gordon, he would have seen what was right in his face all along.

32

Zachary was relieved to finally be making his way back to his apartment. He would go back to Kenzie's Monday night, after he'd had a chance to pursue his investigations. And maybe by that time, he would have everything wrapped up and would be able to tell her a few choice, non-identifying details. She would be curious how the case had turned out.

At his apartment, he showered, shaved, and changed into a neat shirt and pants, looking better than his usual just-short-of-homeless look. It might even be an interview that he should have worn a suit to, but he didn't have a suit, and he was afraid that might be too much.

Despite his certainty that he was right and the urgent need to find out, he was anxious.

It had been years since he had seen or spoken to Bridget's parents.

And she had undoubtedly had plenty to say about him during that time. She would have vented about Zachary and his issues regularly. He was going to be working against a wall of preconceived ideas about him.

Hence the upgraded clothing and clean shave.

Both were now retired. Zachary was sure they were still active in social circles. Like Bridget, they had always been very concerned about appearances and about people knowing how they were serving their community. So there was no guarantee they would be home when Zachary rang the doorbell. But it was still early in the day, and he didn't think they would be gone yet. Most fundraisers didn't start earlier than brunch. Not the ones Bridget had dragged Zachary to, anyway.

Mr. Downy opened the door. After a moment of blankness, his eyes widened when he saw Zachary there and realized who he was. He took a step back as if Zachary were being aggressive. His first reaction to seeing Zachary was that he shouldn't be there. They shouldn't be talking to each other. Mr. Downy hesitated, thinking about this instinctive reaction.

He looked past Zachary, as if he expected to see Bridget there. But when they had been together, Bridget had never stood behind Zachary. She was always out in front, self-confident, wanting to be the first one in.

"Zachary. What are you doing here?"

Zachary cleared his throat. "I'm worried about Bridget."

Mr. Downy considered this. Then he stepped back, opening the door wider to usher Zachary in.

"Honey, who was at the door?" The diminutive woman who was Bridget's mother came out of the living room to see. She stopped short when she saw Zachary, then looked at her husband. He nodded to the living room and they all went in and sat down. Zachary shifted anxiously, wanting to be standing or walking around rather than sitting still. But he needed to look calm and reasonable. He couldn't afford to let them see his wild imaginings and how fast his brain was turning. They would write him off as just being mentally ill and not worth listening to. Any drama or emotion would just be proof that all of the things Bridget said about him were true.

"What's this all about?" Mrs. Downy asked uncertainly. She looked out the window like she too was searching for Bridget's yellow Beetle. If Zachary was there, then Bridget must be too. That was how they had been conditioned.

"I came here because I'm worried about Bridget. I know you probably don't want to see me, with the way that things turned out. But I needed to talk to you… to figure this out."

"Worried about her how?" Mrs. Downy asked. "Bridget is okay. I just talked to her yesterday. She said she's starting to feel better."

"I don't mean about her physical condition… the pregnancy."

"Then what?" As far as Zachary knew, Mr. Downy had never served in the military, but that was always how Zachary pictured him. As a captain or sergeant. Crisp and in control, commanding and demanding exacting behavior from everyone around him.

"Gordon called you before?" Zachary suggested, "To ask you about some family medical history questions?"

"Yes," Mr. Downy agreed. He looked at his wife, then back at Zachary. "What does that have to do with anything?"

"Did you know why he was asking?"

"Because of the pregnancy. He wanted to know what diseases might run in the family. To be prepared for any issues the babies might have." Mr. Downy shrugged. "I don't really see the point. Parents today are so paranoid about the future. But they have to wait and see what happens, just like we did. Nothing has changed."

"A lot has changed as far as medical care and being able to predict problems," Zachary countered. "And a lot of diseases, if you can catch them early, they are much more treatable. The outcomes are much better. Look at Bridget's cancer. A generation ago, it would have been a death sentence. Now she is in remission."

"So the babies might have a predisposition toward ovarian cancer. That's good to know," Mr. Downy admitted. "But you can't predict everything that's going to strike. It's not all genetic."

"But some things are. Some things, they can find in DNA testing."

"If they can find it in DNA testing, then what is the point of a family medical history?" Mrs. Downy put in. She was small and pretty, like a china doll. She always looked perfectly made up and turned out. Zachary supposed that was where Bridget got her good looks.

Zachary rubbed his palms along his pants, trying to dry the sweat and make himself feel more calm and prepared for the conversation.

"Did Gordon tell you that they had done prenatal DNA testing on the babies?"

They both looked shocked at this revelation. They didn't need to tell Zachary 'no' audibly. Their widening eyes and exchanged look told him everything he needed to know.

"How can they do that?" Mrs. Downy asked. "Do they… put a needle into her belly? And into the babies? That sounds very dangerous and unnecessary."

"I'm not sure what method they used," Zachary said. "They can get cells from the amniotic fluid, or from Bridget's bloodstream. They don't have to take it directly from the babies. But I don't know which method they used."

"They should just wait and see," Mr. Downy asserted. "That's how it's always been done. Just enjoy the anticipation of the birth and see what happens after the baby is born. Chances are, everything is going to be just fine. Why spend all of that time worrying?"

Zachary wasn't there to argue the morality of finding out the babies' genetic issues before birth. It had already been done. There was no point in discussing that particular issue any further.

"Bridget had the DNA testing done already. They got the results back, and that was why Gordon was asking you about family medical history."

"We don't have any family history of anything bad," Mrs. Downy said. "Most of our relatives have lived long lives. They die of old age. Heart, I suppose. Eventually, things just wear out."

"You haven't had anyone die young?" Zachary challenged. "Maybe due to accidents?"

"How would that be relevant to family medical history?" Mr. Downy put in, shaking his head. "Accidents aren't genetic. You can't inherit them. You can't get anything from people who died young, before they had a chance to get any diseases."

"But if they died young, you don't know what they might have carried that would develop later in life. If they have a disease that they wouldn't show symptoms of until they were sixty or seventy, and they died when they were fifty, you wouldn't know what they carried."

"And what would it matter?" Mr. Downy asked.

"Because it might mean that there was a predisposition to a disease hidden in your family tree that had never been recognized."

Mr. Downy waved this idea away. "We haven't had a lot of people die young. I don't think that's relevant."

Zachary looked from one to the other. "Does either of you have dementia in your family? Even if it's never been diagnosed. Someone who was experiencing confusion or mood swings before they died? Or having difficulty walking?"

Neither offered any suggestions. No 'Aunt Mary' or 'Great Grandma Downy.' They both just looked at him.

"I don't see how this is an issue," Mr. Downy said. "You said that you came here because you had concerns about Bridget. What business is it of yours what diseases we have in our family?"

Zachary attempted to move the conversation forward. "I am concerned about Bridget right now. That's why I came. I haven't had a lot of contact with her the last couple of years, of course, just chance encounters now and then. But it seems like... she's been getting angrier at me rather than less. I kind of figured that she would start to ease off after we'd been apart for a while. Sometimes she seems... like her old self. But other times... have you noticed more mood swings?"

"That's just the hormones," Mrs. Downy dismissed. "You don't know what it's like. The hormones when you're pregnant are so brutal. I don't think a man can understand it."

"I understand mood swings. I know what it's like to feel out of control. But... I think her behavior was changing before she got pregnant. Don't you?"

Mr. Downy shook his head resolutely. "I don't know what you're talking about."

"Even before we got divorced... she had changed. I thought at the time that she had just decided she couldn't deal with my issues anymore. You don't really know how many problems a person has until you live with them for a while. But now I wonder..."

"Wonder what?" Mrs. Downy demanded. "I think it's just like you said. She didn't know how hard it was going to be until she'd been with you for a while. She knew in her head, but she hadn't experienced it. She didn't know how stressful it was going to be."

"And she was so sick after that," Mr. Downy said. "She was just so sick and weak with cancer and the treatments. She needed to live for herself. Not for someone else. If she hadn't been focused on her own emotional health, she would never have survived it."

"So you don't think that anything has changed, over time. You think she's still the same woman as she was before she and I met."

"People do change," Mrs. Downy pointed out. "They change because of their experiences."

"I don't think that's it," Zachary said slowly. "I'm worried that... she has Huntington's Disease."

33

Mr. and Mrs. Downy's reactions were different. Mr. Downy looked angry, furious that Zachary would suggest such a thing. Mrs. Downy looked terrified. She alternated between looking at Zachary and at her husband, waiting for one of them to speak.

"There is no Huntington's Disease in our family," Mr. Downy finally said in a tight voice, his anger barely controlled.

"There are rare occasions where a child can have it even though the parents didn't. Or there may have been cases in the family that only had a few symptoms, or didn't occur until much later in life, so it was never diagnosed." Zachary swallowed, looking into Mr. Downy's cold, angry eyes. "There are cases where the parents didn't have it," he repeated. "Where it was a first-time mutation."

"You are not a doctor."

"No, I'm not."

"You can't make a diagnosis like that. And even if you were a doctor, you haven't examined her. You haven't run any tests. You can't just know out of the blue that she had something like that."

"No," Zachary agreed. "But it *isn't* out of the blue. Her babies have the gene for Huntington's Disease."

"So it is like you said, they have this mutation, she did not."

"Both babies?"

"If they are identical twins, they would both have it, wouldn't they?"

Zachary wasn't sure. He considered, and nodded slowly. "Yes... maybe. But look at Bridget. Look at the changes over the past few years. Look at how she has become more moody and angry. Her personality has changed."

Mr. Downy shook his head, but Mrs. Downy was not shaking hers. Her eyes were wide with fear, but she didn't deny it like her husband.

"She *has* changed," Zachary said to Mrs. Downy. "You can see that too, can't you? She's different than she was before we got married. And it isn't just bitterness from the marriage. There's been something else going on. Don't you think so?"

Mrs. Downy looked at her husband as if she needed his permission to agree with Zachary, and when he didn't give it to her, she looked down at her folded hands in her lap and didn't agree or disagree with Zachary. He thought he detected a slight tremor in her cheek. She was trying to keep her emotions under control. Staying calm and collected in front of her daughter's ex. Trying not to crack and show any weakness.

"I think it's time for you to leave," Mr. Downy said, rising to his feet.

"You haven't had any concerns about her?" Zachary asked helplessly, sliding forward in his seat to get up. "If she's diagnosed, they might be able to help her, to slow its progression. Give her a normal life for a few years longer..."

Mr. Downy glared down at him. But Zachary could see that his eyes were shiny with tears. He wasn't quite as angry and confident as he pretended to be. Of course he was worried about his daughter. Maybe he had been raised not to show any un-manly emotions, but that didn't mean he didn't have feelings. If Zachary could see Bridget's changed behavior as clearly as he did, Mr. Downy must be able to see it even more clearly. Unless it was one of those things that was harder to notice when you saw the person every day. Maybe he had been too close to her to notice the gradual progression.

But Zachary was sure that Mrs. Downy, at least, recognized the truth of what Zachary said.

He stayed sitting where he was, giving it a few more seconds to see if they were going to send him on his way or whether he could draw out the conversation and get them onside.

"I don't want it to be true either," Zachary said. "And if you really can't see it, if you really haven't seen any changes in her over the past couple of years and it is just me… then so be it. Maybe I'm just more sensitive to her moods after being away from her. But some of the things that she's done in the last little while… have been very out of character." He pushed himself to his feet. "That's what I think, anyway."

Mrs. Downy rose as well. She looked at her husband and put her hand on his arm. Finally, Mr. Downy nodded, giving in.

"Fine," he said with a long sigh. "Maybe there have been changes. But people do change over time. They decide they're not going to put up with being pushed around anymore. They act differently when they're under stress, or when they've had a serious illness or a near-death experience. They even said that some of the cancer treatments could have an effect on her personality. Things can change; that doesn't mean she has Huntington's Disease."

"No. But if she does, it's better she gets diagnosed now, isn't it? So they can treat it and help her."

Mrs. Downy shook her head. "There isn't anything they can do. It's not something they can fix."

"They might be able to slow down its progress. And they say that a cure isn't far away. Maybe not soon enough for Bridget…" He tried to swallow the painful lump that swelled up in his throat. "But what about the babies? There could be a cure in time for them."

"She won't keep them," Mrs. Downy said. "If she thinks there's something wrong with them, she won't risk it."

"Maybe if she knows there will be a cure… or at least that there's a good chance…"

"She won't," Mrs. Downy repeated with certainty. "I know she won't. I'm surprised she hasn't had an abortion already." She sniffled and touched her hand to the end of her nose as if trying to stifle a sneeze. But Zachary knew there was far more behind the gesture than the tickle of a sneeze.

"Sit down," Mr. Downy said, and they all sat again. Zachary rubbed his palms on his knees, thinking.

"She needs to be tested. She needs to go to the doctor and be tested."

"I'd like to see you talk her into that," Mr. Downy said with a sharp bark of laughter.

"I'm probably not the best person to talk to her. But you…"

Mr. Downy shook his head. "*Him*, then. Gordon."

Zachary nodded. "He's a lot better at managing her than I ever was."

"He's nothing like you," Mrs. Downy agreed. She gave a little shake of her head. "I wish that things had worked out between the two of you."

Zachary was surprised. He'd never felt like he had the approval of either of them. Bridget kept trying to mold him into something that would be more acceptable to her family, but hadn't been able to change him like she wanted to. So he'd always known that he didn't fit in with them. That they probably wished every time they saw him that Bridget had picked someone else.

Someone more like them. Someone more like Gordon.

"Gordon is very successful," he said to Mrs. Downy, unable to understand why she would say such a thing. "He's patient and persuasive and wealthy. And handsome. All the things that I am not."

"And you are many things that he is not," she pointed out. "And could never be."

Zachary could think of a lot of his traits that Gordon would never have. Nor would he ever want to have them.

"I can't understand Bridget not wanting to have children," Mrs. Downy said, smoothing wrinkles from her pants as if it were a job that required her close attention. "The pull of motherhood is very strong. It's a woman's natural inclination. I can't understand her attitude about not wanting to have children. She says she doesn't want to ruin her body with pregnancy, but it isn't that. It's much more than that." She shook her head thoughtfully. "I always wanted children. When we got married, I was so excited to become a mother. Every month, I waited for the signs that I was with child. Every time I wasn't, an ache grew in my heart. It became unbearable."

Zachary nodded. That was a feeling he could understand. He longed for children himself, and most women seemed to have an even stronger instinct for nurturing.

"There weren't clinics like this when I was a young woman," Mrs. Downy went on. "All of this technology is new. IVF... it was so new; it wasn't something that you could go to the doctor for. It was brand new."

"That must have been difficult for you."

Mrs. Downy nodded. She continued to look down. The conversation lagged. Zachary looked for a way to carry it forward.

"And it has been scary for you, seeing the changes in Bridget, wondering what was going on. Huntington's Disease is a terrifying prospect. I don't know if you know anything about it..."

She didn't move or answer.

Zachary looked at Mr. Downy. He was staring at a thick book in the bookcase closest to him. Zachary had seen books like that before. He remembered Burton's foster mother pulling a thick volume off of the shelf and leafing through the pages of pictures of all of their foster children.

He had seen pictures of Bridget with her parents. Pregnancy shots of Mrs. Downy. Bridget as a newborn, cuddled in her mother's arms, Mrs. Downy looking at the camera with sparkling eyes and a contented smile.

At their wedding reception, there had been a long picture montage of Bridget growing up, going through all of the different ages and stages, from infancy up through to adulthood, growing lovelier all the time. Her parents were always doting on her. It was the kind of life that Zachary could only imagine. A life where there was plenty to go around, parents who cared for her physically and emotionally, one consistent home from the time she was a baby until she was grown. Even now, as a grown woman, her parents were still there for her, fighting her battles and standing by her side.

Zachary got up and retrieved the photo album. Neither of them stopped him. He paged through it, looking at Bridget's life in reverse, starting at the back and working his way toward the front. There were no ultrasound pictures, but there was that first picture of Mrs. Downy, looking down and her baby bump, two hands wrapped around it as she thought about the baby kicking inside of her.

"We didn't have all of those options they have today," Mrs. Downy said. "Every month that went by…"

Zachary looked at her, blinking. He looked down at the photo album in his lap. Mrs. Downy was there, holding her pregnant tummy. Anticipating the birth. Clearly, something had worked. He looked back up at her. What was it she was afraid to tell him? Had they used a sperm donor? Maybe Mr. Downy hadn't been able to produce children himself, and she had been forced to go through other channels, seeking out someone who was willing to father her child. Maybe *that* was where the Huntington's Disease had come from.

"What happened?" he asked her softly. "You eventually managed to get pregnant."

She shook her head slowly.

"But you did," Zachary repeated, indicating the picture. "You were pregnant here."

"No. I wasn't."

He stared at the picture, not understanding.

"It was a prop," Mr. Downy said gruffly. "Back then… that's what some people did. Pretended. Then one day… came back from the hospital with a baby." He ducked his head. "But… it wasn't what it looked like. There were private adoptions. It was shameful not to be able to have children of your own. So you did what you had to to convince everyone that you did. That the little blond-haired baby you brought home one day really was your own."

Zachary let his breath out in a whoosh. He stared at Mr. and Mrs. Downy in disbelief. "Bridget is adopted?"

"Things were different back then. They were changing, but… there were still circles… people who would look down their noses if they thought that you had done something like that instead of being able to conceive a child of your own."

"So this whole conversation…" Zachary made a circular gesture to indicate what they had just finished talking about. "About your medical history... none of that matters. Because Bridget isn't your biological child. She doesn't carry your genes."

Mrs. Downy nodded, looking shamefaced. "She doesn't know."

"Bridget doesn't know she's adopted?"

"No."

Zachary took several deep breaths, feeling like he couldn't get enough oxygen. Not a panic attack. He was just so shocked he couldn't seem to work his diaphragm properly anymore. Breathing didn't feel natural.

"Bridget doesn't know that you adopted her. She thinks she is your biological child."

They both nodded this time. Mr. Downy looked studiously out the window. Mrs. Downy was staring at the photo album still in Zachary's lap.

"So Bridget didn't lie about it. She has no idea."

"We have meant to tell her..." Mrs. Downy started, "but it has never worked out. The time has never been right. Just when we get ready to tell her... something will happen. And it doesn't feel right. Now that she's older... it feels like the time has passed. And to tell her while she's pregnant... and struggling with this pregnancy... I just can't do that to her now."

"She needs to know now. She needs to understand the DNA results she got back on the babies and to know what it means for her. And to know that she could have Huntington's Disease herself." Zachary shook his head in disbelief. "Why wouldn't you tell her that when she was going in for her IVF? Explain to her that you don't know her genetic heritage. She could have had counseling and testing before she got pregnant."

"I didn't see what good that would do."

"And when Gordon asked about predispositions to diseases that run in your family? You never thought that maybe it was important for him to know the truth instead of the lies you had been telling all these years?" Zachary knew his words were harsh, but he couldn't understand how they could have gone for decades without ever revealing what they knew about Bridget's heritage. "Why did you lie to him? Why didn't you tell him then?"

"We couldn't tell him and not her. It's our responsibility to tell Bridget..."

"But you didn't. You never told either of them that there was more to it."

"We've tried," Mrs. Downy said.

"You don't know how hard it is," Mr. Downy chimed in. It was strangely incongruous to have this man who Zachary had always seen as a confident, competent man, complain that it was too hard to tell his daughter where she had come from. His protest was strangely childlike.

"I've never had to do it," Zachary agreed. "I can't judge you. I don't know how I would have handled it in the same situation. But you have to tell her now! You have to explain to her that she's the one carrying the Huntington's gene, and she needs to be tested herself."

Neither of them jumped up and volunteered to be the one to break the news to Bridget. Zachary sat, looking at them and looking at the little girl in the pictures.

He had told her about his own tragedies, how he had lost his biological parents and been raised in foster care. And she'd had no idea that their lives were parallels. She thought her life was the complete opposite, having been born as Mr. and Mrs. Downy's natural child and raised by them from birth.

In the end, they agreed to call Gordon. Not Bridget. They couldn't yet find a way to break the news to her. But they would talk to Gordon, explain that they had lied to him. Gordon needed to hear that and to know that it wasn't any wrongdoing on the part of the clinic that had led to the two babies carrying the Huntington's gene. He needed to know that it wasn't Forest McLachlan.

Nor had his wife cheated on him. Instead… a fraud had been perpetrated on all of them. They had been lied to by Bridget's parents right from the start. And then, they would discuss how to best approach Bridget with the revelation.

Bridget was not going to like it.

Zachary was glad that it wasn't going to be up to him to break the news to his ex-wife. If he told her something like that, he would deserve the wrath she poured out upon him. She needed to hear it from the people she loved, not from her ex-husband. He didn't need to be her target anymore.

And after they told her that she was adopted, they needed to tell her the rest.

3 5

Gordon sat on the Downys' couch like a statue, his face as gray as stone. He could have been a sculpture sitting there. He didn't move. Zachary couldn't even see him breathing. It was like he had been frozen in time.

Zachary couldn't imagine what was going through his head. He had believed that there had been a switch made at the clinic. To hear now that his wife was not only adopted, but that she might have Huntington's Disease must have been devastating.

Not only his babies, but his wife too.

And if she was already having symptoms, then they didn't get to wait until she was seventy years old. They didn't have the luxury of waiting for a cure to the dreadful disease. If she had it now, her days were already numbered.

"Then it wasn't that man," Gordon said finally. "That lab worker at the clinic."

"No," Zachary confirmed. "I guess he got spooked by our investigation and ran, but he wasn't the one who had the Huntington's gene."

"It was Bridget." He looked at Mr. and Mrs. Downy. "It was Bridget all along."

"We don't *know* that," Mr. Downy pointed out. "Not until further tests are done." He shot a look at Zachary. "Just because she's been moody lately, that doesn't mean she has Huntington's Disease. That hasn't been established."

"No," Gordon agreed. He swallowed and looked at Zachary. His eyes said it all. He had seen the changes too. He was more aware than any of them of the emotional changes that Bridget had been going through. And maybe he was aware of other symptoms he had not acknowledged before. The Downys had said that there was no Huntington's Disease in their family, and he had believed what they had said, because it was what he wanted to hear.

Like Bridget's parents, he wanted to believe that there wasn't anything wrong with Bridget. That she was just emotional. Stressed. Hormonal. That it was because of the cancer treatments.

The alternative was too heartbreaking.

"What does that mean to the girls?" Gordon asked bleakly. "If Bridget has symptoms now, what does that mean for them?"

"They've inherited an expanded Huntington's allele," Zachary said. "They'll likely get it around the same age."

"But she'll abort," Mrs. Downy said. "There won't be any babies."

"Can she do that?" Gordon looked at Zachary. "Is she competent to make a choice like that?"

Zachary looked into Gordon's dark brown eyes, feeling like he was drowning in the depths. Could Bridget even make that decision for herself anymore? And if it fell to Gordon to make that decision, what would he decide?

Gordon put his face in his hands and shook his head.

They sat for a long time. Consoling each other and trying to help each other through the terrible news. Zachary wasn't sure what he could do for Gordon to help him keep it together. If Zachary was still Bridget's husband, he had no idea how he would have handled the news. It would have been impossible. And making the medical decisions for everyone would be overwhelming. Even stoic Gordon was shaken to the core.

Eventually, Gordon left. He would pick Bridget up. Inform her that they had been invited to dinner at her parents' house. And when she got there, they would find a way to break the news to her.

Zachary sat there, watching Gordon's car drive away. It was time for him to leave. He didn't want to be there when Gordon and Bridget returned. He wouldn't be a welcome guest at that conversation.

He had been fiddling with his notepad in his pocket, and he pulled it out now. He flipped through the pages, looking at all of the questions and scenarios that he had scribbled down when it occurred to him that Bridget herself was the one with Huntington's Disease. Not just carrying the gene, but showing symptoms. He flipped through the pages slowly.

"What do you know about Bridget's biological parents? Do you have any background information? Their medical history? There are laws that will allow an adoptee to find out important medical information..."

Mr. and Mrs. Downy looked at each other. Mrs. Downy turned back to Zachary. "Her biological parents are dead."

"Both of them? How do you know that? She was an orphan when you adopted her?"

The two of them nodded in unison. Zachary wondered whether it was the truth or just another lie of convenience. It would be easier for them if there were no medical history? They would only have to reveal the absolute minimum—that Bridget had been adopted. They wouldn't have to share anything else about what kind of people her biological family had been.

"What happened to them?" Zachary drilled.

Parents of infants didn't just conveniently drop dead. There had to be some backstory. They had to know something about how they had died.

"I don't see how that is relevant," Mr. Downy said. "There is no way for us to get their family history. It's a dead end."

"You must have been told something about them. What kind of family she came from, if she was born in the United States or overseas. Even if her parents are dead, there could be extended family members. We might be able to find grandparents or cousins and start building a family tree."

"What does that matter?" Mrs. Downy asked, her voice teary. "If she has Huntington's Disease, what else do you need to know? What does it matter how many people in her biological family might have had it?"

She had a point there. "What if Bridget wants to know where she came from? She might want to know more about her biological ancestry. Or to meet blood relations while she still can. You've kept all of that from her."

"She doesn't need to know anything about them."

Zachary knew better. While some adopted children were not interested in knowing where they came from, most of those he had met felt that there was something missing from their lives if they didn't know anything about their biological family. They felt incomplete without it. They longed to meet someone who was related to them by blood, even if it wasn't a parent or sibling.

"She came from somewhere. You've denied her heritage."

"She won't want to know."

"What if she does?" Zachary was thinking about how he could help Bridget. He knew a genealogist who worked with DNA. She could search public ancestry databases, find her relatives, and then start building them into a family tree. Even without Mr. and Mrs. Downy's cooperation or Bridget being able to unseal her records, they could find out something about the people she had come from.

"You can't search," Mrs. Downy said, clearly reading Zachary's expression. "You can't do that to her."

"To her? I would be doing it *for* her. I would be helping her."

"No, you wouldn't. You can't… it would be cruel to do that to her."

Zachary frowned at this. Researching Bridget's heritage would be cruel? How did that make any sense? He would be giving her what she needed. A sense of where she had come from. The comfort of biological family supporting her through her decline. Knowing her whole self.

Mr. Downy shook his head at his wife. "Don't. Don't say anything else."

She rubbed her eyes. Her makeup was getting wiped away. She looked older and more vulnerable. Like a child and an old woman at the same time.

"He's going to look. And you know he can find things. He'll… he'll ruin everything."

Zachary sat forward in his seat. What was she so worried about? Was the adoption not legal? She couldn't just be concerned about the revelation that she was infertile. Not anymore. Society had changed since then.

"You can't hide the truth forever. I can figure it out. If you have a good reason Bridget shouldn't know, then tell me. Because otherwise, I'm going to assume that it's just to cover your own errors."

"What gives you the right?" Mr. Downy demanded, color suffusing his face.

"I want the best for her. Especially… if she has Huntington's Disease like I think she does. I want her to be happy for what time she has."

"She's perfectly happy without knowing anything about what happened before she came to us," Mrs. Downy put in. "She's our daughter now, it's like nothing ever happened. Sometimes I even forget that I didn't give birth to her. When Gordon came and started asking about family medical history, I didn't even remember at first that Bridget doesn't share our genes. It was just so natural to think of her being a part of us."

Zachary shrugged, irritated at their insistence. "Fine. If she asks for my help, you know I will help her. And I can do it. I can find out what family she came from. Help her to meet her extended family. Whatever she wants me to do."

They knew that was true even without his saying anything about it. He had always been devoted to Bridget. He would always do whatever she needed him to.

The two of them looked at each other. Zachary waited, sure they would break. If Bridget really wanted to find out about her biological family, she would. There was no point in their becoming estranged from her because they wouldn't give her the answers she wanted.

Mr. Downy rubbed his forehead slowly. "It was a very tragic story," he said slowly. "I haven't had to think about it for years."

36

Zachary went back home to Kenzie. He felt wrung out. Enervated. It had been an emotional day. On the one hand, he was glad that he didn't have to be there when they told Bridget the truth about her birth. On the other, he was sorry he couldn't see her. Even just a fleeting moment, passing on the street as he left and she arrived. He'd been watching for Gordon and Bridget as he left, hoping to catch a glimpse of her.

Some day in the future, she wouldn't be there anymore. There would be no chance of running into her in town, at the gas station, or her favorite restaurant. No flash of her yellow bug in traffic. No outrage if he pocket-dialed Gordon. She would be gone from his life forever. Something that he had never believed. She had always come back, asking him a favor, checking in to make sure he was still alive, telling Kenzie that she was making a mistake.

"Hey." Kenzie greeted him with a kiss and searched his face, looking concerned. "How are you? What's going on?"

He shook his head. "It's been quite a day."

"Come on in," she ushered him into the living room. He noticed that she did not have anything cooking. Either she had just gotten home, or she'd had something light to eat without him. He sat down and she sat sideways on the couch so her legs were across his lap and she could see his face as they talked.

"So what's been going on?" she asked. "Is it your case, or did something happen at the Petersons?"

"Things went pretty well for dinner with Pat's family. They went home last night; I didn't see them today. But I sort of... missed the latter part of the meal."

She raised an eyebrow.

"I suddenly... had an insight into the case. I had to focus and follow up on it. So I kind of ducked out for the end of dinner."

Kenzie rolled her eyes, grinning. She'd had to deal with him getting distracted like that enough times. At least she knew it wasn't just her. He did it to other people too. "I'm sure Pat and Lorne understood."

Zachary nodded. "Yeah, Lorne said that it was okay... Pat understood. I didn't plan to do that to his family, though. I'm sure they thought I was being really rude."

"Well, they might as well get to know the real Zachary right from the start. No false assumptions."

"I suppose. Pat seemed to be okay the next day... I just wonder if he was covering up how upset he was."

"Like Dr. B says, if you don't tell someone what you're thinking, don't expect them to read your mind."

"Yeah. I don't like to disappoint Pat. He's been through enough lately."

"None of that is your fault either. But that was yesterday. What happened today? It was your investigation, then?"

"Yeah. I had this idea that I needed to follow up on today."

"And how did that turn out?"

"Well... some testing will need to be done, but I think I was right."

"You got your culprit? The fertility clinic employee who contaminated the samples?"

"It turns out... the Huntington's came from the mother."

"I thought she was tested."

"No, she didn't want to be tested. We just had her negative family history. There weren't any cases of Huntington's or possible Huntington's in her family."

"So you think she has the intermediate allele? But how could you know that?"

"No. I think she has Huntington's." Zachary closed his eyes and for a few minutes, just let his mind swim in the darkness behind his lids, trying to come to terms with what he had discovered. The whole process that he had started in motion.

Kenzie bent closer to him and rubbed his shoulder and back. "That's sad. I'm sorry. One of her parents, then, was intermediate. And they passed the expanded gene to her."

"She was adopted."

"Oooh…" Kenzie thought about that. "Wow, okay. She was adopted, so the family history was wrong. Did she not understand that she could have inherited it from her bio family? I know people have disconnects, sometimes, but…"

Zachary pressed his palms to his eyes.

"You need something for your head."

"No. Nothing tonight."

She didn't press. Zachary needed to be in control of his own medications. She had learned that he was better at anticipating what he might need and avoiding interactions than she was, so she needed to leave that to him.

"Do you want to put something on the TV? Chill out for a while?"

He should probably do as she suggested, just put the case out of his mind and relax with her for the rest of the evening. But he couldn't. It was just too upsetting.

"Kenzie… it's Bridget." He pulled his hands away from his eyes and blinked at her.

Kenzie frowned, studying him. "What's Bridget?"

"It was Gordon who came to me. It was her twins that tested positive for Huntington's Disease."

Kenzie's eyes widened. "Bridget's twins?" She started to connect the dots. Her jaw dropped open. "Bridget was adopted? You think *she* has Huntington's Disease?"

Zachary nodded. His chest hurt, like a heavy weight was being pressed down on it. As much as he had wished to be able to get over Bridget and to put his relationship with her behind him, he had never imagined that it would be this way.

He wanted her to be happy. He wanted himself and Kenzie to be happy. He didn't care so much about Gordon. But he had still wanted Bridget to be happy and the thought that she might have Huntington's Disease was a crushing blow.

Kenzie's face was a mosaic of emotions. Shock, anger, sympathy, all fighting for a place.

"Oh, my..." Kenzie trailed off and blew out a puff of air, thinking about it. "Do you really think so?" Her mind was going rapidly through what she knew of Bridget, both what she had experienced and Zachary's history with her. "You think that all of her drama, her anger, that's because of Huntington's?" She pressed her feet against his leg, digging in her toes, wiggling them. "Oh, Zachary."

"What do you think? Am I way off base? I mean... all along, you've been saying that she's the one who is unbalanced, that it wasn't a rational response to my... mistakes. Do you think that she could be... having episodes because of Huntington's Disease?"

"Yeah. She'll have to get in to be tested to confirm it."

Zachary nodded. "Gordon was going to... talk her into getting tested. He knows someone. He wouldn't have to wait; they could get it done right away. I guess they need to do more than just do a DNA test to see if she has this expanded gene. There are other things they need to do to confirm that... she has active Huntington's Disease."

"Yeah. I don't know all of the ins and outs, but of course just having the gene doesn't mean you have the disease yet. But with her behavior... if you're right and all along she's been getting worse because of Huntington's Disease..." Kenzie shook her head. "You know the prognosis is not good. You know how the disease progresses."

"Yeah. I know. Like having dementia and Parkinson's and Lou Gehrig's all at once. And eventually... she won't be able to communicate. Won't be able to swallow. Or to get around."

Kenzie nodded grimly. "I wouldn't wish it on my worst enemy."

"Even Bridget?"

"How can you think that? Of course not. I wouldn't wish it on her or anyone else. Ever."

Zachary massaged his head again, hoping to be able to relieve the headache.

"Have you had anything to eat?" Kenzie asked.

"No. I don't think so."

"Low blood sugar isn't going to help the situation. What do you want?"

"I'll just heat something up. You don't need to make anything special."

"I'm not offering to make anything special. I'll warm you up some left-overs or pull something out of the freezer. Or a sandwich, if you want."

"You're tired too. I can make it."

Kenzie got to her feet. "You're so stubborn sometimes. I'm getting you something to eat. You can speak up now and say what you want, or I'll surprise you."

Zachary thought he should get up and help her, or at least move to the kitchen table where it was easier to talk to her while they waited for the microwave and while Zachary ate. But he didn't have the energy to move from where he sat.

He didn't offer any suggestions. Kenzie opened the fridge and checked the contents of the various bowls of leftovers before selecting one. She put it in the microwave and started it warming.

Zachary closed his eyes and was surprised when she sat down next to him again. He hadn't felt the passage of time. He opened his eyes and looked at Kenzie. She handed him a bowl of leftover frozen lasagna.

"Thanks." Zachary put it onto his portable desk so that he wouldn't spill, and took a couple of bites. He loved lasagna, but he could barely taste it.

"Why would Gordon involve you?" Kenzie asked, her voice betraying anger. "Of all of the private investigators… why did he have to pick you? He knew you would be too close to the issue. That was really rotten of him."

Zachary was surprised by the strength of her words. Was it really that bad? "He knew that I already knew Bridget's schedule, that I would see if there was anything out of the ordinary. Remember that at the beginning, we were looking for evidence that she'd had an affair, thinking maybe the twins had been conceived naturally."

"That was always a long shot. He had to know that it was more likely to be tampering at the clinic."

"I guess. But we thought… at least I thought… there would be safe-guards in place at the clinic to ensure something like that couldn't happen. I just figured… that it wouldn't. That there wasn't any way an employee could swap his own sperm in."

"Gordon didn't suspect that Bridget had Huntington's?"

Zachary thought back to Gordon's shocked expression when they had told him everything. His ashen complexion. The way he sat there, frozen, not wanting to believe what they had told him. Was that the face of a man who had suspected it all along?

"No. From his reaction today… I don't think there's any way he thought she might have it. He was… as white as a sheet. He could barely talk. And Gordon is never in that state. He didn't know. I'm sure of it."

"What a horrible shock. I can't imagine how it must have hit him. This woman that he's been living with for a couple of years… that he was hoping to start a family with…? It's just too tragic. I don't know how she could have hidden it from him. It should have been obvious that something was wrong."

"I didn't pick up on it. Neither did you. We all just thought… that she was overwrought. I thought she had good reason to be as mad as she was. I wasn't a very good husband."

"Not being a very good husband doesn't make a woman completely unhinged. The things that Bridget has been doing—the tantrums over you being someplace by coincidence, acting like she cares and wants to be involved and then dropping you again once she has what she wanted, just the intensity of her anger—that wasn't because of something you did."

Zachary turned that over in his mind, trying to figure out if what Kenzie said made sense. He had already been over it a hundred times in his mind in the past twenty-four hours. He had worked it through in his note-book, thinking about the various scenarios, trying to weigh Bridget's behavior against some kind of standard of normal responses.

It was hard for him to do. He'd faced a lot of anger and emotional behavior in the past. Much of it felt undeserved or like an overreaction to him. To the point that he no longer trusted his own judgment over what was normal.

He poked at his lasagna and mused, "What would I have done if I'd figured it out while we were still married?"

"She's just here in the hospital as they run the tests," Gordon informed Zachary gravely. "She's had a couple of falls that she hadn't told me about, and they're concerned with the possibility that she could do harm to the twins if she falls again. After the testing… we'll see."

"You didn't know?" Zachary asked.

"I know she's been clumsy lately. Just chalked it up to being pregnant. I've read that a lot of women bump into things, drop things, trip over things. Their bodies go through so many changes; it's only natural. I knew she'd had a couple of accidents. Tripping before sitting on the couch or bed. Catching herself on a wall. She would laugh it off, say that she was getting as big as a house. Even though, of course, she isn't."

"But she told the doctor that she's fallen down?"

"No." Gordon rolled his eyes. "Her assistant. The girl who comes to help her with things she wasn't strong enough to do after the cancer treatments. She knew but hadn't told me. Bridget wouldn't let her."

"Ah." Zachary nodded. Of course Bridget wouldn't want Gordon to know about it. She would keep it quiet. Write it off as just being clumsy because she was pregnant. And when she was no longer pregnant and was still bumping into things and falling down, there would be another excuse. Being tired. Getting up too fast. Having a bit of anemia. Something innocuous to cover up the increasing difficulties she was having.

"How did she... take it? Hearing that she might have Huntington's?" Zachary had problems forming the words, but managed to get them out. He hated that Bridget had to go through this.

"As well as can be expected... she was angry. Said that we were all interfering with her life. Didn't know what we were talking about. That everything is fine and she hasn't been experiencing any difficulties or changes in behavior. But in the end... resigned, I guess. She'll let them run the tests. She says that will prove that she doesn't have Huntington's. I hope to heaven she's right... but I think you and I both know..."

Zachary nodded. He swallowed hard. Since reading that people with Huntington's Disease often had problems swallowing, it seemed like every time he swallowed, he was going to choke. Sympathetic symptoms.

He badly wanted it not to be true. He wanted Bridget to be well.

"The prognosis isn't as bad as all that," Gordon said bracingly. "She could live another twenty years after diagnosis. It's not like it's going to take her in a year, like with cancer."

But what would those years be like? Bridget was already declining. She would need care. Gordon would pay for some sort of care worker at home. For as long as they could make it work. But eventually, it would be too much for home care. Bridget would have to go to a nursing home. She would gradually lose control of all functions. She would be a prisoner in her own body.

"She knows that I'm coming?" he asked Gordon.

Gordon nodded. "She wants to talk to you." He rolled his eyes heavenward and gave a wide shrug. He didn't mention anything about how Bridget had ranted after Zachary had mistakenly called Gordon at home. Bridget didn't want Zachary until she wanted him. She would scream and harangue and tell him that he had to stay away from her or she'd have him put in jail, until she wanted him to do something for her, and then she would be sweet as honey again, talking him into doing something he knew he shouldn't. Just as Gordon himself had done.

Zachary stopped before they got to Bridget's door. "So, Gordon..."

His eyebrows went up.

"We never really had a chance to talk about McLachlan. I know I left you messages, but..."

Gordon shrugged. "He ran. Maybe he wasn't involved in anything to do with Bridget's pregnancy, but he still bolted when you started asking questions. That suggests that he's guilty of something."

"I just wondered… whether you had anything to do with that."

Gordon gazed at him. "I hired you to investigate. So, yes, if asking questions prompted him to run, I guess I'm responsible for that."

"I meant… personally. Did you go over there to talk to him?"

Or to try to get answers out of him another way. Or maybe he hadn't even tried to get any answers. Maybe he figured he knew enough already and just took action. Or hired someone else to do that part.

"Of course not," Gordon said blandly. "You didn't even give me his address."

It would have been easy enough to find. Heather hadn't had any trouble getting it. The receptionist at the clinic had it and verified it over the phone.

"So you didn't do anything when you thought he might have been the one tampering with samples."

Gordon shook his head. His face was smooth. There was no sign that he was lying. There never was.

"The police haven't been able to find any sign of him yet," Zachary told him.

"I suppose he left the state again. Maybe he went somewhere warmer this time. Florida or California. Who knows? He'll ditch his car, take on a new identity, and forge references to get himself a new job. None of us will ever see him again."

His words had the ring of finality. *None of us will ever see him again.*

Zachary couldn't think of anything else to say. If Gordon had anything to do with McLachlan's disappearance, he would never admit it.

He walked with Gordon into Bridget's hospital room.

Bridget was sitting in bed. Zachary's heart gave a tug as he approached her. She was still so beautiful. Cancer and treatment and the early stages of Huntington's Disease had not taken that away from her. She looked more fragile, and yet she glowed with radiance from the pregnancy, as she sat there with one hand over her pregnant belly.

Zachary was reminded of the pictures of Mrs. Downy, pretending to be pregnant, cradling her fake stomach in her hands. But Bridget wasn't faking. The lives of those two babies depended on her decisions.

Her blond hair fell in waves around her face. She was wearing makeup in spite of being in a hospital bed. She wore one of her own nightgowns rather than a hospital johnny. She looked at Gordon, and then at Zachary, a quick movement, analyzing them both.

"Zachary. I didn't know if you would come."

Of course she had known he would come. He would always come when she called.

Bridget smiled sweetly at Gordon. "Could I talk to Zachary alone, Gordon?"

"Of course, sweetheart." He bent to kiss her on the top of the head. "Don't tire yourself out."

"I can talk to him without tiring myself out."

"You don't have a lot of energy with the pregnancy. You need to be careful."

She waved him away. Gordon nodded to Zachary and walked out of the room. There was a man with self-confidence. Zachary couldn't imagine letting an ex-lover sit alone with his wife.

As if anyone could prevent Bridget from doing what she put her mind to. Zachary sat down in a metal and plastic chair near the bed. Not too close to her. Maintaining a respectful distance so that everyone would know that he wasn't doing anything improper.

"So... I guess all of this was your idea," Bridget said, indicating the room around her. "*You* decided that I have Huntington's Disease."

"I don't know," Zachary said. "It was only a thought; I can't prove it. I hope I'm wrong. But if you do... they can give you medications that can help you feel better..."

"Nothing is going to make me feel better right now. Would you feel better if you knew you were going to lose control of your body and your mind and die? Just how would that make you feel?"

"I'm sorry."

Thirty seconds, and he was already apologizing to her. Not for something that he had done wrong, just for generally being in her line of fire. For guessing before anyone else had what was wrong with her.

"They don't know for sure yet, do they?" he asked tentatively.

Gordon had said that she didn't believe she had Huntington's, but she seemed remarkably resigned to having it.

"We'll see what they find out."

Zachary nodded. "I'm sorry. I wanted to help. I never wanted this."

"Gordon should not have involved you in... our mess."

Zachary looked away. He already knew that. Everybody involved knew that. But he felt like it was partly his mess too. He still wanted to be a part of Bridget's life. Even thought they were divorced, he still felt like they would be a part of each other's lives forever.

"Zachary." Bridget put her hand on the rail of the bed. Closer to him. Like she was going to take his hand and hold it as they talked intimately about the whole thing.

He swallowed again. His throat felt stretched out and dry. He should have bought a water bottle at the cafeteria. Nothing felt natural. Like it was his own body that was shutting down instead of Bridget's.

"Zachary, I need you to do something for me." Her expression was soft. Her eyes doe-like.

"Anything," Zachary assured her. Though he already knew what it was, and he already knew that he would never do what she wanted him to.

"I need... I need to find out more about my biological parents." She shook her head in wonder. "I can't even believe I'm saying that. I never knew I had any other parents. I never thought that I wasn't a Downy at birth. It's a shock."

"Yeah. I imagine it would be quite disconcerting."

"You're telling me. Anyway... you're good at research and background and hunting down information and missing people. I want you to find out about my parents. Their names, what they did, why they ended up giving me up for adoption. Mom says they are dead, but I don't know if that's true. I need to find out. Soon."

Zachary nodded. "Okay. Let me look into it."

"I want to know while... I'm still myself. I need to know all about who I am."

"Yeah. That makes sense. Well, you know me... how many different places I lived. But I always knew where I came from. I at least knew my biological parents, even if they weren't a part of my life anymore."

"Yes. And I need that. I need that connection to the past."

"Of course."

"I'll give you all of the information I can. Don't talk to Mom and Dad about it. I'm sure they'll just tell you lies. But I want the truth."

38

*Z*achary would never tell Bridget that he already knew what she was looking for.

He had known that it wouldn't be before-bed reading material, but he couldn't stop himself from a series of internet searches which he had hoped would turn up the tragic story of Bridget's biological parents. She was nearly forty, so he would only be able to find anything about the incident online if someone had digitized the papers it was reported in at the time or someone had used it as a case study for some research project.

He sifted through various stories that had similarities to what Mr. Downy had finally described to Zachary. He discarded them all, searching deeper and deeper. He might have to go to the library or some hall of archives to find hard copy papers from the time. But he would find them. He would get them somehow.

Then he found a medical paper. A student who had done a survey of similar cases. Michael Webber had described it in detail. He had covered their backgrounds, the events that had led up to it, and the incident itself. The bare, cold facts. Zachary sat looking at the screen, oblivious to everything around him, for some indefinite period of time. Until Kenzie was tapping on his leg again, trying to bring him back to a conversation that he had not been a full partner in.

"What are you reading?" she asked, looking at his screen. "Looks like a medical journal from here."

Zachary nodded. "Yes."

"Need some help with it? I can interpret for you."

He adjusted his screen a little, unsure what to tell her. "It's a case I was looking for. Sort of a tragic one…"

Kenzie nodded. She worked in the medical examiner's office. She'd heard more than her share of tragic cases.

"It's an account of a murder-suicide." Zachary let his eyes run down the columns, catching a word here and there. He'd already read it through a couple of times and, in spite of the medical jargon, he understood perfectly what had happened.

"Murder-suicide in a medical journal? Why? What is so interesting about it?"

"Just a few months before the murder-suicide took place… the husband had been diagnosed with Huntington's Disease."

"Oh." Kenzie shook her head. "I know that the suicide rate for Huntington's Disease is pretty high. It's a terrible disease; people don't want to face it, knowing what's going to happen to them. And depression is a big part of Huntington's. They don't know whether the suicidal ideation is because of the prognosis, or because of what's going on in the brain with the neurotransmitters."

"It's pretty bleak. I don't think *I* would want to go on, knowing I was going to face that."

"But murder, I don't think that's as common. I know there is aggression, sometimes assault of caregivers. But that's not the same as murder."

"The medical paper breaks it down. Number of cases, how common it is. Attempted murder is more common than murder itself. Because of the movement disorder, they often don't succeed."

"Still, tragic," Kenzie commented.

"Especially in this case. They left behind an infant child."

"Oh. Poor thing."

"A little blond girl. They didn't have a genetic test for Huntington's back then, so she was never tested to see if she inherited it."

"Whatever happened to her, I wonder."

Zachary looked at Kenzie, surprised that she hadn't picked up on the connections. "She was adopted. Raised without ever knowing what had happened to her biological parents, or even that she had been adopted. So she never knew that she had a fifty percent chance of having inherited Huntington's Disease from her father."

Kenzie's eyes widened. "Bridget?" she asked gently.

Zachary nodded and closed his eyes. "Yes. Bridget."

Did you enjoy this book? Reviews and recommendations are vital to making a book successful.

Please leave a review at your favorite book store or review site and share it with your friends.

Don't miss the following bonus material:
Sign up for mailing list to get a free ebook
Read a sneak preview chapter
Other books by P.D. Workman
Learn more about the author

Sign up for my mailing list at pdworkman.com and get Gluten-Free Murder for free!

JOIN MY MAILING LIST AND

Download a sweet mystery for free

PREVIEW OF UNLAWFUL
HARVEST

1

M ACKENZIE REACHED FOR THE ringing phone, trying to drag herself from sleep, but her hand encountered only the empty base of the phone, the wireless handset missing.

She pried her eyes open while feeling for it on the bedside table, knocking off keys and a glass and an empty bottle and other detritus. She swore and blinked and tried to focus. Where had she left the handset and who was calling her so early in the morning? The phone rang five times and went to her voicemail. Too late to answer it. She sank back down onto her pillow and closed her eyes. Whoever it was would have to wait.

But no sooner had it gone to voicemail than it started ringing again. MacKenzie groaned. "Are you serious? Come on!"

She turned her head and squinted at the clock next to her. It was hard to see the red LED display in the bright sunlight. It was almost eleven o'clock. Certainly not too early for a caller, even one who knew that she would sleep in after a party the night before. She rubbed her temples and scanned the room for the wireless handset.

There was a man in the bed next to her, but she ignored him for the time being. He wasn't moving at the sound of the phone, so he'd probably had more to drink than she had. She slid her legs out of the bed and grabbed a silk kimono housecoat to wrap around herself. The caller was sent to voicemail a second time. MacKenzie took another look around the bedroom without spotting the phone, then went out to her living room, also bright with sunlight streaming in the big windows. Outside, the pretty Vermont scenery was covered with a fresh layer of snow, which reflected back the sunlight even more brilliantly. MacKenzie groaned and looked around. The newspaper was on the floor in a messy, well-read heap. The remains of some late-night snack were spread over the coffee table. Some of their clothing had been left there, scattered across the floor, but no phone.

It started ringing again. Now that she was out of the bedroom and away from the base, she could hear the ringing of the handset, and she kicked at the newspaper to uncover it. She bent down and scooped up the handset. She glanced at the caller ID before pressing the answer button and pressing it to her ear, but she knew very well who it was going to be.

No one else would be so annoying and call over and over again first thing in the morning. She couldn't just leave a message and wait for MacKenzie to get back to her, she had to keep calling, forcing MacKenzie to get up and answer it. Her mother didn't care how late MacKenzie might have been up the night before or how she might be feeling upon rising. It was a natural consequence of MacKenzie's own choices. MacKenzie dropped into the white couch.

"Mother."

"MacKenzie. Thank goodness I got you. Where have you been?"

Her mother had been calling for all of two minutes. Where had MacKenzie been? She could have been in the bathroom, having a shower, talking to someone else on the phone, or at some event. Granted, she didn't go to a lot of events at eleven o'clock in the morning, but it *could* happen. Mrs. Lisa Cole Kirsch had a pretty good idea where MacKenzie had been. In bed, like most any other morning.

"What is it, Mother?"

"It's Amanda. She's sick."

MacKenzie nodded to herself and scratched the back of her head. One of the things that would definitely set Lisa into a tizzy was Amanda being sick. She worried over every little cough or twinge that Amanda suffered. She had good reason, but it still made MacKenzie roll her eyes.

"What's wrong with Amanda?"

"I don't know. Maybe it's just the flu, but I'm really worried, MacKenzie. The doctors said to just wait and see, but they don't understand how frail Amanda is. They think that I'm just overreacting and being a hypochondriac. You know that I'm not just a hypochondriac."

"I know. So, how is she?"

MacKenzie had to admit that even though her mother worried about Amanda, her worry was well-justified. Amanda's health could get worse very quickly, and with the anti-rejection drugs suppressing her immune system, she was prone to picking up anything that went around.

"She's not good. She was up all night, throwing up, high fever, she's just not herself. I called an ambulance at eight o'clock. She just can't keep anything down and I don't like the way she's acting. So… weak and listless."

MacKenzie felt the first twinge of worry herself. Amanda had spent much of her life sick, but she was a fighter. She usually did her best to look like nothing was wrong, not letting on unless she was feeling really badly. She would laugh and brush it off as just a bug and smile and encourage MacKenzie to tell her about what was going on in her far-more-interesting life. MacKenzie closed her eyes, focusing on Lisa's words.

"But the doctors don't think that there's anything to worry about?"

"No, but you know… they never do. She has to be at death's door before they'll admit that there might be a problem."

"Have they given her anything or did they just send her back home again?"

"They've got her on an IV and have said that they'll keep an eye on her. But you know they don't really think there's anything wrong. They're just humoring me."

"Yeah. Do you want me to come?"

"Would you? I'm really worried."

"Okay. I'll need a few minutes to get myself together. I'll be there as soon as I can."

"Thank you, MacKenzie. I don't know what I would do without you."

The sad thing was, Lisa would do just fine without MacKenzie. Even though she said that she needed MacKenzie, MacKenzie wouldn't really be able to do anything that Lisa couldn't do herself. She'd been dealing with doctors for a lot of years, and though she didn't pick up on the medical jargon as quickly as MacKenzie did, she could hold her own very well and was stubborn as a mule when it came to Amanda's care. She would protect her baby at all costs, and Amanda would get the best of care whether MacKenzie were there or not.

But if Lisa wanted the extra comfort of having MacKenzie around, who was she to argue? She didn't have anything else going on that prevented her attendance, and even if she did, it was easy enough to beg off of any event with an excuse, especially if the excuse were that Amanda was sick. MacKenzie had used it as an excuse even when it wasn't true. Although technically, even when Amanda was feeling well, she was still sick, so it wasn't really a lie.

MacKenzie hung up the phone and put it down on the brass and glass side table. She scrubbed her eyes with her fists, and when she opened them again, Liam was standing in the front of her.

"What's up?" he asked. "Everything okay?"

He hadn't yet recovered anything more than his boxers and, for a minute, MacKenzie just let her eyes rove over the piece of eye candy, remembering the night before through a slight haze of alcohol. They had gone to the Cancer Society fundraiser, had made the rounds there and let themselves be seen, and then had returned to MacKenzie's apartment for more drinks, some real food, and private entertainment.

"MacKenzie? What's up?"

"Amanda. She's in the hospital and Mother wants me to go over there and reassure her." MacKenzie yawned.

Liam bent over to pick up the various items of clothing he had dropped the night before. "Is she okay?"

"I'm sure both Amanda and Mother will be just fine. But she sounded pretty worried, and she said that Amanda was listless, which isn't like her. A really bad flu, maybe. I hope that's all it is."

"I was going to have a shower before heading out. Do you want it?"

MacKenzie weighed the options. Amanda was in the hospital, so she would be getting the best of care. Did it really matter whether MacKenzie had to wait an extra ten minutes for Liam to shower before she got herself ready?

"Or," Liam suggested, a dimple appearing in his cheek, "we could shower together and be done twice as fast."

"I have a feeling I wouldn't be out of here very quickly if we did that," MacKenzie laughed. They could easily be another hour, and Lisa would be on the phone again, ringing insistently, demanding to know where MacKenzie was and why she wasn't at her sister's side yet.

"Okay," Liam agreed. "So, do you want it?"

"Yes. I guess so. I need to pull myself together even if I am just going to the hospital." Lisa would not want her to show up looking bedraggled. She'd expect MacKenzie to be well turned-out even if it were the middle of the night, which it wasn't.

Liam nodded agreeably. He pulled on his white shirt from the night before, but didn't put on the pants or the rest of his outfit. "Shall I make you some breakfast while you're in there so that you can get out more quickly?"

"Would you? Just a couple of pieces of toast and some juice," MacKenzie requested, heading toward the bathroom. She looked back over her shoulder at him. "And coffee."

He smiled. "I think I know by now that you don't start any morning without coffee."

"Well, I need to fortify myself with *something* this morning before facing my mother."

She had a quick breakfast while Liam got into the shower, but he wasn't out by the time she was finished. She poked her head into the bathroom.

"Will you be much longer?"

She could see his shadow through the shower curtain as he turned his head toward her. "Oh... I can just lock up when I leave. You can go ahead."

MacKenzie shook her head. "I don't like to leave people here when I'm not around. Sorry. Can you be quick?"

"Yeah, sure." His tone was agreeable, but clipped. He obviously didn't appreciate that she didn't trust him enough to leave him alone in her apartment. But MacKenzie had been burned in the past by people who didn't respect her privacy, and she wasn't about to leave him there without supervision. She didn't know him well enough. Just because she could go with him to an event, and maybe bring him home afterward, that didn't mean she knew enough about his essential character to leave him there alone. She valued her privacy and there were a few things around the apartment that were quite valuable. Not that she thought Liam Jackson was going to steal them. She knew where to find him if he did. But it just wasn't good policy. If she didn't notice that something was missing right away, she might never be able to track it down again.

"I'll just be two more minutes," Liam promised.

"Thanks."

She went back to the bedroom and, since she had the time and couldn't leave until he was finished, she actually went ahead and pulled her bed into some semblance of order. It didn't look as good as when the maid did it, but it was better than leaving it all rumpled. She would appreciate it when she got home later.

If Lisa could only see her now. Twenty-seven years old and actually making her own bed. On a roll, she went into the living room and picked up the newspaper, which she threw in the garbage, and her clothes, which she threw in the laundry. Liam was out of the shower but not yet out of the bathroom. She threw a random assortment of dishes into the dishwasher and had the place looking pretty tidy when Liam made an appearance, dressed, hair wet but neatly combed, and his face still stubbly, not having taken the time to shave. She stood on her tip-toes to give him a kiss. "Thanks. Sorry about having to rush you out of here. It's my sister. Mother wants me there, so I have to make sure she's okay."

Liam nodded, looking down at her and letting his fingers linger on her jaw for a moment. "That, or you got one of your girlfriends to call to break up the party so that you could get rid of me."

"Ugh. I wouldn't do that when I was still in bed."

He smiled. "Give me a call later, then. Let me know how it goes. And we'll see each other again… soon."

They didn't have anything lined up, no dates, no fundraisers, nothing on the horizon. Liam was a nice guy, good looking, and MacKenzie might add him to her regular coterie of admirers, but she hadn't made up her mind yet. She wasn't one hundred percent sure that he was her type. Whatever that was.

After seeing him out the door, she put on her coat and winter gear and headed for the hospital.

When she managed to find her way to Amanda's hospital room, not in the renal unit where she usually was, Amanda was asleep. Lisa sat next to the bed, watching her sleep. Not reading a book. Not looking at her schedule for the week. Just watching her sleep. MacKenzie would have gone crazy. She couldn't stand to have people staring at her.

"Hi, Mom," she said softly.

Lisa looked over at her, automatically making a motion for her to be quiet before she evaluated MacKenzie's voice and the deepness of Amanda's sleep and decided that she probably wasn't being too loud after all.

"How is she doing?" MacKenzie looked over her kid sister. Amanda was twenty years old, but when she was asleep, she looked about ten. She was shorter than MacKenzie, and MacKenzie wasn't exactly an Amazon herself. Amanda was small and elfin, and people often mistook her for a kid if they weren't paying attention. She had a beautiful face, when she was feeling well. She wasn't looking too bad. Her weight was good, her cheeks round rather than sunken like they had been when she'd been through her worst times. She had long, dark hair that got tangled if she didn't take care of it, which was hard to do when she was in a hospital bed all day, but she didn't like to cut it short so that it would be easier to take care of. She said she needed her strength, like Samson.

Amanda was pale, and that bothered MacKenzie. But if she had the flu and had been throwing up for hours, then of course she was going to be pale. It was just a virus. She would be feeling better soon.

"She's sleeping," Lisa stated the obvious. "She's been so sick all night... I'm glad she was finally able to drift off. Maybe she's on her way to feeling better."

"Probably just a bug."

"Yes. Hopefully."

There was an IV hanging, but Lisa had said that Amanda needed it to stay hydrated. It didn't necessarily mean that she was back on some treatment again.

MacKenzie pulled the other chair in the room closer to her mother's and sat down. Amanda had been given a private room, of course. There was no way she was going to be left in some hallway or emergency room curtain. Lisa would see to that.

"Do you want to go get something to eat?" MacKenzie suggested.

"Well..." Lisa's eyes flicked over to Amanda. "I don't know. I don't want to leave her alone."

"I'm here. And you haven't had anything to eat, have you? You've been with her since last night?"

"Yes, you're right."

"Well, you're not going to be any good to her if you're fainting from hunger or all angry and irritable from low blood sugar. So go. I'll be with her if she wakes up. She's not going to be alone."

"Are you sure?"

"Why don't you take advantage of the fact that I'm here, because I'm not going to be here all day. Go have something to eat."

"Okay," Lisa agreed, but she still made no movement to get up, watching Amanda with worried eyes.

"She'll be fine for now. I'll have them page you if something happens."

"Would you?" Lisa brightened at that suggestion. She could go have something to eat and still be sure that Amanda hadn't taken a turn for the worse. She clutched her purse on her lap, then nodded and got up. "Thank you so much, MacKenzie, I appreciate you coming and being here for your sister."

"And for you," MacKenzie reminded her. "Don't you try saying that I never do anything for you."

"I would never say that."

MacKenzie raised her eyebrows as her mother left. She might say it and she might not. But she would certainly imply it the next time she wanted MacKenzie to do something for her and MacKenzie had something else going on or didn't want to be there.

Lisa's heels clicked sharply as she walked away. MacKenzie watched her go. She leaned back in her chair and looked over Amanda once more. The hospital chair was far from comfortable. She was going to have to get used to it if she were going to be there for a few hours.

"I should have brought a book," she murmured to Amanda. She hadn't thought to bring anything with her. She'd just gotten herself together and headed over. And she couldn't go down to the gift shop to pick something up. Not after dismissing her mother and saying she'd stay with Amanda while Lisa was eating. MacKenzie sighed and resigned herself to just sitting there and napping while she waited either for Amanda to wake up, or for Lisa to return from lunch.

2

SHE HAD NODDED OFF, and when she opened her eyes and rubbed the stickiness away, she realized that Amanda was awake, her head turned to look at MacKenzie.

"Oh, hey sleepyhead," MacKenzie greeted.

"Hi," Amanda said in a soft little voice. MacKenzie waited for the rejoinder about how MacKenzie had been falling asleep in her chair. But Amanda didn't tease her. MacKenzie bit her lip. That was what Lisa was so worried about. Amanda might look like she was just a little tired, but that shouldn't change her personality. Her lassitude suggested that there was something more wrong, not just a twenty-four-hour flu bug. She shouldn't have been experiencing that level of fatigue with just a virus.

"How are you feeling?"

"I think I'm better now," Amanda said faintly.

MacKenzie waited for her to go on, but she didn't. "I guess you had a pretty rough night of it,"

Amanda nodded. She turned away from MacKenzie again and her eyes closed. MacKenzie frowned watching her. It was just the flu. Just a fever and throwing up. It could be any number of viruses. They had her on IV. She was going to be just fine.

. . .

Lisa returned, and looked worriedly over to Amanda lying in the bed, as if she had expected her to be sitting up talking by the time she got back.

"She was awake for a minute," MacKenzie said. "She didn't throw up, so that's good news."

"I think they put something in the IV to stop her."

"Oh. Well, that's good. At least they're taking it seriously."

"She really does need to sleep," Lisa said, but MacKenzie knew she was trying to reassure herself. They were all used to Amanda's high energy level. Even when she was sick, she still joked and teased and tried to keep everyone around her in a good mood. She didn't like long faces around her hospital bed.

"If she was up all night throwing up? She sure does. I was up half the night and I could still use a few more hours of sleep. And I wasn't throwing up."

"You were up late?"

"I was at the fundraiser."

"Oh, the one at the Phelps's house?"

"Yeah. That one."

"Who did you take?"

"Liam Jackson."

"He's a nice boy."

"He seems that way," MacKenzie agreed. She focused on looking out the window on the opposite side of the room. She didn't want to blush and have Lisa detect it. MacKenzie smiled and raised her eyebrows as if she weren't thinking immoral thoughts about Liam Jackson.

"How is Daddy?"

"You know your father. Always occupied with very important meetings with very important people."

MacKenzie nodded, smiling. Lisa hadn't said it in a way that was sarcastic or critical, but with a little bit of humor, as other women might talk about their husbands' interest in cars or collectibles. *Boys and their toys*. Was that how her mother saw Walter's lobbying? As a hobby that occupied her husband and kept him out from underfoot?

"Does he have anything interesting going on right now?"

"I'm not sure what he's working on. I don't really pay much attention, unless it is something that could have an impact on one of my causes."

Lisa always had plenty of causes on her agenda. There were an infinite number of foundations, societies, and fundraisers that needed her attention and support. Lobbying kept her father busy and fundraising kept her mother happy. MacKenzie just didn't know what it was that kept *her* happy. When was she going to find her way in life? She didn't want to be a lawyer, lobbyist, or politician. But she didn't want to be a socialite or drum-beater either. She had done well enough in school and had taken enough classes in college to get herself a degree, but that hadn't helped her to find her place in the world. She wasn't passionate about anything.

Lisa's eyes were quick and perhaps took in more than MacKenzie had expected. She reached over and patted MacKenzie's hand. "You'll find something," she said. "You're just a late bloomer. You need to be patient and give yourself some time."

"When you were a kid, what did you think you would be when you grew up? Did you have any dreams?"

Lisa shrugged and looked away from MacKenzie. "I don't know. I wanted to be a wife and mother. I was never really interested in a job. I felt like children were my avocation." She shrugged. "I know that's not a very popular answer these days. We're supposed to think big and take the bull by the horns, to make our mark on the world. But I can't help but think… that the marks being made on the world wouldn't amount to very much if it weren't for the mothers."

MacKenzie gave her a smile. "The hand that rocks the cradle, and all that?"

"Yes. Exactly. Mothers shape the thinkers and the soldiers. The scientists and the astronauts and the Nobel laureates. They all had mothers. They all had people to help them along the way and give them support at various parts of their lives, like a mother would, even if they didn't have a mother. I happen to think that's a very important position."

"Of course," MacKenzie agreed. "I never thought that you should be required to give up your family and have a high-power job."

"I could have, you know," Lisa said. She obviously didn't want MacKenzie thinking that she had only stayed home to be a mother because she couldn't do anything else. She had chosen to be there and not to hire a nanny to raise them. That had been her choice, not a fallback position.

"I know, Mother. You have a brain. You're very organized and I'm always amazed at what you can accomplish. I know you could have chosen to do other things."

Lisa nodded, satisfied.

MacKenzie looked back at Amanda. They had been lucky to have a mother who stayed home to look after them. Amanda probably wouldn't have survived without a strong, proactive mother watching over her. How many times had Lisa been the one to take her to the hospital and insist to the doctors that something was wrong, and she wasn't taking Amanda home until they had figured out what it was? She had insisted that Amanda wasn't just a whiner or a hypochondriac, but that she was really ill. She could have died if they hadn't been forced to dig deeper for the answers.

MacKenzie and Amanda hadn't really been playmates. MacKenzie had been too much older than Amanda to consider her a real friend and peer. Instead, Amanda had been MacKenzie's baby as much as she had been Lisa's. MacKenzie had been fascinated with her care and had happily fed and changed her. It was like having a living doll. MacKenzie had never even liked dolls. But she liked having stewardship over the tiny new person in their home. Lisa had encouraged her interest rather than shooing her off to go play or insisting that she diaper her dolls instead of her sister.

At first, no one had known that anything was wrong. Amanda got sick a lot, but children picked up viruses everywhere, it wasn't really that unusual. As she got older, she didn't outgrow it, and MacKenzie realized that she was sick a lot more often than MacKenzie or her friends, or little Amanda's other friends. She remembered the day when she had been out at the playground with Amanda, about nine years old by then, and MacKenzie a teen. Amanda had been playing tag or grounders or some other schoolyard game on the climbing equipment with her friends, but she had to sit down at the edge of one of the platforms, her face white, trying to catch her breath and get up the energy to go back to the game. The other girls teased her for calling timeout too often and told her that she couldn't be safe, but there wasn't any point in tagging her while she sat out, because she wouldn't run after the rest of them and the game would grind to a halt.

MacKenzie walked over to Amanda.

"Mandy-Candy," she singsonged, "what's wrong? Don't you want to play anymore?"

Amanda was breathing shallowly, too fast. "I want to play," she protested, her arms folded across her stomach, "I'm just too tired. I need a break."

"Do you want to go home?"

Amanda looked at the other girls still playing and having a fun time on the playground equipment around her. She looked sad. Not just sad, but desolate, as if they had all run away and left her behind where she could not follow.

"I guess so," she said finally. "I can read, I guess."

"Do you really want to?" MacKenzie pressed. "I'm not saying you have to. If you want to stay and play…"

Amanda shook her head. "I can't," she said hopelessly. "I don't know how they can run around all day."

MacKenzie sat looking at her as the seconds ticked by, a knot growing in her stomach. She walked home slowly with Amanda, back to the big house on the hill. It was a long way for a child who didn't have any energy left. Partway there, MacKenzie boosted Amanda up onto her back and carried her piggy-back to the house. Amanda lay against her, body limp, arms around MacKenzie's neck.

When they got home and MacKenzie settled Amanda in bed with a book, she went looking for Lisa. Lisa was, luckily, home for the evening and not on her way out to some fundraiser.

"Mother… I think something's wrong with Amanda. I mean… really wrong."

Lisa looked at her for a long time, then finally nodded. "I do too. And I think it's time we found out what."

So many doctors had said that Amanda was just a girly girl, that she didn't want to participate in activities and was overly sensitive to every little ache and pain that came along with growing up and roughhousing with friends. There wasn't really anything wrong.

But when they had insisted that it was time to figure out what was really wrong with Amanda and that they weren't going away until they got some answers, everything changed.

And it would never be the same again.

Unlawful Harvest, Book 1 in *A Kenzie Kirsch Medical Thriller* by P.D. Workman takes you back to before Zachary and Kenzie met. It can be purchased at pdworkman.com

ABOUT THE AUTHOR

Award-winning and USA Today bestselling author P.D. (Pamela) Workman writes riveting mystery/suspense and young adult books dealing with mental illness, addiction, abuse, and other real-life issues. For as long as she can remember, the blank page has held an incredible allure and from a very young age she was trying to write her own books.

Workman wrote her first complete novel at the age of twelve and continued to write as a hobby for many years. She started publishing in 2013. She has won several literary awards from Library Services for Youth in Custody for her young adult fiction. She currently has over 60 published titles and can be found at pdworkman.com.

Born and raised in Alberta, Workman has been married for over 25 years and has one son.

———

Please visit P.D. Workman at pdworkman.com to see what else she is working on, to join her mailing list, and to link to her social networks.

———

If you enjoyed this book, please take the time to recommend it to other purchasers with a review or star rating and share it with your friends!

facebook.com/pdworkmanauthor

twitter.com/pdworkmanauthor

instagram.com/pdworkmanauthor

amazon.com/author/pdworkman

bookbub.com/authors/p-d-workman

goodreads.com/pdworkman

linkedin.com/in/pdworkman

pinterest.com/pdworkmanauthor

youtube.com/pdworkman

CPSIA information can be obtained
at www.ICGtesting.com
Printed in the USA
LVHW011555040221
678386LV00007B/244